Breaking the Beast

The Redemption of Joe Branch

By Steven C. Bird

Breaking the Beast

Steven C. Bird

Breaking the Beast
The Redemption of Joe Branch

Published by Steven C. Bird at Homefront Books

Illustrated by Hristo Kovatliev

Print Edition 7.9.19

ISBN: 9781078103411

www.homefrontbooks.com

www.stevencbird.com

facebook.com/homefrontbooks

scbird@homefrontbooks.com

Twitter @stevencbird

Instagram @stevencbird

Breaking the Beast

Table of Contents

Disclaimer

The characters and events in this book are fictitious. Any similarities to real events or persons, past or present, living or dead, are purely coincidental and are not intended by the author. Although this book is based on real places and some real events and trends, it is a work of fiction for entertainment purposes only. None of the activities in this book are intended to replace legal activities and your own good judgment.

Breaking the Beast

Dedication

Breaking the Beast: The Redemption of Joe Branch is my thirteenth book, and along the way I've had the help and support of so many people that naming all of them would simply be impossible.

Of course, my prime motivator is and always will be my loving family. Each word I type is another step toward supporting them and working hard toward making their dreams come true. To my wife, Monica, thank you for helping me throughout this project. Thank you for being my sounding board and my support system. To my children, Seth, Olivia, and Sophia, thank you for being my anchor and giving me a reason for...well, everything. You are truly my world.

To my parents, thank you as well for all of the support you have given me throughout my writing career and thank you for your continued support throughout the development of this book.

The writing community, in particular the indie-author community, has also been instrumental in my development as a serious writer. Your continued support, advice, and mentoring have made each book I write evolve a little further from the last, and I thank you all from the bottom of my heart for that.

I'd also like to make a special shout out to my author colleagues with DD12, who have been my real and online friends for the past year and make one heck of a team! Franklin Horton, Chris Weatherman (Angery American), Boyd Craven, L. Douglas Hogan, Lisa (L.L.) Akers, W.J. Lundy, Patti Glaspy, Jeff Motes, Chad (C.A.) Rudolph, Jeff Kirkham, and Jason Ross, thanks for your continued friendship and support!

Breaking the Beast

Also, I'd like to make a special shout out to real-life friend and award-winning audiobook narrator Kevin Peirce for doing such a fantastic job on the audio version of this book.

Chapter One

I pushed the CD into the old Pioneer Super Tuner III car stereo, and after a few whirring sounds... ahhh, there it was, that blues riff that always got me going. I turned the volume up so loud that it nearly drowned out the rumble of the four-hundred-and-twenty-eight cubic inch big-block Ford as I mashed the accelerator to the floor and shifted into third gear.

"Man, this car's got some pull," I said as I watched the tachometer rev past fifty-five hundred RPM. "Boom boom boom boom...(guitar riff)... gonna shoot you right down...(guitar riff)... off of your feet... (guitar riff)...yeah, yeah!" I sang as I accelerated past one hundred miles per hour and shifted into fourth. "Damn, I love this car!" I couldn't help but say aloud. The visceral feel of a true American muscle car with some good ol' John Lee Hooker blasting through the speakers almost made me feel whole again. Almost...

You may wonder why I chose a 1967 Ford Mustang Shelby GT500 as my getaway vehicle with so many out there to choose from. Well, that's a long story, but one worth telling. You see, my father had a '67 Mustang when I was a kid. It was nothing like this. It was just your basic off-the-dealer-lot working man's car. He may not have had deep pockets, but man, did he put some work into it, and over time, he turned it into something special. I've had a soft spot in my heart for Mustangs ever since. Especially the old ones.

Besides, I couldn't just leave this beauty sitting unattended and covered with dust in that old garage. No, she deserved better. She deserved to tear down the road and go down fighting in a blaze of glory, rather than rotting away in an abandoned town in a forgotten place.

Breaking the Beast

This girl, she's something special—a near perfect restoration of an original Shelby. She's raven black with a grey Shelby stripe—simply drop dead gorgeous. Her four-hundred-and-twenty-eight cubic inch big block Ford is fed by two Holly carbs through a mid-rise aluminum intake and shoves all that power through an old-school four-speed transmission, and a bulletproof nine-inch rear end.

On the inside, she's got the original black leather bucket seats up front with a bench seat in the back, all with a classy grey inset to match the Shelby stripes on the exterior. This is the car I'd have had in my garage if I had won the lottery before it all went down. This car is the perfect symbol of that good ol' American attitude for me, and she was a survivor. A driver, not a trailer queen. It was really the only choice.

In addition to my affinity for Mustangs and her needing to be rescued from her neglected state, she's also old school, with a breaker-point ignition system and no computers. Yep, this baby is EMP proof, which makes her EMWS proof.

You may be wondering what EMWS means. EMWS stands for Electro-Magnetic Weapon System, and now that the One World Alliance has them, well, they own the electromagnetic spectrum. They use their EMWS arsenal to deny the rest of us the use of modern technology containing circuitry unless such use benefits the alliance, which these days, is damn near everything.

Sure, I could have found a vehicle that was EMWS safe that got better fuel economy, and I do realize fuel will be an issue, requiring me to do a lot more scavenging, but if I'm gonna go down, I'm not only gonna go down swinging, I'm gonna go down swinging in style.

Go down? Go down for what, you ask? First, let me introduce myself. My name is Joseph Branch, but you can call me Joe. They, "they" being the One World Alliance (OWA), call me Lieutenant Joseph Branch of the OWA Defense Force, or ODF for short. Well, they used to call me that. By now, I'm sure they call me traitor, in addition to many other colorful and derogatory terms.

Do I deserve such treatment? That depends on who you ask and how you view the world. If you're loyal to the Alliance and to the cause, then I'm sure "treasonous bastard" fits the bill as well. But if you're one of the others out there, hoping to be delivered from this hell on Earth the Alliance has created, well, you'd probably call me a friend. At least, I hope that's what they'll call me... if I survive long enough to meet any of them.

What hell on Earth did the One World Alliance create? I'm glad you asked. You may want to have a seat and grab a cold drink and some popcorn for this. It's a hell of a story.

Nearly five years ago today, the Sembé outbreak began to sweep the globe. It was first discovered in a small village just outside the town of Sembé in the Republic of the Congo. Christian missionaries from the U.S who had worked with the village the year before had returned as planned, only to find the entire community dead.

They described it as a wrath of God. Bodies were stacked in a large pile, seemingly positioned for a mass cremation by the remaining villagers, but it appeared no one lived long enough to light the fire. Several other villagers were found with eyes that had filled with blood as their capillaries hemorrhaged. Blood could be seen seeping out of every orifice on the villagers' bodies.

To make things worse, the local wildlife seemed to have discovered the macabre human buffet before the missionaries arrived. Predators and scavengers large and small were feasting on the decomposing corpses and seemed to have been doing so for several days before the missionaries arrived.

The missionaries fled and traveled back to Sembé to notify the local authorities, and as a result, the disease began its journey around the world, hitching a ride on several of the missionaries as well as the local authorities who had responded to their plea for help. Like they say, "No good deed goes unpunished."

As the virus spread like wildfire throughout the world, seeming to jump from place to place quicker than some medical experts felt was the likely path of or the timeline the natural spread of the virus would have taken, accusations as to the source were thrown around in all directions. The favorite root-cause theory of most of the major world governments was, of course, climate change.

They claimed the changing climate was having even more significant effects on microbial ecosystems than they had feared, causing rapid mutations in microbial life and even viruses. There were, of course, no studies or solid numbers to back those claims, but that didn't deter the state-friendly media from regurgitating their scripted talking points twenty-four seven.

There seemed to be nothing the scientific and medical communities could do. Death tolls in some of the poorer countries reached nearly ninety-five percent within the first year, with developed nations suffering losses of up to seventy percent. Simply put, the spread of the Sembé virus made the black plague of the middle ages look like a common cold. It was a true apocalyptic event like the modern world had never seen.

As populations dwindled, and food production and distribution systems around the world crashed, even more people began to die from starvation and the resulting chaos that followed. Desperate people are one of the most dangerous animals on Earth, and everyone was quickly becoming desperate.

Halfway through the second year of the pandemic, a group of international scientists discovered a wonder drug that promised to save us all. Unfortunately, it didn't cure victims of the Sembé virus, it merely suppressed the symptoms, meaning, as long as you had a steady supply of their wonder drug, you would live. Without it, if you had been exposed, you would begin to feel the effects of the virus within a few days, with death coming in several weeks to a month.

That was when the One World Alliance was born. With populations dwindling around the world, and with economies and production and distribution systems bordering on total collapse, the United States, along with the member states of the United Nations and the European Union, formed the One World Alliance in the name of saving the world and all of humanity. By saving the world, they, of course, meant ruling it.

Globalists had finally achieved their long sought-after goal of a New World Order. They now had a global government that was above all nations. After all, who could resist their governance? They controlled the drug that would keep everyone alive. Well, everyone who had access to the drug, of course. That's where things started getting a little shifty.

Where was I in all of this? When the Sembé outbreak began, I was a Capitol Police Officer serving in Washington D.C. Once the OWA was formed, the Capitol Police Department was conscripted into service as part of the newly formed One World Defense Force (ODF), which was the military-style law enforcement organization founded by the OWA.

And how could we say no? The benefits plan was better than anything else out there. They offered us food, and most importantly, survival. They promised us a lifetime supply of their lifesaving antiviral drug, Symbex, if we would serve for at least ten years while the world recovered.

Breaking the Beast

It wasn't long after joining the ODF, having been persuaded with the choice between the good life on the inside and certain death on the outside, that I found myself deep inside the U.S. Capitol. Well, what was previously the U.S. Capitol.

Washington D.C. was now nothing more than an outpost for the OWA, with its main headquarters located in Brussels, Belgium, a town where politics and bureaucracy have always seemed to control the agenda. It should be of no surprise, I guess, as it was also the former home of the European Union, which was immediately rolled into OWA upon its founding. Imagine that: a multi-state political organization hell-bent on open borders and globalism being a key ingredient in a globalist organization that seemed to be poised to launch as soon as an opportune time arose.

The U.S. and other major powers soon quickly followed suit and joined the OWA. Here in the states, politics had been trending toward open borders and globalism for quite some time, almost seeming to parallel the direction Europe had taken, even though the results were rarely positive for the citizenry or for the stability of their society. So when the crisis struck, and a ready-made answer presented itself, well, the president and Congress fell right in line as if they were acting out a script—a script written in Brussels.

But enough about politics, let's talk about me. You're probably still asking yourself, "who the hell is this guy, and why should I believe a word he's saying?" I quickly advanced through the ranks within the ODF. Life was good. I mean, it's not like I had anything else to do with my time. There wasn't much of a world left to recreate in.

I started off as a basic security officer, then based on my experience with the Capitol Police, I was quickly promoted to sergeant, and then to lieutenant. I had just recently been promoted to lieutenant and was excited at first, but things felt as if they began to fall apart as soon as my butter bars were pinned to my collar. You see, that's when I found out about a dirty little secret, one that would change the course of my life forever—or end it. It's still up for debate as to how that will turn out.

As a Lieutenant, my duties took me deep into the inner sanctums of the OWA. I was no longer patrolling the streets around the capital: I was now deep on the inside. I began to overhear things. Things that just didn't sit right with me, nor would they sit right with any decent human being. Sometimes, when I would get back to my OWA provided apartment after a day spent in the bowels of global government, I felt as if I needed to take two showers instead of just one, to scrub the filth off me that I'd accumulated just from being around the snakes who were in charge. It didn't take long to realize the OWA wasn't an organization formed in the wake of a global emergency situation to bring stability to the world. No, it was much more than that.

What was that dirty little secret, you ask? The One World Alliance was an organization born from the conspiracy of all conspiracies. In the years leading up to the Sembé outbreak, people often said out of disgust that the medical industry no longer created cures, only treatments. Treatments that would create lifelong customers who provided a lifelong flow of money to the medical and pharmaceutical industries, which of course, flowed into the right political coffers. With the help of corrupt government regulators and lawmakers who were on their doles, this became quite the racket, one that placed a heavy burden on people who found themselves perpetually medicated, but never cured.

Many of those government officials and world leaders who had helped create the environment that protected such unethical behavior seemed to devise a plan to take that perpetual dependency to an entirely new level. Not only would they set out to control the entire world's food production and distribution, but all other industries, and most importantly, the global financial industries.

It seemed over recent decades that people around the world were being trained to turn to the government every time there was a disaster. People stopped looking to themselves and their neighbors when catastrophe struck. Instead, they turned to the government. As that trend continued to grow, people fell far too easily into the hands of the OWA as the pandemic swept the globe.

But I digress; back to the dirty little secret. It seems those decades of developing drugs that would suppress viruses, but not cure them, was merely the field-testing phase of their dirty little secret. I'll bet anyone who took a viral suppression drug to suppress a virus such as herpes or HIV, often asked themselves, "If they can make it go away as long as I take the pill, why can't they just make it go away for good?"

In more cases than we would like to know, they could have. But like I said, why sell one bottle of pills to cure someone when you can sell them pills for life? Anyone with a soul would know deep in their heart that doing such things are wrong at every level. But when politics no longer serves the people and joins forces with big business and the world's elite through cronyism, and then when you add the mainstream global media to that team as well, and... you've got a monopoly on creation, control, and communication. That's a combination that's got some teeth.

As this unholy alliance crept its way into every facet of our lives, taking more of a hold on political power while using our own medical treatment as a testing ground for the ultimate endgame, the OWA was set up to be our savior from their self-created boogieman. Yes, that's right. They are responsible for the Sembé virus that has killed more people around the world than any other single cause in human history. It wasn't some accident from a lab, either. They developed it based on their viral suppression research activities buried deep within our very own healthcare system, and then unleashed it on an unsuspecting village in Africa. Once it was released, they orchestrated its spread throughout the world, all while protecting themselves and their allies with a wonder drug they already had in place.

Yes, that's right. The dirty little secret was the conspiracy of all conspiracies. It was the most heinous and evil act ever perpetrated on humanity, and it wasn't done by some psychotic religious cult or terrorist group hell-bent on the destruction of all non-believers. No, it was perpetrated by an elite order of globalists: The New World Order, if you will, who had set out to establish themselves as not just the ruling class of their own nations, but of the world. A world they could rebuild and repopulate as they saw fit.

Just as a former White House Chief of Staff once said, "Never let a crisis go to waste." I guess since a big enough crisis wasn't going to come soon enough for them, they decided to make their own.

Chapter Two

Once I had put together all the pieces of the puzzle, it became clear to me just how many of my fellow ODF members were onboard with team tyranny. The sergeants and below, who were mostly sheltered from the truth, were just doing their jobs. At that rank, they were still the disposable front-line security personnel, managing the day-to-day operations of policing and security on the streets in and around the capital, as well as the OWA's other areas of interests and bases.

Lieutenants and above were placed in positions of command over those operations, as well as providing security inside the hallowed halls of government, protecting the elite inside their inner sanctum. That part of the job really started getting to me after a while.

I knew serving the OWA was wrong. I began to feel as if I was a storm trooper carrying out the bidding of the Empire. When I looked at my fellow citizens on the street, even though they didn't know what I knew, I felt guilty. I felt guilty that I was the muscle for the organization that had destroyed their world, and killed so many of the people they once held so dearly. I had to do something, but what?

I decided to bide my time, learning as much as I could about every facet of OWA and ODF operations. I figured a plan or idea on how I could help my fellow man and stand against the tyrants I served would eventually present itself. I just had to be patient, and not let any of my superiors or the elite themselves begin to question my loyalty. The penalty for that was clear.

Even though there wasn't a written policy on such things and it didn't get carried out as common knowledge, there was a reason I had advanced through the ranks as quickly as I did. Clearly, there were voids to be filled above me, and the longer I stayed and the more I learned, the more certain I was as to how those personnel shortfalls at the senior ranks came to be.

The captain directly above me in my chain of command was Captain Ronnie Wilks. Ronnie was a likable fellow who had served with me before the outbreak hit as a Capitol Police Sergeant back when I was just a new recruit. I did my best to ignore the fact that at his level, he was surely more 'in the know' than I. The understanding of the level of knowledge he was likely to have, created a conflict within me. At any other time in my life, I would look at Ronnie as someone I could trust without question.

He would have been the guy I'd have drunk beer with while grilling steaks on our days off. He would be the guy I'd invite to my wedding. Hell, of all the people left alive, he'd probably be my best man. If I was getting married, of course—which I was not. I knew my life was going to take a sharp turn at some point in the near future, so there was no reason to complicate things with entertaining the possibilities of a relationship. Although it was very tempting at times. Being 'in the know' had created a very lonely world for me.

Ronnie's likeability allowed me to lower my guard with him, behaving more like my real self than with anyone else. He seemed to look at me in the same way. We never spoke of the OWA other than in terms of its operational control over the ODF in which we served. Not many people around me did, either.

In the past, before the outbreak, people would express their political ideology to their coworkers, even if they knew it would result in an argument that could never be settled. Now, though, everyone remains silent on their view of the world. The OWA simply *is*, and no one questions it. I guess we all had the same feeling deep down inside us about how the staffing shortfalls above us came to be. We were like horses wearing blinders. We would just keep pulling the wagon and concern ourselves with the next obstacle directly in front of us. Nothing more.

One day, I visited Ronnie's office on the first floor of the Capitol building to provide him with the weekly written reports of my assigned areas of responsibility. There was generally nothing new in the reports. If anything out of the ordinary had happened during the week, he would have known about it immediately. This was just one of those repetitive tasks that seemed to add an unnecessary cog in the machine. I suppose someone higher up in the food chain liked keeping us all preoccupied with menial tasks. Either way, I saw it as a routine visit to Ronnie's office, and I rather enjoyed that break in the week's monotony.

As I approached Ronnie's office, I noticed his door was closed, which meant someone was already there. Ronnie hated having his door closed. He always said something about not liking the still air since his office didn't have an HVAC vent of its own. If his door was closed, it meant someone was in there, and whatever was going on, it was something that couldn't be shared.

I stood in the hallway and waited patiently for his meeting to conclude. As I looked around the elaborately adorned former U.S. Capitol building, I thought of all of the patriots who'd first walked these halls early in the nation's founding. I thought of how they'd given everything they had in order to create a nation that would ensure the freedom of their children and of future generations.

I guess you could say I was an unofficial history buff. I wasn't a history buff in a scholarly sense, I just liked to read books about earlier times. I was especially fascinated with the founding of the United States, as well as the U.S. Civil War and from the expansion into the West through the World Wars.

I wondered what they would think of us now, having consistently strayed further and further from their original objective of a government established of the people, by the people, and for the people. We were now anything but that. The United States, or at least the scoundrels occupying halls of government at the time, had surrendered our sovereignty to tyranny so widespread the founders could have never imagined it.

As my mind wandered on, Ronnie's office door opened, and I heard him say, "Ah, there he is. Lieutenant Branch, could you join us, please?"

Stepping into Ronnie's office, I carefully glanced around the room to see three individuals in suits, who appeared to have no interest in my joining their conversation, as well as our ODF sector chief, Chief Hildebrandt.

"Yes, Captain Wilks," I said with a smile toward Ronnie and a nod toward the three stiffs in suits. "Good evening, Chief," I then said to Chief Hildebrandt with a nod and a smile, removing my hat and placing it under my arm, maintaining my professional bearing, of course.

Seeing my weekly reports in my hand, Captain Wilks quickly said, "Just put those right here," motioning to his inbox. "We've got more important things to discuss. Please, have a seat," he said with a gesture toward the only remaining unoccupied seat in the room.

"Thank you," I said, as I took a seat, extremely curious about what may be going on.

Ronnie turned his attention back to the men in suits, and said, "Lieutenant Branch here is the best we've got. I'd trust him with my life and the lives of my family any day."

Without even looking my way, one of the stiffs told Ronnie, "There's no need to rehash what we've discussed. We'll leave

Lieutenant Branch's briefing up to you, with discretion, of course."

"Of course," Ronnie replied, seeming a bit put off by their lack of regard for my presence.

As the three men stood, both Chief Hildebrandt and Ronnie rose smartly as if snapping to attention. Following their lead, I stood as well, understanding such behavior highlighted the authority and status of Ronnie's visitors.

Once they were gone, Ronnie looked at me nervously and said, "Get the door, please."

"Sure thing," I replied, pulling the heavy oak door shut. As I walked back to my seat, I could see that both Chief Hildebrandt and Ronnie were relieved that the suits were finally gone. "Who were those guys?" I asked.

"OWA Special Service," Chief Hildebrandt replied.

The OWA Special Service (OSS) was what you'd get if you crossed the U.S. Secret Service with the CIA, and maybe sprinkle in a few clandestine organizations that we didn't even know about. They weren't people you wanted to mess with. No one was closer to the OWA elite than the OSS. In my eyes, they were the equivalent of Hitler's SS, which was ironically part of their acronym.

"That can't be good," I said, seeing both Ronnie and the chief showing clear signs of stress.

Ronnie sat back in his chair and loosened his tie. Ronnie was a few years older than me and would have been the ideal actor to play a stereotypical Hollywood police precinct captain. He was the captain who, although beloved by his men, was always ready to explode on them at any given time whenever their actions made the local news, bringing the heat down upon him from city hall.

Sector Chief Hildebrandt, on the other hand, was more like your typical career focused coworker, who just wanted everything to keep running smoothly so they wouldn't miss out on their next promotion. He'd paid his dues on the street, and for lack of a better way to say it, was done with it. He hoped to never find himself outside the highly protected walls of government again.

Before Ronnie could say a word, the chief stood and adjusted his uniform, saying, "I've got to brief my boss. He's gonna be pissed enough that he wasn't involved in this conversation. I can't let him catch wind of this before I tell him. You can handle this, Ronnie," he said as he turned to leave the room.

"Absolutely," Ronnie replied. Waiting until Chief Hildebrandt closed the door securely behind him, Ronnie looked me in the eye and said, "You're about to get some fresh air, my friend."

"Fresh air? What?" I stammered, confused by his statement. I mean, I was too senior to be a patrol officer on the streets, so how was I going to be getting some fresh air when I worked entirely within the confines of the Capitol building? Was I being demoted? "What the hell is going on?" I asked.

Leaning back in his chair, Ronnie explained, "There are some high-value prisoners en route to the Central Detention Facility down on D Street."

"Why are high-value prisoners going to a basic detention facility?" I asked. "Why not take them somewhere more appropriate? D Street is more for your average street trash."

"The optics of it," Ronnie replied.

"The optics of it? How do you mean?"

"As far as they know, they may or may not end up being prisoners. They could end up being defectors."

"Defectors from what?" I asked, assuming there were no more governments out there to be defecting from, based on my own limited personal knowledge of the outside world, that is.

Looking me dead in the eye, Ronnie seemed as if he were sizing me up before answering. "Insurgents," he declared. "You know how it goes. There are people out there who want to fight for their share of power whenever some sort of reorganization of things occurs. We've seen it over and over again throughout history, and our present day is no exception."

Staring at me, Ronnie looked deeper into my eyes than I'd ever seen. He was usually the kind of fellow that huffed and puffed, spouting off but not putting too much of his own personal feelings into things. "How do you feel about such things?" he asked.

"About insurgents in general?" I said with a shrug, attempting to get him to clarify his question. "Or someone specific? I don't know who you're referring to. This is the first I've heard of them, whoever they are."

Leaning back in his chair, Ronnie looked around the room and said, "Let's go for a walk."

"A walk?" I repeated.

"Yeah, a walk. I've got to get out of this stuffy room."

Ronnie and I then proceeded out of his office, and through the Capitol building toward one of the rear entrances. "How's it going, Mark?" he asked the security officer on duty at the door.

"It's going good, Captain," Mark Sutton replied. "A slow, uneventful day. Just the way we like it."

"Well, don't work too hard," Ronnie said as we continued through the door, smiling at Mark.

"There's no danger of that," Mark replied. "My shift is almost over, and I've got a hot date tonight."

"Right on," I said with a smile.

Once outside and on the wide concrete sidewalk that wrapped around to the right, following a tall, stone retaining wall leading away from what used to be the Capitol Building

Visitor's Center, Ronnie gazed off in the distance as if he was in deep thought. "It's a shame our world has gone to hell, isn't it?"

"Yeah... Yeah, it sure is."

"You weren't married, were you? Before, that is?"

"No. No, I was lucky and had gotten out of a rocky relationship the year before. I was in pure bachelor mode. I didn't want to get hurt again. I guess that jaded attitude kept me single, and avoided the potential heartbreak of losing someone when it all started going down and people starting dropping like flies around us."

"Well, I was married and had two kids," he explained. "My wife, Margaret, died when the virus first reached us here. She was a charge nurse in the emergency room at Sibley Memorial Hospital. That damned virus swept through the hospital staff like a wildfire. Margaret was one of the first to become ill, and one of the first to pass."

Struggling to retain his composure, Ronnie cleared his throat and continued. "My oldest daughter, Alicia, was twenty-two years old and was saving the world all on her own as a member of the Peace Corps. She was in Cameroon when first reports of the Sembé virus started coming in. When they locked down travel in and out of Cameroon, we lost contact with her. I... I don't know what happened, but I can only assume the worst.

"My youngest, Ron Jr., was in his sophomore year at the U.S. Naval Academy at the time. Given the national state of emergency, he and his classmates were deployed throughout the fleet as Midshipmen. He was doing well the last I heard, being meritoriously promoted to Ensign and given a field commission. Our line of work isn't the only one where you can move up quickly these days."

"Where is he now?" I asked.

"He's on the Bunker Hill, CG-52. It's a Ticonderoga-class cruiser. They were homeported in San Diego, and have been deployed for quite some time. Where they are now, I have no idea. You know how it goes; you can't really email or call someone outside of the local area these days.

"The last time I spoke with him, he was disgusted about how they were forced to man the rails for a ceremony where they lowered the Stars and Stripes and raised that big, damn ugly OWA flag with the O and a globe in the center in its place."

As we continued walking, Ronnie mumbled, "I'm not okay with how things are these days, Joe."

"Who could be?" I said, not knowing where he was going with this.

"Oh... there are those who are quite happy. Quite happy indeed," he replied. "I'm having a hard time dealing with it, too."

"Be careful Ronnie; they'll promote me to captain to fill your vacancy if you say stuff like that in front of the wrong people," I said, attempting to sound as if my cautionary statement was in jest, but we both knew it wasn't.

"That they would, Joe," he replied, looking at me out of the corner of his eye. "That's why I would only say it in front of you. I feel like I can trust you, Joe. I know where you came from. I know your roots. We both came into this place from the Capitol Police. I don't share much in common with others around me. I can trust you, can't I, Joe?"

"Of course, Ronnie," I replied. My curiosity was killing me. He obviously wanted to tell me something. That, or he wanted to try to trap me into admitting something. Of which it was, I couldn't be sure just yet, but I was dying to find out.

Looking around, Ronnie said, "If you stay in this little world, this... fake world, you'd likely forget how bad it is outside this city. It's a wasteland out there. With the exception of OWA farming and production facilities, all you'll see in any given direction is the remnants of what was. Fields that used to be full of crops are now full of weeds and small trees as nature is wasting no time taking it back, now that the local farmers are all dead and gone.

"Cities that were once bustling now look like scenes from apocalyptic movies, with abandoned cars parked all about, broken windows, and burned ruins from the panic and mayhem of the initial stages of the collapse.

"The bodies of all those people... all the ones who weren't properly dealt with by loved ones or local EMS, well, I'd imagine the animals had quite the time with that buffet. I'm sure by now the coyotes and other predators that once kept their distance are roaming the streets like they own the place."

Stopping in his tracks, Ronnie turned and looked at me, saying, "It's an absolute hell out there, Joe. And the worst part is, it's a man-made hell. They planned it, Joe. They did it on purpose."

I knew precisely what Ronnie was saying. The things I'd learned since being on the inside had totally shattered my world, far beyond that of the collapse itself. Feeling like I was part of the problem, rather than the solution... or the revenge, I'm not certain which it was for sure, was eating at my soul. I wanted to agree with Ronnie. I wanted to let him know he wasn't the only one feeling this way, but was he testing me? How was I to know? Did I really know Ronnie all that well? Or did I just feel like I did?

I could see him staring into my soul. I'd never felt that analyzed by another man before. He was reading me, almost as if he, too, was desperate to find someone who agreed with him— someone who felt the same as him, and was willing to admit it.

Just then, I heard a sound overhead, and instinctively looked up. It was a surveillance drone flying at around one thousand feet. D.C. was full of them these days. They were as common as birds, or perhaps even more common.

Looking back to Ronnie, I said quietly, "I bet those things can pick up the sound of a voice a long way off."

Nodding, Ronnie began walking once again. I could tell he wasn't done saying his piece. It was eating at him like it was eating at me. I didn't know if he was planning to tap out or planning to make a move.

"This way," he said, leading me toward a nearby construction site.

Just up ahead, there were several hard hat-wearing workers who were using air-powered jackhammers to break up some old concrete. Between the air compressors that were running to provide air to power the hammers and the clattering of the hammers themselves, it was quite a racket.

Stopping just short, trying not to get too close, Ronnie said, "This should help."

I nodded, anxious for what he was about to say next.

"Joe," he said, pausing while searching for his words. "These insurgents. I don't think they're the bad guys. Not all of them, anyway."

"Where do you get that idea?" I asked. "You're as cooped up in this place as I am."

"I'm privy to a little more intelligence than you are, Joe. My last position with the Capitol Police was with the Anti-Terrorism Unit. I would spend my days sifting through a plethora of data and intelligence reports from all of the alphabet agencies. I learned how to read between the lines and make up my own opinion of the situation, not just the opinion the analyst who wrote the report wanted me to have.

"Anyway, I've been doing the same thing here. There is a large insurgent group out west. They're well equipped and have a large number of veterans and military personnel who defected from the OWA when it was initially being formed. Too many people in the military intelligence community put two and two together. Word got out, and thousands of people disappeared before being assimilated into the ODF."

Looking me in the eye, he said, "Do you remember when the Capitol Police was rolled into the law enforcement branch of the ODF? How many times did someone ask you if you wanted to come along? They gave you the low-down, and that was that, right?"

"Pretty much," I concurred. "It was basically 'work for us and receive suppressive therapy, or die an agonizing, painful death from the virus'. It wasn't a tough decision to make. At least, it was the only option I had at the time."

"Right, well, the armed forces received similar, um, offers, if you can call them that. Well, the surviving armed forces, that is. Many, it seems, were allowed to die from the virus while they awaited shipments of the Symbex anti-viral drugs. I guess the OWA felt they could only support a force of a specific size, so they intentionally let the virus run its course in some areas to, well, downsize.

"But like I said, not all of them took the bait. Some who left their units may have just gone off to help their families and loved ones back home. Others, well, maybe they just wanted in on the melee. You know as well as I do that not everyone who puts on a uniform is a fine, upstanding citizen.

"But some," he continued, "some, defected to a militia organization, one of the organizations we've labeled as insurgents, who vowed to fight the OWA and either find a cure or find a way to manufacture their own anti-viral treatment medication."

"They've got the resources to do medical research?" I asked. "That sounds like more than just a ragtag militia with stockpiles of guns and ammo."

"It is," Ronnie confirmed. "They've got some very bright minds with them. Their only weakness is that without the anti-viral suppressive therapy drug, they're being forced to live like rats, avoiding contact with others and remaining as low key as possible.

"The OSS operators the OWA sends out on strike missions are all carriers, so something as simple as hand-to hand-combat, even if they win the fight, could be a death sentence for them all. Those who are exposed are forced to leave the group to protect the rest. They voluntarily die alone to keep from risking the cause.

"All they need is to get their hands on a batch of the Symbex therapy drugs so their medical team can attempt to study it, break it down, and replicate it. Once they have the ability to suppress the virus, they can crawl up out of their holes in the ground and really start to give the OWA a hell of a real fight.

"Higher-ups in the OWA are very worried about that. Their grip on the people depends on their monopoly of the Symbex anti-viral drugs.

"There have been some, even within the OWA, who have tried to obtain classified data on the drug's formulation, or merely argued to have the data released, who were swiftly dealt with. Not everyone is in on the agenda. Some are just useful idiots, like us, slaving away for those who inflicted this on us. The saddest part is, most don't even know it. They still think they're working for the greater good."

I stood there, speechless. I knew what he was saying was true. I could feel it in my bones. Ronnie had just confirmed my worst fears. He had confirmed my own theories based on everything I had seen and overheard since being on the inside, only Ronnie had much more information and evidence to go on, making the case even stronger.

As I stood there and pondered everything he had just said, Ronnie calmly asked, "So, are you going to sell me out, Joe? You could very easily tell the sector chief everything I just said. I'd be gone and out of your way before tomorrow if you did. You'd have my office and my job. But then you'd also have my cross to bear. You would know what I know, and you would be forced to continue to serve those who killed millions—no, not millions, billions, along with their future progeny and everything they could have ever achieved. Could you do that, Joe?"

"No, Ronnie. No, I couldn't, and of course, I won't," I stammered, still unsure of what to say.

"Good. That's why I picked you, Joe. And there are reasons I picked the others as well."

"Picked me? Others?"

"Yeah, there's a reason I picked you, along with several others for the detail Chief Hildebrandt and the OSS suits assigned to us."

"What exactly is this detail all about?" I asked.

"The OSS is spread a little thin due to a sharp uptick in insurgent activity to the south. With that in mind, they've asked the ODF to carry out a detail they would normally do themselves. They'll have an OSS unit on site at the Central Detention Facility where the defectors are being transported. The defectors say they will provide the OWA with critical intelligence information in exchange for a two-hundred-dose supply of the Symbex anti-viral drug for them and their families to use while traveling to their assigned OWA facilities, and immunity from prosecution. They want to be able to live out in the open, and be provided with the same level of anti-viral care as the rest of the people who actively support the OWA."

"People like you and me," I quipped.

"Exactly, people like you and me. Anyway, I'm done rolling over. I'm done being a part of the problem, rather than part of the solution. We've got to break the back of the beast, Joe."

"What do you propose?" I asked.

"Our assignment is to transport the two hundred doses from Walter Reed to the Central Detention Facility. We are to hand it over to the OSS on site, and they will complete the negotiations."

"Why would the OWA want the OSS to give insurgents access to the drug. Aren't they afraid they'll just use it for the research purposes you mentioned? Wouldn't that be against the OWA's best interests?"

"Of course it would. And you'd be nuts to think they'll actually let them get very far with it before taking them out. These aren't high-level personnel we're dealing with. They aren't the best and the brightest. These defectors are low-level individuals who see an easy way out, or what they *believe* is an easy way out. They're damn traitors is what they are.

"The OSS can handle them. I'm sure the refrigerated case we'll be transporting the drugs in will have a tracking device somewhere inside. Those bastards will get just far enough to lead the OSS back to whoever it is they're trying to help with the medication before they're taken out.

"The way I see it, those traitors, those Benedict Arnold's, don't deserve the drugs, and I don't plan on giving it to them," Ronnie proclaimed.

"What's your plan?" I asked.

"The rest of the detail consists of the last people I would consider my fellow countrymen. Lieutenant Don White, Lieutenant Jose Perez, Sergeant Hamid Houbbadi, and Sergeant Franco Capelli. They're *all in*. They know the score, and they're totally okay with the fact that they're sleeping with the devil.

"There are two kinds of people serving the ODF. There are people like you and me, who came onboard thinking we were doing the right thing, and when we find out the truth, we're appalled by it. And there are those who find out exactly what's going on and are okay with it. They're just glad they're on the team with all the guns, the drugs, and the power."

Confused, I asked, "Then why put them on the detail with us?"

"Because I don't want us to have to take out someone I like, like you, Joe," he said with a smile. "Or someone who doesn't deserve it. I'm trying to do a good thing here, Joe. I don't want to take more innocent lives.

"None of our guys, whether they're in on the lies and corruption or not, would just let us walk away with the drugs. They'd all do their duty and try and stop us, knowing that deadly force is more than authorized regarding the protection of the Symbex drugs. So, I picked guys I wouldn't lose sleep over if I had to kill them."

Pausing to gauge my reaction, he added, "And you're not one of those guys, Joe. I can't do this alone. You and I can work as a team. We can use our knowledge of the system to get those two hundred doses far away from here and into the hands of someone who can do a service for humanity and break the OWA's monopoly on granting life to people in exchange for their servitude. It may even lead to a cure, Joe. How do we not at least try to make that happen?"

Looking Ronnie squarely in the eye, I said, "I'm in."

"So, you've got no reservations about this?" he asked.

"No, sir. Not one," I assured him.

"Good. Now, once this goes down, the sand will be running out of our hourglasses. We'll be able to keep the virus suppressed if we take a dose every other day at a minimum. We've got to move quickly, though, in order to get the drugs somewhere fast enough that we'll have enough left to provide to their researchers, as well as keep ourselves alive while they race to replicate it. If not, we'll die whether the OWA catches up with us or not. It's like lighting a fuse. Once it's lit, there's no turning back."

Looking around, I said with a smile on my face and confidence in my voice, "I knew I liked you, Ronnie."

Chapter Three

Later that evening when I arrived home, I almost expected to have a few OSS thugs waiting inside my apartment for my... um, early retirement from the ODF. No one in the new world of what D.C. had become had any expectations of privacy.

Before the Sembé outbreak began, we had voluntarily conditioned ourselves to constant surveillance. Our phones tracked our every move, listened to every sound, and tracked every selection made on touchscreens through every app and browser. We had installed internet-connected listening devices in our homes for the sake of convenience. Add to that, every internet-connected device we owned had a camera installed, and we gladly gave every application we installed permissions to both the camera and the microphone. Privacy was officially dead.

The difference in the post-outbreak world was merely that we didn't personally authorize the surveillance, but it was still there. The OWA didn't operate under something as restrictive as the U.S. Constitution. The global state of emergency had allowed them to capitalize on the philosophy of "Never let a crisis go to waste" like never before.

The absolute horror of the situation, a situation that many truly believed to be the end of the world for humanity, an extreme level of desperation felt by nearly everyone, led to an environment where an authority operating under the guise of providing aid or stability, did so without question or oversight. And the next thing we knew, we had a new, all-controlling government. But hey, they were here to help, right?

And now there I was, sitting in my apartment that was undoubtedly under surveillance, planning, the very next morning, to turn against the beast I had been serving since it all began. A plan I'd only known about for several hours, yet I felt as if it was something I was put on this earth to do.

Not once did I have to convince myself to join Ronnie in his suicidal plan. Not once did I have to weigh my options in my mind. It was something I was going to do. Period. I had never been more certain about anything in my entire life. It was as if everything I had ever done had led to that moment, that time, and that place.

To say it was a sleepless night was an understatement. As frequently as I remember looking at the clock throughout the night as I tossed and turned, I couldn't have slept for more than a few minutes at a time.

The next morning, I laid there staring at the alarm for what felt like an eternity, counting down the seconds for it to commence its painfully annoying series of beeps to tell me it was time to crawl out of bed and walk away from it all.

Just as the alarm began its plea for me to get up, I silenced it and crawled out of bed, still exhausted and desperately needing sleep. I walked over to the coffee maker and began brewing a pot of my favorite dark roast coffee blend. I couldn't help but chuckle, in some sort of demented, guilt-ridden kind of way, as to how I was able to enjoy the luxuries of a climate-controlled apartment and a hot cup of coffee, all while many others outside of this center of power and influence suffered every day, struggling to survive in the hellish world my masters had created.

I wanted to pack a few things, you know, just in case this harebrained scheme actually worked. I couldn't likely keep up any sort of successful escape and evasion if I couldn't blend in, and wearing the uniform of the ODF was no way to blend in. But, if Ronnie and I were going to be able to pull it off without anyone raising any eyebrows, I couldn't do anything out of the ordinary. No, that day had to be just like any other day.

Donning my dark grey uniform shirt and black pants, I slid my badge and identification into place and slid my belt through my belt loops. Looking in the mirror, I chuckled to myself and thought, *Yep, you're a damned stormtrooper alright.*

I went to the weapons storage locker the ODF had installed in my apartment to keep my government-issued weapons, and I opened it to see my PX40E 9.5mm enhanced service pistol, and my CX91E 6.2x40mm enhanced patrol carbine.

Shortly after the OWA's assumption of authority in the states, an emergency order was given that outlawed the private ownership of weapons and arms of any kind. Knives were even heavily regulated. Again, much of this seemed like a replication of what had already occurred in Europe and much of the world in the days leading up to the outbreak.

Once traditional weapons had been taken off the streets and destroyed, the OSS, as well as the law enforcement and military branches of the ODF, were then issued advanced combat weapons designed, engineered, and produced by a multi-national conglomeration that had sprung up out of Belgium, called GDI, or Global Defense Industries. They were now the only manufacturer allowed to produce weapons under the authority of the OWA, which, of course, meant everywhere. It was a complete and utter monopoly—cronyism and corruption at its finest. Or should I say filthiest? That, of course, depended on which side of the corruption you stood.

When the private ownership of arms and ammunition was banned, the OWA, via their friends at Global Defense Industries, developed a new line of weapons that used proprietary cartridges and used smart weapons technology to prevent them from being used if they were to find their way into the wrong hands.

The PX40E 9.5mm enhanced service pistol was the first of the new designs to be deployed. Using a polymer-cased proprietary round and an electrical impulse ignition system, rather than the ancient use of percussion-fired primers, they ensured that existing weapons in the hands of insurgents could not be simply rechambered to fire the new round.

The power source for both the ignition system and the integrated advanced holographic sighting system were two very slim but powerful batteries concealed within the sides of the grip, with the double-stack seventeen-round magazine extending through the center between them. The location of the magazine seemed to be the only similarity between this new design and the traditional designs of the not-too-distant past.

All of that advanced technology made for an effective combat and defensive weapon, however, the most essential aspect of the enhanced weapons platform was the use of an identification chip implanted in the soft tissue of the hand, between the forefinger and the thumb, which interfaced with the electronics built into the weapon. This integration rendered the pistol useless in the hands of someone who hadn't been authorized by the ODF or OSS to use them. Not only would the weapon refuse to fire, but it would also begin to sound an ear-piercing alarm that could only be silenced by another authorized user.

The CX91E enhanced patrol carbine and the RX91E enhanced service rifle were designed around all of the technology used to produce the PX40E handgun, yet were chambered in the compact but effective 6.2x40mm, polymer-cased smart round. The CX version had a compact, collapsible and side folding stock, as well as a relatively short thirty-centimeter barrel, which was just under twelve-inches, while the RX91E was more of an infantry-style weapon with a sturdy fixed stock that could double as a blunt weapon and a fifty-centimeter barrel, which came in at just a shade under twenty inches.

In addition, the CX91E and RX91E both had a digital zoom feature built into their holographic sighting system, with the CX model zooming out from zero to 4X, and the RX model reaching a maximum of 10X of magnification, all without the weight and bulk of a traditional rifle optic or scope.

As I pulled my pistol from its charging station in the safe, I looked at the now empty charging port and thought, *I guess I've got a day or two at most with this thing before the batteries are depleted, depending on how much I have to use it, that is.*

After I holstered my pistol, I removed my CX91 from its charging port as well. Although we didn't typically carry our patrol carbine at my level, its use would not be out of the norm today, considering the fact that we were assigned an escort mission of one of the OWA's most valuable and closely guarded assets.

Looking at my watch, I realized I had wasted enough time contemplating the day ahead. It was time to get to work and get on with things.

I took the employee shuttle from my apartment complex to the capital building as I usually did, yet on that day, with my patrol carbine slung securely over my shoulder, I felt the eyes of everyone on the bus staring right at me. Maybe I was just paranoid, but I felt as if everyone around me knew something was different, that it wasn't just another day at the office for ol' Joe Branch.

Once I arrived at work, I followed my typical morning routine of grabbing yet another cup of coffee from the ODF break room, and then took my place in line to receive my daily dosage of Symbex, metered out by medical personnel assigned to the facility.

Though not required to be taken daily, the powers-that-be had determined that a smaller dose given more frequently had the same effect as a much larger dose every two or three days, saving the OWA some of its most precious resources. No one would come right out and tell us how long we could go without the drug before signs of the virus first appeared, but I had never personally gone more than two days without a dose.

I arrived at Ronnie's office ten minutes before my required report time. "Cutting it a little close, aren't we, Lieutenant Branch?"

"Sorry, Captain, the line was long this morning," I muttered as the others assigned to the detail looked me up and down as if I somehow didn't measure up. Seeing the cup of coffee in my hand, they knew I had my priorities.

"No longer than any other day," Ronnie replied in a grumpy, dismissive tone.

Present in the room, in addition to Captain Ronnie Wilks and myself, also onboard for the escort detail were Lieutenant Don White, Lieutenant Jose Perez, and Sergeant Hamid Houbbadi.

"At least you're not last," Ronnie chided. "Sergeant Capelli isn't here yet, either."

I couldn't help but look at each of them and wonder if they had any idea they could be seen by their Captain as being expendable. I also couldn't help but wonder if I was the only one Ronnie had briefed in such a way. Maybe I was the expendable one? Perhaps someone else in the room thought they were there to kill me and follow through with some insane defection plan?

Don't get me wrong, I wasn't a paranoid guy, riddled with self-doubt. I was, at that point in my life, quite the opposite. I had complete faith in myself; it was everyone and everything else around me that gave me pause. A lot had happened in the preceding years, and most of what I had seen, heard, and read about, shook my faith in humanity to its core.

"Captain Wilks," Sector Chief Hildebrandt announced as he walked into the room, accompanied by an ODF officer unfamiliar to me.

Standing, Ronnie replied, "Yes, Chief."

"Officer Hanson here will be joining your detail in lieu of Sergeant Capelli. He's been detained elsewhere. Besides, Officer Hanson here has a bright future ahead of him, having recently been promoted to Sergeant." Patting Hanson on the shoulder, Chief Hildebrandt added, "He's not been officially promoted yet, but he may as well start getting in on some higher-level assignments to get ahead of the game."

I gazed at Ronnie's facial expression. I could see fear and confusion in his eyes. He hadn't expected this. I could see the conflict going on within him.

"Is this a problem, Captain?" Chief Hildebrandt asked.

"No. No, sir," Ronnie replied. "I'm sure Officer Hanson, whom I'll soon be referring to as Sergeant Hanson, will be a great asset to us today."

"Congratulations, Sergeant," Ronnie said to Officer Hanson, shaking his hand to welcome him aboard.

"Very well," Chief Hildebrandt said. "I'll leave you men to your work. I'll be expecting your report once the delivery has been made, Captain."

"Yes, Chief. You'll have it by the end of the day," Ronnie replied as Chief Hildebrandt turned to leave the room.

"I'll have it as soon as you're back," Chief Hildebrandt demanded loudly enough for everyone in the vicinity to hear, affirming his authority over the operation.

"Could you get the door, Lieutenant Branch?" Ronnie mumbled quietly.

"Of course, Captain," I replied, taking the knob and pulling it shut.

After Ronnie went through the motions of our standard security escort detail pre-brief, we walked as a group to the rear entrance of the capital, where we would be met by Sergeant Evans of the ODF vehicle and equipment division.

Once outside, we saw a Navistar Defense MRAP (Mine Resistant Ambush Protected Vehicle) pulling up just outside the vehicle access zone.

As Sergeant Evans exited the vehicle, Captain Wilks approached him and asked, "Where did you get that old thing?"

"Hell, Captain, this thing is one of the best we've got. They're old by today's standards, but they were built right in the first place. Besides, you're only going a few miles right here in the city, right? What more do you need?"

"If you knew what we were transporting, you'd have sent one with a gun on top," Ronnie replied with a wink.

"Ahhh, you're haulin' some juice," Sergeant Evans chuckled, referring to the slang name of the Sembé virus anti-viral treatment medication formally known as Symbex.

"I didn't say that," Ronnie replied.

"That's okay, Captain. Your secret is safe with me," Evans said with a grin. "Well, you boys have fun, and try to bring her back in one piece."

"It'll be a walk in the park," Ronnie said as he turned to me and said, "Lieutenant Branch, you drive. Houbbadi, you ride shotgun. White, Perez, and Hanson, you guys can sit in the back with me. I'll be carrying the... juice, as Evans so professionally put it."

Ah, great, I thought. *Right where I can be shot in the back of the head.*

Working our way across town toward the Walter Reed National Military Medical Center, or the Walter Reed World Medical Center as it was now known, a few of the guys in the back chatted with Ronnie while Houbbadi and I kept our eyes peeled on what was out in front of us. We weren't necessarily friends, so keeping up the charade of a friendly chat wasn't expected by either of us. We were each content with our silence as we watched the city go by out the thick, bullet-resistant windshield.

Reaching Walter Reed, I looked back and asked, "Captain, where are we picking up the objective?"

"We're being met at the Command Duty Office. It's just off Palmer Road South," Ronnie explained.

"Roger that, Captain," I replied as I negotiated the sizeable armored truck through the foot traffic surrounding the facility. One can imagine just how hectic things would be around a major government medical facility in the wake of the largest medical disaster of human history.

Pulling to a stop, I set the parking brake as Captain Wilks said, "All right, you two stay up front and keep the truck running. The rest of us will meet with station security personnel and take possession of the objective. Keep your heads on a swivel."

After a few minutes inside, Captain Wilks and the others exited the main Command Duty Office door with the case in hand. Ronnie was carrying a specially designed case that would withstand moderate impacts while suspending the contents safely inside. The case also contained a cooling system that regulated the internal temperature to ensure the greatest possible longevity for the contents. Battery power provided the necessary support for the electronic lock, the onboard tracking system, and the cooling system. The unclassified answer was that the case could remain at an adequate temperature for up to four days without recharging, but who knows what it's really capable of.

Climbing back into the truck, everyone took their seats in the back as Captain Wilks ordered, "Let's move."

As I drove the MRAP on the prescribed route toward the Central Detention Facility, we'd reached what I felt was the halfway point when Ronnie shouted toward the front, saying, "Hey, Joe! Let's take the alternate route we discussed."

Hearing mumbling amongst the others in the back, I looked to my right to see Houbbadi turning around, confused at what Ronnie had just said. I looked back to Ronnie and said, "Sure thing, Captain."

Looking me dead in the eye, Ronnie nodded, then drew his PX40E and shot Lieutenant White directly in the forehead, causing the back of his head to explode, splattering its contents onto the interior wall of the armored vehicle. The sound of the round hitting the wall as it exited White's head was almost as deafening as the muzzle report.

Seeing Houbaddi begin to reach for his weapon, I immediately drew my sidearm as well, shooting him in the head while his attention was focused on the ruckus occurring in the back of the MRAP. If I had it to do over again, I would have fired several shots into his torso, attempting to avoid his body armor under his arms or around the bottom of his neck. The splatter of blood and brain matter from the exit wound in his head obscured my vision on the passenger side window, as well as the portion of the front windshield directly in front of Houbbadi.

Dividing my attention between keeping the vehicle on the road and the conflict occurring inside, I heard Ronnie shouting, "Stand down, Hanson! Stand Down!"

"Damn it, Captain! What the hell?! What the hell is going on?!" Hanson shouted with fear and confusion in his voice.

"You weren't supposed to be here. It wasn't supposed to be you!" Ronnie shouted. "Now lower your damn weapon, and you'll make it out of this. Don't make me do it."

Glancing back, I could see that both of the men had their sidearms extended, pointing them at each other. Ronnie had a calm and collected look on his face, but Hanson was in total panic mode. His gun shook uncontrollably in his hand as he struggled to steady it.

"Lower it, Hanson," Ronnie said calmly.

Looking forward, swerving to avoid an oncoming vehicle, I heard two shots being fired in rapid succession.

"Damn it to hell, Hanson!" Ronnie shouted.

I quickly swung my sidearm toward the rear, only to see Ronnie pointing his pistol directly at me. I struggled to remain focused on him while I kept the large vehicle between the lines, narrowly avoiding several collisions in the process.

Lieutenant White lay dead in the back of the MRAP. Ronnie had managed to catch him sufficiently off guard while I dealt with Houbbadi. However, Hanson had reacted in a split second, complicating the situation.

I glanced to Hanson, then back at the road, and then back to Hanson, who lay there twitching and bleeding.

Multiple scenarios ran through my mind. Was I set up just as the others were? Was the only reason he hadn't shot me yet because my hands were on the wheel and he needed me to bring the vehicle to a stop first? Was I just a pawn in his game?

"He's alive," Ronnie said. "I tried my best to avoid a kill shot."

I could hear Hanson begin to moan and grunt, confirming what Ronnie had said. "He wasn't supposed to be here, Joe. Chief Hildebrandt screwed everything up. That bastard always screws everything up. Hanson wasn't supposed to be here. He's not one of them. He's not like them. At least, not yet."

With a nod, Ronnie looked me squarely in the eye and said, "We're good, right, Joe?"

Slowly lowering my pistol, I said, "Yeah, Ronnie. We're good."

Breaking the Beast

"The bastard got me right under the collar bone," he said as he placed his gun in his lap and reached into his vest and shirt, removing his hand to reveal blood on his fingers. "The damned bullet glanced off the edge of my vest and got me right under the damned collar bone. I don't think it's broken. It feels like it passed straight through. I'll live, but we've gotta get him some help. I've got an idea. Just drive."

"Roger that, Captain," I replied as the full weight of the situation came bearing down on me like a ton of bricks.

Chapter Four

"So, what now?" I asked as Ronnie pulled Houbbadi's body from the front seat and shoved it into the back of the vehicle.

"Take a left off of Wisconsin Avenue onto Yuma Street," he said as he wiped Houbbadi's blood from the window with Don White's jacket. "There, see that construction site? They got started on that years ago. It was supposed to be an expansion for American University. But when the Sembé virus outbreak reached us, construction simply ceased."

As I exited onto Yuma Street, he pointed and directed, "There, pull around between those two buildings. We don't have a lot of time. They'll be on us before we blink."

"Don't they have drones in the air watching us?" I asked.

"Not this time," Ronnie replied. "They planned on it, but... hell, I'll explain later," he mumbled.

As I rounded the corner between the two buildings, he again pointed, "There. Pull up next to that Tahoe. That's our ticket out of here. While I'm transferring the doses from this case to a container I have waiting, grab the clothes in the back seat and put them on. I guessed about your sizes. Hopefully, I was close."

Pulling to a stop alongside the Tahoe, I quickly grabbed my CX91 carbine, climbed down from the truck, and began changing out of my uniform as Ronnie had directed. I was starting to settle into the fact that Ronnie and I were definitely a team. All of my doubts and misgivings were brushed aside at the sight of Ronnie's foresight and planning, which obviously involved me for more than just taking out the other officers.

Once I had changed into the denim jeans, hiking boots, and the brown pullover sweatshirt, Ronnie said, "That leather jacket is yours, too. Once you're all squared away, go back to the truck and gather the extra ammo from the others."

Doing as he had asked, I exited the MRAP to see him opening the transport case via the digital keypad adjacent to the handle. Once the case was open, he began transferring the contents into a backpack that contained a small twelve-volt powered, soft-sided electric cooler.

"This thing was made for road trips, camping and such," he explained. "It will work perfectly for our needs as well. I've got one of those fold-out solar charging systems to keep its batteries topped off during our journey, especially since we have no idea how far we'll have to go or for how long we'll have to travel."

"I was starting to think you had every detail worked out," I replied in jest.

"There's more," he said with a grin. Reaching into the pack, he produced a container made for breath mints and slid it open. Inside was a USB data storage device. "Remember when I said some people tried to obtain data on Symbex and were dealt with accordingly?"

"Yeah," I replied, thinking back to our first conversation on the subject.

"One of them was a dear friend and confidant. She worked deep inside the belly of the beast as a researcher. Though security was far too tight to sneak anything out of the lab, she was able, over time, to memorize and then transcribe some vital data obtained from their years of research, trials, and error. She put together a Cliff notes version that could be used to jumpstart the reverse engineering process and get other makers of the drug up and running in far less time."

"That's all on there?" I asked.

"Yeah," Ronnie replied. "So, if you find yourself separated from me at some point, and you have the pack, don't forget about this. It will be critical to the success of the drug's replication."

"So, what happened to her?" I asked, curious as to how Ronnie could have avoided being identified as one of her contacts. "How did she get the data to you without you being exposed as well?"

Pausing and placing his hand on my shoulder, Ronnie avoided the question of what had happened to his friend, and instead explained, "I read a book once where the author said, 'every job you ever do should be to train you for something else, either for a promotion, or a new venture, something. Don't just sit there idly by collecting a paycheck and not putting what you do every day to some important use'. For example, if you're gonna be an HVAC technician, you should be using that time to learn the business from the ground up so you can go into business for yourself someday. Well, I've tried to live my life that way, and my time with the anti-terrorism unit, well, let's just say it provided me with a vast education that is now paying big dividends. I didn't just learn what my 'persons of interest' were doing, I dug deep and learned *how* they were doing it as well. Not only did that help me shine in that position, but it helped me to be able to put all of this together without ending up simply being another unplanned job vacancy."

He then added, "But as much as I may seem to have things nailed down tight, what I couldn't do was reach out and make contact with the right people on the outside from my office. We're just going to have to wing it from here."

Getting back to the task at hand, he said, "Get the truck warmed up and be ready to go. I'll be right back." He tossed me the keys as he turned and opened the back of the MRAP, pulling Hanson out and slinging him over his shoulder. He had just begun to shuffle toward the building when he paused and quickly waved for me to join him.

"What's up?" I asked, running to his side.

"I underestimated my injury. You're gonna have to help me," he grunted from the pain of supporting Hanson on his good side.

"Sure thing," I answered as I took one of Hanson's arms and helped pull him off of Ronnie's shoulder.

Hanson was unconscious and sweating profusely, but his breathing and pulse were strong.

With each of us holding him up with an arm under his, Ronnie held the ODF case in his free hand and gestured with his head, saying, "In there. Hurry."

We dragged Hanson through a set of unlocked double doors and into the building. "That way," Ronnie again instructed, gesturing down the hallway.

Reaching the bottom landing of a set of stairs that led up to the second floor, Ronnie grunted, "Up there."

Upon reaching the second level of the building, we traveled halfway down the hallway before Ronnie said, "In there. This will do."

Reaching out with my free hand, I turned the knob and opened the door to reveal a utility closet of some sort. "Are we just gonna leave him in here?" I asked.

"With the case," Ronnie quickly replied. "They'll find the MRAP any minute now, and the tracking device in the case will lead them here to him where he can begin to get the help he needs. They'll assume that we, or whoever they think took the case are in here, and they'll make a careful, deliberate entry into the building, clearing it as they go. That'll take a little time, allowing us time to be long gone before they put together an idea of exactly what went down."

As we carefully placed Hanson on the floor, Ronnie checked his vitals once more and whispered, "Sorry, bud. Good luck."

Turning to me with a serious expression on his face, Ronnie said, "Now, let's get the hell out of here while we still can. Go straight to the Tahoe and get her running. I'll be right there."

After I ran back down the stairs and out of the building, I climbed into the driver's seat of the Tahoe, started the engine and shifted the transmission into gear. Holding the brake with the transmission in gear and the engine running, I waited nervously for Ronnie. "C'mon! C'mon!"

Seeing Ronnie round the corner of the building, he ran up to the passenger door and quickly climbed inside. I immediately noticed that he, too, had changed out of his uniform and was wearing a pair of khaki work pants, hiking boots, and a black nylon jacket.

"Where to?" I asked.

"Just get us the hell out of here," he grumbled.

"Which way?" I asked again, not at all knowing what he had in mind.

"West!" he declared with a smile.

"That's kind of vague," I sarcastically replied.

"Yes, it is. Now, drive!"

"Whatever you say, Ronnie," I acquiesced as I pressed the accelerator and drove away from the construction site.

What seemed like only a few minutes later, several helicopters flew overhead at rooftop height in the direction from which we had just come.

"Looks like they're heading for the MRAP," Ronnie noted. "I'm surprised it took them this long. Not only did they know the exact time we should have arrived, but that case also had a tracking device built in."

"What did you do with Hanson?" I asked, remembering how he had stayed behind as I exited the building.

"I didn't do anything with him!" Ronnie exclaimed. "What, do you think I offed him after you left?" Shaking his head, he said, "He's still hanging in there. And like I said, I figured that would buy us some time while they track the case's location and make an entry. We'll be miles away by the time the building is cleared, and then Hanson will get the help he needs."

"Won't he be able to tell them everything? Who was in on it? They'll know what we did!" I exclaimed.

"Yes," he sighed. "He will, just as you or I would if we were in the same position. But I just couldn't kill him. He's an innocent. I had reconciled what was necessary with the others as they were, like I had explained, *all in* for the OWA, despite the evils that have been perpetrated on all of humanity. They were willing accessories to the guilty party. I can deal with that. But Hanson, he's just like us, before we really knew what was going on. He's just a guy who got caught up in it all."

"Did you know him?" I asked.

"Enough," Ronnie replied.

Opening the glove compartment, he handed me a pair of sunglasses and an old, well-worn Washington Nationals baseball team ball cap. "Facial recognition software," he said as he, too, donned a pair of glasses and a tan cap with a trucking company's logo embroidered on the front. "Keep your hat pulled down low. It will defeat facial recognition from cameras that are scanning from a downward angle. The glasses have a reflective coating on them that reflects NIR light, which will help from other angles."

"What the heck is NIR light?" I asked.

"Near Infrared," he explained. "It's light we can't see with our naked eyes, but when it's bounced off our glasses, it distorts the view of a camera, adding one more layer to our anti-facial recognition defense strategy. It won't be a big deal once we get out of and away from the city, but you know as well as I do, there's almost nowhere around here where you aren't being watched.

Impressed with his foresight, I nodded and said, "I'm glad you've put so much thought into this."

"I don't take committing treason lightly," he chuckled.

"So...," I asked with hesitation. "What's next in your plan?"

"Next?" he quipped. "We've got one more stop to make before trying to get out of town."

"What's that?" I asked, seeking a little more information than his vague statements were providing me.

"It's an impromptu stop. It wasn't really planned, but I had it in the back of my mind in the event one of us was injured," he explained. "An old friend of mine is handy with gunshot wounds. He was a Navy hospital corpsman... on the green side."

Seeing that I didn't exactly follow, he explained, "Fleet Marine Force. He was a Navy corpsman assigned to a Marine unit as a combat medic. This will be like putting a Band-Aid on a scratch for him. He's seen it all."

"Good," I replied. "Are you sure he's home? It is the middle of the day and all."

"He called off sick today," Ronnie said with a smile. "He felt like he was coming down with something."

"Gotcha," I grinned, again relieved that Ronnie had put so much thought into things.

After carefully driving through town, we began to reach the outer edges of the still-populated D.C. area, beyond which was a vast expanse of uncertainty that neither Ronnie or myself had much experience with, as we'd spent virtually all of our time since the collapse inside the safe confines of global government.

"Just up ahead," he grunted as the pain was beginning to take its toll on him. "Take a right. Here. This one."

Turning onto a street in a suburban neighborhood, Ronnie looked at his notes and said, "It's the third street down. Yeah, that's it. Wilshire Circle."

As we approached Wilshire Circle, he said, "Stop here."

I looked around the upper-middle-class neighborhood for signs of activity. All of the homes appeared to still be occupied. "They seem to be doing okay around here," I commented.

"Yeah, well, the people living here now aren't necessarily the people who lived here before," he explained. "My buddy is one of the few original occupants. He owns his place. The rest are loyalists who were given the homes of those who died or fled, as part of their compensation packages. Let's just say, he's not too fond of his new neighbors. He's a kindred spirit of both you and me."

"Who are we here to see?" I asked.

"You'll meet him soon enough. I'd rather you not have any beans to spill if our visit is stopped before we arrive."

Simply nodding in reply, both Ronnie and I exited the vehicle with our CX91 stocks folded, making them compact and concealable by our jackets.

With the backpack slung over his good shoulder, Ronnie mumbled, "Don't look around too much. Let's just fake a conversation while we walk."

Chuckling, I said, "It's funny how it's virtually impossible not to look suspicious when you're trying not to look suspicious."

"You're looking through the eyes of a seasoned cop. Things like that are more obvious to you than most," he replied. "There," he pointed. "The white house."

"That's where he lives?" I asked.

"Of course not," he chided. "What kind of fool would meet two fugitives wanted for treason in his own home? No, this place is supposed to be currently unassigned. My guy just happens to be the 'community manager' for the ODA's housing authority. To the average onlooker, it'll look like he's merely showing the place to a prospective resident."

As we approached the front door, Ronnie said, "We'll just knock and wait to be let in like everything is normal and routine."

Stepping up onto the porch, Ronnie reached out to knock on the door as it began to open before his knuckles even touched the glass. "It's good to see you, old friend," a voice said from within. "Come on in."

Once inside, a man who appeared to be of Native American descent quickly closed the door behind us. "Let me introduce you two gentlemen," Ronnie announced. "Hey You, this is Him. Him, this is Hey You. Any questions?"

Ronnie could see my confusion, and said, "I'd rather you two not know each other's details. I've seen one too many people crack under... um... interrogation, who never intended to speak. The less each of you know, the better."

Nodding that I understood, I followed the two men down the stairs and into the basement, where Ronnie's friend had an array of first aid supplies spread out on a folding table. "Who's hit?" the man asked.

"Me," Ronnie replied as he removed his jacket, revealing a blood-stained shirt underneath. "I think it went all the way through. It hurts like hell, though."

"Lucky you," the man chuckled. Looking me in the eye, he then said, "Hey You, why don't you go back upstairs and keep an eye out. This may take a while, and we don't want any surprises."

"Of course, Him. I'd be glad to," I said with a nod as I turned and worked my way out of the basement and up the stairs.

Once I reached the first floor, I took a seat on a chair by a window with a good view of the street. I unfolded the stock on my CX91, locking it into place, and positioned the weapon across my lap. Pulling the curtains back just enough to get a good field of view, I sat back and tried my best to calm my nerves as the events of the previous day and up until that moment flooded my mind.

I understood why Ronnie was being so secretive, and why he wasn't letting me in on such details as the name of the man who was helping us, but I couldn't help but worry if I was being used as a patsy. It would be easy for them to slip out while I kept watch, only to have the ODF's OSS surround the house, taking me out before I even knew what was going on. Any feeble attempt to defend myself against what would undoubtedly be an overwhelming force would give them the perfect cover to get away.

I didn't want to think that way, but I had to face facts. The guys that we took out in the MRAP didn't see themselves as disposable, either. They thought their mission was one thing, but in reality, they were pawns in Ronnie's game. Just because I believed in Ronnie's game, didn't mean I wasn't a pawn as well.

After what seemed like an hour of paranoid thought and worry, I heard footsteps coming up the stairs. I gripped my gun, preparing for the notification that my services were no longer needed, only to have Ronnie and his friend appear, both smiling and pleased by how things downstairs had gone.

"Are you about ready to get the hell out of here?" Ronnie asked.

"Absolutely," I replied.

The other man handed Ronnie a set of keys, and said, "It's a blue Toyota pickup truck with a matching fiberglass canopy on the back. You'll find it two blocks over. The tank is full, and there are four six-gallon gas cans in the back, as well as other provisions I thought you may find useful. I'll take care of the Tahoe. Did you leave anything important in it?"

Thinking it over for a brief moment, Ronnie answered, "Nothing we need, but you may want to scrub it."

"I'll take care of it," his friend assured him.

"Thanks," Ronnie said, reaching out to shake the man's hand.

Disregarding the handshake, the man leaned in and embraced Ronnie, giving him a hug. "Take care, old friend," he said. "What you're doing... it's... it's much bigger than anything any of us have done. I... I just don't have the words."

As they released each other, Ronnie looked him in the eye and said, "Thanks. And thanks for everything. You're a big part of this, too. If it all works out, whether I make it or not, well, you'll know you were key to making it happen."

The man then turned to me and said, "Take good care of Ronnie. He'll push himself too hard if you let him. He needs to heal up. We're all counting on you. Even people who don't realize it just yet need you to succeed."

"I will," I said as my paranoid fears began to wash away.

Ronnie patted his friend on the shoulder, then turned and walked out the front door, saying, "Let's get going," as I nodded to his friend and dutifully followed along behind.

Chapter Five

Walking down the sidewalk of the abnormally well-kept suburban neighborhood, I couldn't help but think of the alternate universes that existed, now that the OWA had seized control of the governments of the world. If you're loyal to the cause, and they continue to find your loyalty of use, you'll live in a nice neighborhood surrounded by other loyalists. You'll eat well, receive medical treatment, and most importantly, you'll receive your regular dosage of the lifesaving medication needed to fight off the virus they themselves inflicted upon the world.

In the world's other reality, if you're either deemed to be unimportant to the OWA, or you stand against them and what they have done, you live in what is now a hell on Earth. Survivors outside of the comfortable, strictly controlled domain of the OWA face death if exposed to the virus, as well as a daily struggle against hunger, extreme poverty, and a lawless world where brutality is, more often than not, the only law they know.

The world... that other reality, was the one I was about to voluntarily step into. I had turned my back on the comfort and security I'd had in the D.C. area, as well as a career that had served me well and promised to keep the gravy train rolling on along. Like Ronnie, though, once I knew the truth, I just couldn't continue living a lie. My false enthusiasm and my contempt for the beast that was the OWA would've eventually betrayed me.

One day my coworkers would hear that I was no longer there and had been replaced. More than likely, not one of them would bat an eye at my disappearance. It was a comfortable prison without bars. It was a charade I couldn't keep up forever, and I wouldn't have been able to live with myself if I did. No, that dangerous, threat-filled world I was about to step into at least offered me one thing... redemption. I had served the beast, but if I could help bring it down, maybe I could respect myself again someday.

"There it is," Ronnie said, interrupting my internal rambling.

Looking ahead, I saw the blue Toyota pickup truck that Ronnie's friend had described. It was a mid-nineties extended cab with four-wheel drive. It had dark tinted windows, which would come in handy in trying to avoid being noticed, a bumper mounted winch and all-terrain tires.

Good choice, I thought, knowing that what lay ahead was all a mystery and that the additional capabilities it offered compared to the average car, may come in handy in ways we may not yet foresee.

Turning and tossing the keys, Ronnie said, "Here, Joe. You drive. My shoulder is killing me, and the pain meds he gave me are starting to go to my head."

"Sure thing," I replied as I reached out and caught the keys.

Reaching the truck, I unlocked the driver's side door with the key as Ronnie patiently waited on the passenger side. Once inside, I leaned over and unlocked his door because this particular model was economically equipped, with no power locks or power windows. It was powered by the base-model four-cylinder engine mated with a five-speed manual transmission. It was so bare-bones simple it didn't even have air conditioning.

"At least it's an extended cab," Ronnie said as he reclined the passenger seat. "I can barely fit in a regular cab Toyota of this vintage. Not comfortably, anyway."

As I pushed in the clutch and turned the key, the 2.7L four-cylinder engine came to life, quickly idling down and purring like a kitten. "Which way?" I asked.

"West!" Ronnie again proclaimed as he pulled his hat down over his eyes as if he was settling in for a nap.

Exhaling, I conceded, "Okay, then." With that, I released the clutch, and we began the next phase of our journey.

I opted to take the smaller roads, avoiding interstate highways, knowing that it would be much easier to duck on and off the road as needed on the more rural routes than a freeway with limited onramps and exits.

After a while, all was going well as I drove down Lee Highway in Fairfax County. Hearing Ronnie snort and cough himself awake, I asked, "How are you holding up over there?"

"Ah, man. How long was I out?"

"About a half an hour," I replied. "I've seen a few drones flying overhead, but that's to be expected."

"Where are we?" he asked.

Pointing up ahead, I said, "We're on Lee Highway in Fairfax County, heading toward Willow Springs."

Raising his seat back, he looked around and said, "We're nearing the edge of what can be best described as the civilized area. Another half hour down the road and we'll no longer be in the OWA's preferred real-estate. With most of the resources being devoted to the OWA's strongholds, the rest are left to fend for themselves."

"What about access to the anti-viral treatment drugs? Does that stop as soon as we cross out of their controlled area?" I asked, wondering how people in the area could still be alive without them.

"Remember, not everyone out there is infected," he explained. "The ones who keep to themselves, avoiding contact with others. That makes them dangerous to you and me. They'd just as soon shoot us as look at us. They don't want to be infected, and they'll do whatever it takes to avoid contact. The ones who are infected are either dying or have found a way to be useful to the OWA.

"The OWA does have a few locations scattered around the country where the drug is available. They don't really care about the well-being of the folks lucky enough to receive treatment, they just want the OWA to continue to be seen by the unwashed masses as the great savior. The things that you and I are both aware of aren't necessarily common knowledge."

Looking up into the sky, Ronnie said, "There's a drone right there."

Seeing an ODF marked patrol SUV up ahead sitting on the shoulder of the oncoming lane, I pointed and asked, "What do you think?"

Looking the vehicle over and thinking about it for a brief moment, Ronnie declared, "Could be something... Could be nothing. We'll find out soon, I guess."

"I've got a bad feeling," I declared as my heart began to race.

"Turn left, there," Ronnie urged, pointing toward Summit Drive which led into a quaint, suburban neighborhood. "If something's up, we'll find out and maybe keep a little distance between him and us in the meantime."

Turning off of Lee Highway and onto Summit Drive, Ronnie watched the patrol vehicle as he held his CX91 carbine across his lap.

"What's he doing?" I impatiently asked.

"Nothing just yet."

I looked straight ahead as I drove, watching for threats up ahead while Ronnie kept his eye on the patrol vehicle that was now behind us and to our right.

"Ah, hell," he grumbled. "He's on the move. Something's up."

"Damn it!" I growled as I hit the steering wheel with my fist. "I knew this had all gone too easily so far. The other shoe had to drop eventually."

"It's okay. Just keep driving like normal," Ronnie said in a calming voice.

My heart raced, and my palms began to sweat, "Well?"

"He's going on by," Ronnie said with relief in his voice.

As I began to relax, he said, "No... wait. Shit. He stopped. He's backing up. Damn it. He's coming."

"Lights! Damn it! Drive, Joe! Drive!" Ronnie shouted as the patrol vehicle's lights began flashing, and the siren began whaling.

I shoved the accelerator to the floor as the anemic little four-cylinder...well, it didn't do much. Downshifting, I bounced the engine of the little truck off the tach's redline as we sped through the neighborhood with the patrol vehicle gaining on us rapidly.

"Go, Joe! Go!" he again shouted.

"I am, Ronnie! That's all this thing's got!"

Rounding the bend to the right, I got a view of the rest of the road, and my heart sank when I realized it went right back to where we had started. "It's a damn loop!"

Seeing another ODF vehicle enter Summit Drive up ahead, I realized they had us trapped. Thinking quickly, I reached down and pulled the truck's transfer case shifter into four-wheel high and yanked the wheel hard to the right, flooring the accelerator and crashing through one of the many decorative white picket fences that adorned the quaint little neighborhood that once represented a Norman Rockwell style of Americana.

As I turned the truck ninety-degrees to the vehicle directly behind us, Joe raised his weapon and began firing out the passenger's side window, sending a barrage of 6.2-millimeter rounds into the windshield of the pursuing vehicle. "It's them or us!" he shouted, as if needing to justify his actions, perhaps feeling the guilt of opening fire on those who just this morning were seen as his brothers-in-arms.

As the SUV swerved off the road and crashed into a child's swing set, it was clear his well-placed shots had reached their intended target.

With the other vehicle that was now to our left still in pursuit, I steered the truck toward the narrow gap between two of the cookie cutter houses, tearing through yet another fence as we went.

"We're not gonna make it, Joe!" Ronnie shouted as we sped between the tight confines of the homes, breaking off the side-view mirrors as we narrowly maneuvered through the gap.

Clearing the houses, I immediately turned left, crashing through more decorative white picket fences and back onto the section of Summit Drive that we had used to enter the neighborhood.

As the second pursuing SUV attempted to follow us, the vehicle slammed itself between the two houses, crumpling the sheet metal of the fenders and doors as it wedged itself firmly in place, ending the pursuit.

"Hot damn, Joe!" Ronnie shouted as he slapped himself on the thigh in disbelief. "Talk about a square peg in a round hole! Nicely done. Nicely done, indeed," he said with a smile as he pointed up ahead. "Now, let's get the heck out of there and find us some new wheels. Every ODF officer out there will be looking for this truck a few minutes from now."

"That way," he said, pointing toward a side street on the right.

As I drove, Ronnie's demeanor shifted from elation to regret. "I had to do it, Joe. You know that, right?"

Glancing over to him with a nod, I said, "Yeah, Ronnie. I know. If we were in their shoes, running with the information they had, we'd have put our lives on the line to stop the threat the same as they did. We'd have followed our orders, and the information we were given, to our graves if need be. We've all got a choice. They made their choice, and we made ours."

"Yeah, I know, Joe. I know, but it still doesn't make it feel any better. I mean, that officer could have been an outstanding guy. Many are."

"He could have also been *all in*," I reminded him, attempting to get his mind off of the death of the pursuing officer and back to the business at hand.

"There," he said, pointing to a minivan parked on the side of the road. "Let me out here. I'll meet you somewhere along the side of the street on down the road to transfer our gear and supplies. I don't want to do it right here in front of the house where its owner likely resides."

"How are you going to get it started?" I asked.

"I've got a few gadgets that'll come in handy," he assured me with a forced smile.

Stopping and letting him out as requested, I watched him approach the minivan through the rearview mirror as I drove away. Glancing over to the passenger seat, I noticed his special backpack was still in the floor. *He sure must trust me,* I thought.

Pulling over next to a cluster of trash cans, I parked underneath a poorly maintained willow tree whose uncontrolled growth had caused it to reach beyond the boundaries of the yard from which it grew, creating a nice visual cover from prying eyes in the sky. After taking a good look around, I shut the truck off and reached over and grabbed Ronnie's pack. I then exited the vehicle and walked to the back of the truck, ready to begin transferring our supplies as soon as Ronnie arrived.

Within just a few minutes, I looked up to see the champagne-gold Dodge Caravan rounding the corner with Ronnie behind the wheel.

Pulling up alongside the Toyota, Ronnie popped the rear liftgate of the minivan and hopped out with the engine still running. "Let's make this quick," he said as we began transferring the plastic totes full of supplies and provisions that Ronnie's pal had left in the truck for us.

Once it had all been transferred, Ronnie said, "You drive. You've done a bang-up job so far. There's no reason to change things up now. Besides, my shoulder is starting to hurt like hell."

Sitting down in the minivan and adjusting the driver's seat, I noticed a cable running from underneath the dash and to a black box with a small keypad and an LCD display lying in the floor.

"What's that?" I asked.

"That's my key," he said with a chuckle. "The new onboard diagnostics they were putting on these things had a few hidden features that the powers-that-be insisted be included by the manufacturers, all of which were kept quiet from the consumer, of course."

"Of course," I replied sarcastically.

"Big business and big government collusion goes way beyond the pharmaceutical industry," he added. "For far too long, self-serving government officials had been forcing companies to go along to get along. The OWA's tentacles are everywhere."

"Doesn't a car this new have satellite tracking?" I asked.

"I disabled that feature," he replied. "The government wants to track you, but they don't want to be tracked when running their own nefarious operations. Heck, I could use that magic box there to program the car to send false location signals, but that's something they could home in on if they wanted. There is a signature to such things that they can detect. They don't want to be fooled by their own con. No, I'd rather not transmit at all."

"If they can home in on false location signals, what's the point?" I asked.

"The point is, they want to be able to connect all the dots they want when setting someone up to take a fall, or to be ousted from office by something scandalous. They can plant a false breadcrumb trail, showing someone they aim to take down at the scene of some crime or compromising situation. They can tell it's fake, but we can't. If we sent a false location signal, it might throw the local ODF patrol officers off, but the ones who pull their strings could see right through it. You see, they need to be able to fool their own lower-level officers who'd be writing the reports and doing the footwork of the investigations. With not everyone being all in, their cons need to run deep."

Shaking my head in disgust, I grumbled, "The more I learn, the more I feel like a fool for being a part of it all for as long as I was."

"That's why I picked you, Joe. You're the real deal. That's a quality that's becoming harder and harder to find."

After driving for what felt like the next half hour, we passed a sign that read, *You are now leaving a level 2 secure zone. Travel from this point forward is at your own risk. Emergency services will not be provided.*

"Well, here we go," he said. "Off into the great unknown. You know, I've not been anywhere less than a level 2 secure zone since the outbreak began. Heck, most of the time, I've been comfortably inside a level 1 zone. I've definitely not been to anything even close to the no-go zone."

The no-go zone was what the OWA called the areas outside of their immediate control. With such a drastic loss in populations around the world, they simply couldn't adequately rule or control every square inch of it, so they chose to focus their resources in areas where the survivors who required their regular dose of Symbex could be easily cared for, monitored, and put to work.

Chuckling, I said, "Me, too. That's sad, huh? We were safe and sound while everyone out here was suffering and dying. And at the hands of those who fed us and kept us safe."

"What's sad is that the world ever got to the tipping point in the first place, Joe. That blame rests on each and every one of us. It rests on every person who turned a blind eye to corruption in support of their own flavor of partisan politics, every person who voted for them, and every person who simply didn't bother themselves with being more involved with the world around them. You and I couldn't help where we were when it all started. We were in the belly of the beast from the get-go. The way you have to look at it is, our time serving the OWA kept us alive and got us prepared for the mission we're on today. It put us where we needed to be, when we needed to be there. Don't second guess your life. You're doing the right thing now. That's all that matters."

I nodded, understanding what he'd said, but it didn't make it any easier to accept. I had literally been serving the Empire as a stormtrooper. I was like that guy, FN-2187, or Fin, who had finally realized he was on the wrong team, and was now on the run, trying to earn his self-respect back. Now, all I needed to do was find the rebellion.

Chapter Six

Once we were past what remained of Warrenton, Virginia, everything began to look like a scene straight out of a post-apocalyptic film. Many of the homes appeared to have been burned to the ground, and the others looked simply abandoned. Did they burn the homes of the infected? Or was it more of the collapse of our once great and peaceful society that caused conflict on nearly every level, leaving formerly quaint and picturesque neighborhoods looking like a third-world war zone, or a scene from a zombie apocalypse film.

"It's getting late," Ronnie said. "We need to find a place to hunker down for the night and get some rest. Who knows what tomorrow, or any day ahead of us for that matter, will bring? We need to stay on our game the best we can."

"What did you have in mind?" I asked.

"There seems to be plenty of houses available. I've not seen signs of habitation in a few miles now. I saw chimney smoke from one place on the outskirts of Warrenton, but that's about it. I'd say just about any of these homes that remain standing would fit the bill. Let's find one with a garage so we can hide the van."

"Good idea," I said. "This thing will stick out like a sore thumb."

"Tomorrow we'll try to find something else. Something that blends in with the no-go zone a little better."

Chuckling, I said, "Yeah, the soccer-mom minivan doesn't quite go with the area. Something straight out of Mad Max would fit in a little better."

"Turn here," he said, gesturing toward a driveway off the right side of the road.

I could see that the driveway led to a small house nestled in the trees, with overgrown landscaping all around, providing us with a fair amount of natural visual cover.

Picking up his CX91, he added, "Hold up here. Let me check it out on foot, first. When I get out, get yourself turned around so if something goes sideways, you can get our precious cargo out of here."

I brought the vehicle to a stop and Ronnie stepped out, holding his carbine at the low ready. Once he was clear, I began to maneuver the minivan to be in a position to get away in a hurry, as he had recommended. I watched as Ronnie carefully worked his way up the tree line toward the small, single-story home.

There were no signs of occupation, but that may be just what someone else wanted others to believe. The driveway was littered with clothes and other small items as if the house had been plundered and looted in the past. It looked as if everything had been laying out in the weather for quite some time, and from my vantage point, I could see that one of the main front windows in the home had been broken and had not been repaired. *Surely, if someone was living there, they'd have covered that large hole up in some way,* I reasoned.

I watched as Ronnie disappeared behind the home' *I guess he's gonna use the back door,* I thought as I picked up my own CX91 from the floor, placing it across my lap.

A few moments later, I saw the garage door begin to rise, followed by a view of Ronnie's legs as he lifted it by hand. Once the door was raised, he waved me in, urging me to back the minivan inside.

Once the van was parked, I exited the vehicle, and Ronnie closed the roll-up garage door by hand, leaving the small windows in the door to be the only light source as the last rays of the day's light shone through. The light illuminated a nebulous cloud of dust that swirled around the garage. The thick layer of dust that covered virtually everything had clearly not been disturbed in quite some time.

"This place will do," he announced. "There aren't any signs of recent activity, and the original occupants are clearly not with us anymore."

"What makes you say that?" I asked.

"Just don't go in the bedroom on the left at the end of the hall."

"Why?" I again asked. "What's in there?"

"Just take my word for it," he urged.

Nodding, I joined him at the rear of the minivan as he began removing the plastic storage bins filled with our supplies. "Let's take this stuff inside with us. We need to go through it all to see what we've got to work with."

Entering the living room through the side door of the garage, Ronnie said, "Let's put everything on the kitchen table. We can go through it there."

I should have left well enough alone. But I felt as if there was some sort of a force, like a giant magnet, pulling me toward the room where Ronnie had advised me not to go. Maybe it was morbid curiosity? Maybe it was some childish feeling that I didn't need Ronnie to shield or protect me from anything? Who knows? I just know it felt as if I couldn't help myself. I felt like I had to see, whatever it was, with my own eyes.

As I began walking down the hallway toward the bedrooms, I looked at the family pictures hanging on the walls.

Somehow, even though the home had clearly been looted and ransacked, with what was at one time, someone's personal possessions strewn about, the pictures on the walls remained untouched. Perhaps the looters weren't the sort of looters one would think of, taking advantage of the vulnerable after a tragic event or disaster. Perhaps they were just like the rest of us, doing what they had to do to survive, and respected the memories in those photos.

The photos represented a snapshot in time when our relatively safe and modern society was, for the most part, sheltered from the hellish conditions some people faced around the world every day. The pictures contained what was clearly a loving family. There was a father, a mother, and two small children, a boy and a girl, that seemed to age before my eyes as I walked down the hallway. I could watch the children grow from infants to toddlers, and then to adolescents, by merely following the story the photographs seemed to tell so vividly.

Seeing the love and happiness on the faces of the children in the photos filled my mind with apprehension about satisfying my curiosity of what could be found in the room. At this point, I really didn't want to see what was inside, but I felt as if that decision was being made for me. I was being pushed toward the room.

"Joe," Ronnie said softly from behind me.

Pausing for a moment, I declared, "I know," before continuing toward the door.

Once I reached the door, I stared at the knob with dread. As my hand reached for the knob, I could visibly see it trembling. Somehow, I knew I wouldn't be the same after I looked inside. My life had been a good one. I'd worked hard and lived a comfortable, reasonably successful life, and for the most part, had avoided the pain, suffering, and heartache that many had been forced to endure. I had lost my parents to lung cancer, which was something that could be seen coming from a long way off. I hadn't faced the level of suffering and misery that so many had. Up until now, my emotions had been spared the sudden, agonizing loss of a family member.

I looked to my left and saw Ronnie watching me from the living room. He exhaled and gave me a nod as if he understood why it was that I needed to face what was on the other side of the door.

I slowly turned the knob and pushed the door open. The hinges creaked as the door slowly swung open to reveal what was evidently a child's bedroom. It was a girl's room—probably belonging to the young girl in the pictures lining the hallway. My eyes scanned the room that was now barely lit by the sunset through the dust-covered windows. I could see light dancing around the room from the setting sun shining through the branches of the mature trees that surrounded the home.

As I stepped into the room and looked to my right, around an elaborately adorned antique wardrobe painted white with stickers of pink unicorns and puppies and kittens of various types scattered across the front, I froze in my tracks. My eyes fell on the decayed body of what appeared to be an adult male sitting on the floor, leaned against the wall and slumped over against the white, antique child's bed.

The corpse appeared to have suffered severe head trauma, a gunshot wound, no doubt. The wall behind the body contained the splatter of old blood stains and damage to the drywall that would be consistent with an injury from a bullet as it had exited the man's skull.

I looked around the body and saw no weapon. I knew that's the one thing the looters wouldn't have left behind. Even if they had respect for the former occupants of the home, a handgun that had somehow escaped confiscation after the prohibition on personally owned weapons had been enacted, would be far too valuable to leave behind in this horrid new world.

As my eyes left the corpse and looked to the bed next to him, I could see the silhouette of a young girl beneath a white sheet. My heart sank as tears welled up in my eyes. I could now paint the scene clearly in my mind.

The girl, no doubt the light of her father's life, had succumbed to the Sembé virus. She'd died with her father by her side, and it was more than he could bear. My heart ached. I couldn't imagine such a loss. I couldn't imagine mustering the desire or strength to go on after such a devastating, soul-crushing moment.

I had always wanted children, but it just never seemed to come. I had never had a relationship that felt solid enough, or right enough, to settle down and have a family. I had always felt as if something was missing in my life. Perhaps that something was a hole that needed to be filled by the love of a family.

Today, though, I was glad I didn't have to suffer through the agony of such a terrible loss. The pain and suffering that millions of people all over the globe had faced in the wake of the Sembé virus.

My heart quickly turned from pain and sadness to rage and hatred. This scene was a scene that had no doubt played out all across the world as families had watched their loved ones die from the horrible fate brought on by the virus—the virus that had been intentionally inflicted upon the world by the OWA.

I stormed out of the room to see Ronnie standing there in the hallway, waiting for me. He reached out his hand and placed it on my shoulder as I struggled to contain my emotions. I had never felt such rage, such hatred.

"Joe," he said in a soft, caring voice. "This is why we're doing what we're doing. If we can help the ones out there who are left to avoid such losses and potentially break the OWA's stranglehold on humanity's future..."

"I know," I said, trying to shake off the dark cloud that was now hanging over my head. "Where are the others?" I asked. "The others from the pictures."

"I found what appears to be two graves in the back yard. The mother and the son must have gone first, leaving the father and his little girl behind. When the girl passed, it was probably too much for the father to take. She was probably all he had left to live for. She was no doubt his very reason for being, and without her..."

"Yeah," I whispered, wiping a tear from my eye.

Chapter Seven

The rest of that evening was mostly spent in silence. Ronnie and I sifted through the gear and provisions provided by his friend, with only the occasional word spoken between us. I had heard about the horrors of the world outside the OWA's safe areas, and I had thought I'd come to grips with it all. After seeing the heartbreaking scene down the hall, though, it all came back on me like a ton of bricks.

I felt claustrophobia setting in, although I had never had such a phobia before. I felt as if the world around me was squeezing me, preventing me from breathing or escaping. A psychiatric professional would have probably had a good multi-word diagnosis for how I felt that night, but I was at a loss. Throughout the roller coaster of anxiety and the feeling of total helplessness, the one thing I never felt was futility. Not once did I feel as if there was nothing that I could do. Not once did I regret hitching my horse to Ronnie's wagon and undertaking this crazy, suicidal mission to break the OWA's grip on humanity. The realization of that little fact helped me press on through the darkness I felt around me.

Using a small flashlight he had brought along, Ronnie made a makeshift lamp, using a semi-transparent cloth to muffle and soften the light. He didn't want the full-strength beam of a flashlight to inadvertently give away our position to anyone who may be observing the home. When he was happy with the amount of light being omitted, we began sifting through the gear and provisions left in the Toyota for us by Ronnie's friend, the medic.

Once we had finished sorting and inventorying our supplies, we had tallied up a month's worth of MREs, if we ate only two meals per day, that is. They had expired, but as Ronnie put it,

"They'll keep us alive… hopefully. Besides, they probably put bogus expiration dates on them just so the government would have to buy more."

In addition to the MREs, there was a reasonably complete first aid and trauma kit for each of us. We had several lighters, four cans of Sterno fuel for campfire-free/smokeless cooking, two changes of clothes for each of us. The clothing consisted of mostly natural greens, browns, and tans, socks and all. There were also two lightweight day-pack backpacks, two all-weather sleeping bags, and two solar rechargeable flashlights.

He had also provided us with a nice pair of Vortex Kaibab 18x50 high-power binoculars. Those would definitely come in handy during the journey to help us gather intel, as well as helping us to avoid walking into unnecessary danger.

On the more exotic end of the spectrum were several jewels that made us feel as if we had indeed hit the jackpot, at least the jackpot for folks who were on the run, that is. Ronnie's friend had provided us with a Pulsar thermal monocular, as well as several extra battery packs and a portable, solar recharging setup, along with a Faraday bag to store it in and protect it from the OWA's electromagnetic weapons systems capabilities.

The grand prize, of course, was a pair of Glock 22 pistols chambered in .40S&W that were both former police service pistols from before the collapse, as well as a classic World War II vintage M1 Garand.

It had been quite some time since either Ronnie or I had handled conventional firearms. Once the OWA had banned the possession of private arms and weapons, using Symbex as leverage to get people to follow through with their ordered surrender, all we had seen were the newer, advanced weapons platforms such as our CX series weapons manufactured by Global Defense Industries (GDI).

I remember watching Ronnie pick up one of the Glocks, staring at it like a kid who was in awe of his new toy. "Man, I've not seen one of these in years," he said. "Not since we carried them with the Capitol Police, that is."

We both reacquainted ourselves with the manual of arms of the classic law enforcement handguns, and placed them in our day packs, along with three magazines and two fifty-round boxes of ammunition, and then moved on to the Garand.

"My grandfather used to own one of these beauties," I said as I held the rifle, admiring its classic lines while checking its condition and function. "This one was made by International Harvester."

"The tractor company?" he asked.

Chuckling, I explained, "Yes, the tractor company. During World War II, America's manufacturing might was called to arms. GM made airplanes. Ford made tanks. Hell, even IBM and the Smith-Corona typewriter company made rifles. IBM manufactured M1 carbines, and Smith-Corona manufactured M1903 bolt actions."

"How do you know all of that?" Ronnie asked, looking at me as if he had just met me for the first time.

"I've always been an unofficial history buff—mostly military stuff. WWI, WWII, the Civil War, you name it. I'd have been a gun collector if I hadn't lived in D.C. where such things weren't allowed."

"What the heck is this?" Ronnie asked, holding up one of the Garand's enbloc clips.

Taking it from him, I explained, "That's the clip. Just like the name implies, it's just a metal clip that holds eight rounds of .30-06 cartridges in place. The spring-loaded feeding system that's built into a weapon's magazine these days is housed internally in the rifle itself."

Holding the rifle in front of myself, I locked the charging handle back and demonstrated, "Hold the clip in your hand like this, with the blade of your hand against the charging handle. Shove the clip into the rifle with your thumb like this, ensuring that you hold back the charging handle with the blade of your hand, then release."

After the bolt slammed forward, I said, "If you don't guard the charging handle like that, it'll bite you, and you'll get what they called *Garand thumb*."

Continuing, I said, "These things may be ancient technology, but even with mere iron sights, they shoot true out further than most people can see well enough to aim. They'll do what you need them to do, and they'll do it well. These are from the days of the main battle rifle when hard-hitting bullets were fired at distances of hundreds of yards, long before CQB was even a term. And best of all, they don't need batteries."

Handing the rifle to Ronnie, I watched as he went through the motions of the Garand's unique loading procedure. "I can see how this thing could really bite you," he commented.

"Where do you think your friend got these?" I asked.

"I imagine he had them buried somewhere, expecting a day like this to come when he needed to retrieve them.

"Of all the weapons to squirrel away, why an old relic like this?" Ronnie wondered aloud. "I mean, there were a lot of really cool rifles out there before the ban."

Pondering his question for a moment, I guessed, "I'd imagine it was easier for him to give up a few cookie cutter rifles than a war hero and a classic such as this. Just imagine turning over something that has gone through a world war like this rifle has, only to have it destroyed and melted down."

"I imagine you're right," he said.

"How much ammo did he give us for it?"

Quickly counting five twenty-round boxes, I said, "One hundred."

"That's not much," he complained.

"Yes, it is," I countered. "This stuff hits pretty hard on both ends. You won't be rapid firing it very often. That, and you'll only need to hit each guy once with it."

Once we had finished the tasks at hand and had all of our gear packed away and ready to go at a moment's notice, Ronnie said, "We need to get some rest. The sun will be up soon, and we'll have another long day ahead of us. Let's take shifts. I'll take first watch."

"Nonsense, Ronnie," I protested. "You're nursing a wound. I'm not. Get yourself some rest before it gets the best of you. I'll wake you in a few hours, and we'll swap."

Looking me in the eye and seeing that I wasn't going to budge on the issue, Ronnie acquiesced and moved to the corner of the room, where he rolled out his sleeping bag and settled in for a much-needed nap.

Going through the gear had done a good job of distracting me from the dark cloud that had been hanging over me that night, but once Ronnie was asleep, snoring like a poorly tuned chainsaw, I couldn't help but think about the tragic scene frozen in time just down the hall.

Just as my mind started drifting back to that dark, dreadful place, I heard a noise that sounded as if it came from behind the house, just by the kitchen door.

With my senses now focused on the potential threat, all other thoughts vacated my mind. Hearing a faint, muffled sound, I thought, *was that whispering? Holy crap. It is. There's someone outside.*

Verifying the readiness of my CX91 carbine, I stood and started to sneak across the room toward Ronnie, only to realize his snoring may be exactly what I needed. Anyone with reasonable hearing would know someone was asleep inside the home. If I were to wake him, even if I kept him from speaking, they'd sense the change and would be on alert to our knowledge of them, or alter their plans. No, with Ronnie snoring away, they'd maintain the idea that they had the drop on us.

Being outside the safe zones, the threat could be any number of things. It could be a gang of thugs that laid in wait during daylight hours, observing people as they traveled through, only to launch their raid under cover of darkness, it could be someone desperate and hungry, or it could be the OSS, here to put an end to our two-man rebellion. Either way, this wasn't a good way to spend our first night outside the zones.

Hearing the back door knob rock quietly back and forth, I moved toward the kitchen counter and lay down in the prone position just below the sink. This would give me the best opportunity to take a shot while requiring the intruder to rotate all the way around the door to engage me, especially if they were right-handed; this would put them at a severe disadvantage. It would also reduce my visible profile to anyone trying to see in either the front or back windows while their counterpart made an entry.

As a figure entered the room, it was much too dark for me to see any detail. Once Ronnie laid down to take his nap, we had extinguished the small flashlight we had been using previously as a lamp, leaving only a trace of moonlight shining through the gaps between the curtains to illuminate the room.

Evidently, we hadn't done a good enough job with regard to our light discipline. The odds of someone merely stumbling across this house the same night as us were very slim. I didn't like this. I didn't like it one bit. Whoever was here more than likely knew we were in the home, which meant they were ready and willing to fight.

I felt like a bat using sonar to see. I was using the sounds of the soft, carefully placed steps of the intruder to estimate his position in the room. Once I was sure they were all the way inside, I carefully placed my left thumb on the button used to activate the weapon-mounted light built into my CX91, and flicked it on strobe, while shouting, "Down! Down on the floor! Now!"

Hearing the simultaneous scream of what sounded to be a young girl, and the sounds of Ronnie struggling to his feet in confusion, I could see through the intense strobes of disorienting light a small figure that was maybe five feet tall, acting confused and conflicted about what to do. I could tell whoever it was wanted to run, but was frozen in fear.

"Down on the floor, I said!" I again commanded, causing the figure to reluctantly comply.

"D...d...daddy," the figure stuttered, as what I now recognized to be a young girl lowered herself to the floor.

Hurrying to my side, Ronnie knelt and covered the girl with his carbine, saying, "What the hell, man?"

"There's at least one more outside," I said calmly. "She just called for her father, but that may be a ruse."

"Kick the door shut with your feet," I said to the young girl.

Once she had done so, I switched my light to the steady beam setting so we could get a good look at our intruder. Like I had suspected, it was a young girl who appeared to be no more than twelve or thirteen years old.

"Daddy!" she again shouted as she began to sob heavily.

"Are you infected?" I asked.

"N...no..." she replied.

"Well, we are, so you'd better keep your distance," I said in a calm, yet authoritative voice.

Avoiding exposing himself in front of the window, Ronnie attempted to look outside for the father the girl kept calling for. "Where is he? How many are with you?" Ronnie asked.

"It's just my dad and me," the girl replied, beginning to regain her composure.

"What are you doing here? Are you robbing us?" he asked.

"We... we're hungry," she said. "We've not eaten in several days. My father isn't doing well."

"Is he infected?" Ronnie asked.

"No," she replied.

"Then why isn't he doing well?"

"A few nights ago, we were robbed," she explained. "Daddy was beaten pretty bad. They took everything we had. They took the last of our food. We just want something to eat and a safe place to spend the night. That's all, I promise. We didn't know anyone was here."

"Tell him to show himself," Ronnie demanded.

After a moment of silence, he again insisted, "Look, if he doesn't show himself, we're going to assume you're lying and that you meant us harm."

"What kind of father sends his daughter ahead of him to scout for danger?" I whispered.

Merely grumbling in reply, Ronnie again demanded, "I'm not going to ask again."

"Daddy!" she shouted in a trembling voice. "Daddy, they want you to show yourself, or they'll hurt me."

"Now, that wasn't very nice," Ronnie said. "I never said such a thing. Is that to prompt him to take some sort of action against us?"

"Don't hurt her!" a voice shouted from the front yard of the home.

Turning toward the threat, Ronnie said, "You stay on her, I'll check this out."

Slipping through the room and doing his best to avoid the moonlight, Ronnie peeked at an angle through the window to catch a view of a man in his late thirties standing on the front lawn, appearing to be unarmed.

"Please, don't hurt her," he again asked in what sounded like a sincere voice. Whether that was rehearsed sincerity or not remained to be seen. "She's all I have left in this world. Just please, please don't hurt her."

"What kind of coward sends his daughter ahead of him?" Ronnie asked.

The man's head began to hang low. "Yeah, I'd be ashamed, too," Ronnie added.

Turning to me, Ronnie said quietly, "What do you think?"

"I think I don't want to shoot a young girl, that's what I think."

"Don't be blinded by preconceived notions of who the innocent are, Joe. That'll get you killed."

Looking back out the window, seeing that the man was still there, Ronnie shouted, "How many more are with you?"

The man quickly replied, "No one. It's just us. We didn't mean to intrude or to startle you. We're just looking for a place to spend the night, and were hoping to find something to eat."

"You won't find anything to eat around here," Ronnie replied. "You should know by now that waves of people have beat you to it. What are you really up to?"

"That's it, I swear," the man insisted. "Please, just let her go. I'll trade myself for her. Just take me, and let her go."

"Daddy, no!" the girl shouted.

"Quiet!" I demanded. "My friend and your father are having a polite conversation. Let them finish."

Thinking it over for a moment, Ronnie mumbled, "I don't like it, Joe."

"Me, neither, but I'm not shooting a young girl," I again insisted.

In an exasperated tone, Ronnie said, "Against my better judgment, let her go. Just let them go."

"Why is it against your better judgment?" I asked.

"It just doesn't feel right. But I can't argue with you. We can't turn to shooting children this early in the game. That's not who we are. You know it, and so do I. If we take any other action, that's liable to happen."

"Don't move!" Ronnie shouted to the father. "We're sending her out the front door. Don't move until she reaches you. When she does, both of you turn and walk away slowly. Don't be a fool and try anything else. There's nothing else for you here but heartache. That, I promise you."

"Yes. Yes, sir," the man said. "Thank you. Thank you, sir."

Turning to the girl, Ronnie said in a soft voice, "My friend there is going to cover you while you stand and walk across the room to the front door. I know he said he didn't want to shoot a young girl, but he'll choose me over you, trust me on that. Once you're up, walk across the room slowly and don't make any sudden or unexpected movements. If you or your father do anything to make us think we're making a mistake in letting you go, well, it won't end well for either of you. Do you understand?"

"Yes," she replied. "Thank you."

"Okay, then. Go ahead, get up."

The girl got on her knees and then slowly stood. She was trembling noticeably. I couldn't be sure if it was fear or hunger. Likely, it was a bit of both. She looked very worn and weathered for her age. The life she was living with her father had clearly taken its toll on her. It was a heartbreaking sight for me. I could picture her and her father, and what life must have been like for them before the Sembé virus tragically shook their world to pieces, stripping them of everything they had, and of their futures.

Like the horrific scene down the hall, they had likely lost other close family members and were all that remained for one another. Still, they were a threat to us. Desperate times called for desperate measures, and the current state of the world outside the zones was far beyond desperation. Everyone had to be viewed as a threat. It's simply how things were.

Once she reached the door, Ronnie said, "Stop. Stand right there and don't move."

I was confused by his order, but then saw him walk over to his pack and remove two of his MRE's. He then removed his medical kit and removed an anti-bacterial/anti-viral sterilization wipe, and cleaned the MRE's thoroughly.

He then walked over to the girl, being sure to keep his distance as best he could, and offered her the meals, along with several unopened packets of the sterilization wipes in her direction, holding onto them with the wipe he used still in his hand. "Take these. I cleaned them. They should be safe."

Reaching out and taking them, her voice trembled, and she said, "Thank you."

"Now, go. Go on out there to your father and get far away from here. Don't come back. There won't be more charity from us. Get away from us and then use the other wipes to clean your hands and any other part of your body that may have come in contact with anything in this house. Do you understand?"

"Yes," she said as she walked out the front door to her father.

Once the two were reunited in the front yard, they quickly turned and walked away, disappearing into the darkness.

"It's your turn to sleep," he said.

"Yeah, right," I replied. "Like I could go to sleep now."

Chapter Eight

The morning sun soon shone through the trees, illuminating the dust that danced on the breeze that flowed through the broken front window of the house once again.

"I don't think we should take the van," Ronnie said as he gazed out the window, using the edge of the wall as partial cover.

"Why?" I asked.

"Not after last night. We can't assume they were alone. We also can't assume others aren't around either. They could be from a larger group, sent as a probe. If that's the case, they'll be watching the house and us driving away in the minivan will make us sitting ducks. No, I think we need to slip out the back on foot and lose ourselves in the woods. We can try to find other transportation elsewhere. If we got in that minivan now, and simply drove right out of the garage, I'd feel like a soldier on D-Day watching the landing craft door open in front of him, expecting a barrage of machine-gun fire at any minute. No, it just doesn't feel right."

"Nothing feels right anymore," I replied. "Are you sure it's not just paranoia eating away at you?"

"Sometimes paranoia is well placed," he retorted.

Replying with merely a nod, I said, "Whatever you think, Ronnie."

With that, Ronnie slipped his arms through his daypack, wearing it on his back, while strapping his refrigerated pack on the front of his body.

"You carry the extra rifle, I'll carry the Symbex," he insisted. "You know your way around that old relic more than I do, anyway."

"Roger that," I replied, slipping my pack on and slinging the Garand over my shoulder while carrying my CX91 at the low ready in front of me.

Looking into the back yard of the house, I began to feel Ronnie's sense of dread come over me. "Damn you and that D-Day remark," I quipped. "You've got me paranoid now. How do you want to handle this?"

Retrieving the thermal monocular from his pack, Ronnie powered it on and scanned the area, "I wish I would have thought to use this last night when the girl and her father were here. I'm just not used to having it yet, I guess," he said as he scanned the area around the rear of the home.

"What do you see?" I asked. "Not much that looks alive," he replied. "A few small critters, but nothing that raises a red flag."

He then walked to the front of the home and surveyed the area lying in front of the house with the thermal monocular as well. "Ah, ha!" he reported.

"What?"

"Some sneaky bastard is hunkered down beyond those overgrown hedges."

"Is it the girl and her father?" I asked.

"I only see one heat signature big enough to be a person," he responded. Thinking it over for a moment, he decided, "Well, with nothing out back and a possible threat up front, I say let's both just go for it, running across the back yard simultaneously. You go left toward that big maple tree, and I'll go right past the swing set. Once we get into the cover of the woods, we'll meet back up. If we both bolt across the yard at once, if anyone is lying in wait, at least one of us will get through. If I go down, do whatever you have to do to get the Symbex."

"We should have left under cover of darkness," I replied.

"Six of one, half dozen of the other," he shrugged. "You could just as easily run into a knife in the dark as a bullet in the daylight. At least you can see and avoid this way. This monocular is great for surveying the area, but you can't really run with it, holding it up to your eye."

"You always put a positive spin on things," I said in jest.

"Whatever I can do to help," he replied with a grin. "The heat return out front definitely reassures my paranoia about just driving away from here," he added.

I wasn't sure if he was trying to convince himself, or if he was trying to reassure me. Either way, I didn't have a better plan. Up to this point, Ronnie had it all figured out. Now, though, it seemed as if we'd be making everything else up as we went.

"Let's go for it," I said reassuringly.

Positioning ourselves at the back door, I placed my left hand on the knob while holding onto the grip of my CX91 with my right. Ronnie placed his left hand on my shoulder while holding on tight to his carbine with his right hand as well.

"Good luck," he said.

"You, too, Ronnie," I replied. "On three. One... two... three!" I said as I turned the knob and made a break for it across the yard. Reaching the maple tree, I ducked behind it and turned to cover Ronnie as he disappeared behind the swing set and into the bushes.

Quickly scanning the area and seeing no threats, I began working my way through the woods further from the home while Ronnie did the same, working his way toward my position.

Meeting up approximately fifty yards behind the home, on the edge of the woods near the back yard of another house, Ronnie whispered, "See? That wasn't so bad. I don't know why you were so paranoid."

"Yeah, right," I said, rolling my eyes.

"What now, Captain Wilkes?"

Swatting me on the back of the head, he said, "Don't call me that anymore." Looking around, he pointed, saying, "Let's just work our way around this neighborhood through the trees. It almost seems as if they let a buffer of trees grow between the two subdivisions. The only drawback to that is we're probably not the only ones who'd choose to do so."

"I'll take point," I said, leaving my position of cover behind a tree and moving forward in the direction he suggested.

I had barely taken a few steps when a shot rang out behind me. I spun around quickly to see Ronnie falling forward. It seemed like it was all happening in slow motion. I could see the expression on Ronnie's face as he fell. It was one of shock, disbelief, and fear, all rolled into one. Over Ronnie's shoulder, I could see the man from the night before. He had evidently been hiding behind an overturned tree stump that, with the help of the thickly wooded area, had conveniently masked him and his daughter's heat signatures from our vantage point in the home. Once Ronnie had stepped past them and into the open, the father had fired an older revolver, striking him in the side between the packs.

I immediately raised my CX91 and fired several shots directly into his center of mass, knocking him backward and onto the ground. The girl's father was dead before he hit the ground from the very lethal 6.2x40mm cartridge.

Seeing the young girl go for her father's handgun, I shouted, "No! No! Don't..." but it was no use. The girl reacted like a crazed animal, going for the gun to either avenge her father or to finish the job in an attempt to get to whatever was in our packs. She was like a desperate animal, unlike any young teenage girl I had ever seen. My time in the zones had shielded me from such desperation, and it was more than my mind could comprehend or recognize.

Before I had a chance to process it all, my training overrode my thoughts, and I fired two more shots at the threat. Unfortunately, that threat was the young girl, who now lay dead before me, slumped over her father.

Quickly running to Ronnie's aid, I rolled him over just in time to hear his final words escape from his mouth, along with the sound of air escaping from between the frothing and gurgling wound in his side where the projectile had clearly entered his lung. With his eyes seeming to stare off into the distance behind me, he muttered, "Finish it..."

With no time to process it all, not knowing if there were others in the area, I quickly removed both of his packs and ran as hard as I could through the woods. I struggled to keep up the pace with both of his packs across my left arm, my CX91 in my right hand, and the Garand bouncing around, clanging into my carbine as I awkwardly tried to carry it all, as well as having my pack on my back.

I'm not sure how far I ran or for how long. After a few moments, the instinct to flee was replaced by rage. My run was now fueled by a total and complete state of fury. Not only had we let the girl and her father go the previous night, but Ronnie had given them food and took great care to prevent them from catching the Sembé virus from our contact with it.

I felt betrayed by my own feelings from the previous night. I had refused to accept the fact that a teenage girl could be a legitimate threat. I had refused to acknowledge or reconcile the fact that such a world could have driven people to such behavior. Perhaps I'd projected the plight of the father and daughter in the bedroom at the end of the hallway onto them. I'd wanted them to live. I'd wanted them to survive this hell, and someday help to rid the world of the OWA's monopoly on our life and death so they could rebuild their lives.

My emotions had betrayed me. My emotionally-guided view of reality had gotten Ronnie killed, and now I was on this ridiculous mission alone. With no plan at all—only some absurd idea that somewhere out there was a group of people I could reach who could put the anti-viral drug I now carried to good use and somehow save the world. Was that also some ridiculous, emotionally-guided fairy tale of a dream?

~~~~

The rest of that day was a blur to me. My body and my mind must have put themselves into protection mode. I know I must have been in some sort of shock. The face of the little girl that I had been forced to shoot haunted me. Her fragile little voice from the night before, calling out for her daddy, haunted me and echoed through my mind.

I had shot a young girl. She was just a child. I could rationalize the fact that she was presenting herself as a threat until I was blue in the face, but that wouldn't do anything to soothe my aching heart. All my life, I had been a pretty decent guy. But, how does a pretty decent guy shoot a child?

Throughout my tenure as both a police officer and an ODF security officer for the OWA, I had drawn my gun in the line of duty maybe five times and had only discharged it once. That's not to say I hadn't been involved in any in-the-line-of-duty shootings, but with multiple officers on the scene, not everyone has to fire.

The one and only time I'd had to use deadly force and discharge my weapon was during a hostage standoff situation at a local convenient store. It was a robbery gone wrong. A young man, who was more than likely following through with some sort of gang-related initiation ritual, attempted to rob a store and then proceeded to make a scene out of it. He couldn't keep himself from showboating around and trying to be seen as the one with the ultimate power over others, the power to choose life or death.

He taunted people, pointing the gun at the back of their heads, one by one, asking, "Should I choose you? Or you?" all with a few disrespectful expletives thrown around just to help him mentally beat his chest. Male, female, young, or old didn't seem to matter to him. His callousness and complete lack of regard for others was something straight out of a Hollywood movie.

His showboating had prevented him from getting away before we arrived on the scene, and once the pressure was on him, he began to break. His showboating and machismo quickly turned to fear-fueled, erratic behavior. He was on the edge, and we knew if we didn't do something quickly, some innocent person or persons would end up suffering the consequences of his actions.

We chose to make entry into the building and put an end to the situation before any of that happened. I was assigned to enter from the rear with Officer Miguel Rodriguez. Miguel and I were pretty close. I mean, well, we wouldn't have been the best man at each other's weddings or anything, but we were friends, and we had each other's backs.

Upon receiving the command to enter, Miguel went in first with me following closely behind. We quickly worked our way through the stockroom toward the storefront where the hostage situation was taking place. Unfortunately, the officers assigned to make entry through the front of the building rushed in before we were in position, forcing the suspect to turn and run toward the storeroom in our direction.

Just as Miguel began to pass through the door, the young man appeared with his Hi-Point .40 caliber pistol held sideways, and immediately began discharging the contents of his magazine in a very uncontrolled manner, sending bullets flying into two-liter soda bottles and bags of chips everywhere. It was a total spray-and-pray situation.

At some point during the spastic discharge of ammunition, Miguel was hit once in the vest, and once just above the vest, striking him in his throat just above his breast bone.

As Miguel fell in front of me, I immediately discharged several well-placed hammer pairs into the suspect, ending the situation.

I quickly turned my attention to my friend and was forced to watch him drown in his own blood as he gurgled and coughed, struggling to breathe. I didn't know what to do. It wasn't a simple case of CPR or a pressure application.

The officers making an entry in the front of the building quickly brushed me aside and began every attempt possible to save Miguel's life, but it was too late. He was dead before the building was adequately cleared to allow for the entry of the EMTs.

I was interviewed by the department's counselors and was briefed on the different stages of remorse I would likely feel for taking someone's life, but it never came. I actually was glad the man who shot Miguel was dead. He was clearly a threat to the community as a whole, and now that threat had been removed. I often wondered if something was wrong with me because I didn't experience the textbook reactions that I was told to expect. Was I just that cold-blooded and callous? Or was I satisfied with the feeling of revenge for killing the man who had killed my friend? I never really figured that one out.

This was totally different, though. The young girl wasn't some gang-banger wannabe out trying to compensate for a bad childhood or something by terrorizing the neighborhood. She was a young girl, caught up in a horrible situation—a situation created by those I served up until the day before.

Breaking the Beast

I'd imagine that as the world fell apart and people began to become hungry and desperate, many people who would have once been your beloved next-door neighbors, who you'd gladly have over for a backyard barbeque or birthday parties, had now become predators out of sheer desperation. If your children were hungry, and I mean painfully hungry and weak, you'd likely do just about anything to provide for them. Add to that the pain and mental anguish you may have already suffered by watching others in your family die. If you were down to one surviving family member, whether it was your parent or child, would you not do anything you could to provide for them? That's probably what had become of this girl and her father.

I'm not making excuses for what they did. They did, after all, kill my friend and partner, Ronnie. They chose to attempt to take from us to provide for themselves. I'm not sure I'd have been any different if I was outside the zones when it all went down. I'd like to think I would, but none of us could say that for sure.

Chapter Nine

After Ronnie's death, I kept my movements limited to the cover of darkness. I would sleep during the day and travel at night, using the thermal monocular after each bound of movement to clear the way in front of me of any threats. If I saw a heat signature that could have been seen as a threat, I simply altered my course. I chose not to encounter or engage anyone if I could help it.

Having learned a valuable lesson from Ronnie's death, I also didn't give the information gathered from the thermal imager as much credit as I would have previously. I used it as a tool but knew there were objects, as well as tactical methods, that could block or reduce a heat signature, especially for those who were intentionally trying to defeat such a technology. Let's face it. There were a lot of people out there these days that didn't want to be found, and they'd had time to get good at it.

It also seemed as if I wasn't the only one who had learned to travel under cover of darkness. Not only did I pick up signatures with the imager of people on the move at night, but I also noticed more drone activity in the skies during the night. The OWA clearly had picked up on this trend of nocturnal behavior as well. And luckily for me, as long as I could avoid the others, they helped me to blend in with the myriad heat signatures the drones were no doubt observing from overhead.

It had been almost three weeks since Ronnie had died. Steady travel had taken me all the way to the outskirts of Chattanooga, Tennessee. My daily goal had been to travel at least twelve hours per day, on a Trek hardtail mountain bike I had picked up in an abandoned neighborhood in the Charlottesville area.

Breaking the Beast

I traveled in a southwesterly direction for several reasons. First, it was almost November now, and the nights seemed to be getting cooler by the day. The last thing I wanted to happen was to freeze to death, ending my journey in a not-so-glorious manner. Tracking in a southerly direction while continuing to make westerly progress would help to mitigate that risk, as well as getting me more into the areas where I had heard of increased insurgent activity. The greater the likelihood I would encounter some sort of organized insurgency, the greater my chance of finding the people I needed to complete my mission. I was flying blind. I had a very vague, poorly defined game plan, with a clearly defined mission objective. It was like throwing a dart, blindfolded, needing to hit the bullseye, with the only certainty being that the dartboard is somewhere on the wall in front of you, but not knowing exactly where. But hey, play the hand you're dealt, right?

Why didn't I hotwire some abandoned car or truck you might ask? Well, I was on my own now. And without someone else to help keep an eye on the situation, I feared it would be far too easy for me to drive right into a trap or to be spotted by an OWA drone. There just weren't too many people driving motorized vehicles these days. I had seen a few, and each time they had piqued my interest and provoked me to observe them closely. I didn't want to be drawing that same level of attention. Besides, I really wasn't that far from D.C., and stealth would be crucial in successfully evading the beast that close to its lair.

The mountain bike also came in handy by allowing me to avoid roads at times. It was a lightweight model with an alloy frame that made it easy to pack or push when the terrain wasn't bicycle friendly. I had rigged both of our gear packs as a set of saddlebags, while keeping the refrigerated Symbex pack on my person at all times.

Near where I had found the bike, I found a kid's backyard playset that had a green canvas sunshade over what was a clubhouse at the top of the plastic slide. I removed the canvas material, rolled it up into a tube and tied the black nylon cord that used to secure it to the playset around it to form a fabric tube that would serve as a makeshift scabbard for the Garand.

With the batteries in my ODF-issued weapons having been depleted the week before, I had discarded them, now being armed with the Glock pistols and the relic M1 Garand rifle.

One of the Glocks resided at all times in my waistband, and I kept the other in the refrigerated pack. After all, you can't reveal all the cards in your hand at once. That, and I reasoned if I ever had to leave anything behind in a hurry, it wouldn't be that pack. It literally never left my back or my hands. Too much was riding on the contents of it to take any chances of being separated from it.

Chattanooga had been a milestone goal of mine. Reaching Chattanooga would put me on the other side of the Appalachian Mountains, giving my route of travel more flexibility. The mountains created several choke points if one were to travel by road that would make it far too easy to become trapped. Traveling by foot and with the mountain bike gave me the ability to travel overland, avoiding those choke points.

The Trek had served me well, but based on the time it had already taken to get that far, I was ready for a change. I was ready for something that would allow me to log a few more miles each day, and also allow me to get a little much-needed rest while doing so.

Chattanooga sits just west of the Nantahala and Chattahoochee National Forests, marking the end of most of the difficult terrain. There was ridgeline between Chattanooga and me, though. It was located right around Collegedale. It wasn't really part of the mountain range but was a remnant of plate tectonic from long ago that created them. The ridge would serve me well as a position of elevation, allowing me to observe the city for a while before proceeding.

I decided to set up camp under a cluster of trees near the top of the ridge. The location provided adequate elevation for my observational purposes, while also providing visual cover from above, in particular, drones with optical sensors. My heat signature would still be observable to the drones, but I hoped the trees would diffuse my heat signature enough to at least mask the fact that I was a human, even if my presence could still be detected by those technological demons. It's funny, all that weapons technology development seemed like a good idea back when we thought it would only be used against others.

Every time I would set up camp, I treated my precious cargo of Symbex like a backpacker in grizzly country handles their food. The first and most important thing is to keep it as far away from you as possible during the night. Bears have a great sense of smell, and that packet of tuna in your bag is going to send them your way. At night, while you're asleep, you don't want to be cuddled up in your tent with your tuna.

Many hikers would either use a bear can, which is a bear-proof container to put their food inside and stash it a reasonable distance from their camp, or use a bear bag, which is essentially running your food up and over a tree branch with a length of rope or chord.

Now, I wasn't hiding from bears, mind you, so I didn't really need to run it up a tree like a flagpole, but I wanted the Symbex in a safe place should I be stumbled across while I slept. I wanted to be able to potentially talk myself out of a situation if that were to occur, and having one of the most precious items on earth with me at the time would surely make that hard to do. A lot of good people would do bad things to get their hands on that stuff, and I wasn't about to take any chances.

After I had selected my campsite, I would scout the general area for a good place to conceal the Symbex pack. I would hide it, cover my tracks, and then take the extra solar charger and battery pack back to camp with me to charge while I slept during the day. If anyone who happened to cross my path enquired about that, I would simply clump it together with my other devices, such as the thermal, as an explanation. If they stole the thermal, so be it, but I couldn't let them take the Symbex at any cost.

Once I had settled in for the day, I began to glass the area west of my position looking for movement. Though not a large city by NYC or LA standards, Chattanooga had been a bustling town before the collapse, and I assumed that surely some sliver of humanity had remained.

After several hours of steady observation, and having seen no activity, I decided to rest my eyes for a while and take a nap. Lying face down, I simply placed the binoculars off to the side, rested my head on my arm, and my consciousness quickly gave way to fatigue and absolute exhaustion.

~~~~

Awakened by the sudden, harsh jab in my back, I attempted to reach for my pistol as a boot landed on my wrist, with another immediately pinning my head to the ground.

I knew better than to struggle or fight. I was outnumbered by at least a few men who had gotten the drop on me as I slept.

With what I could only assume was a rifle barrel being jammed into my back, I relaxed and awaited the instructions of my captors. The boot on the back of my head began to ease up once someone had reached down and picked up my Glock, removing it from my view. Once my weapon was gone, he reached down and grasped my wrist, twisting my arm around and behind my back, where he began zip-tying my wrists together. As he pulled the plastic tie painfully tight, another man knelt beside me, and asked, "What are you looking for?"

Spitting dirt out of my mouth, I said, "I'm just making sure it's safe to travel through the area. That's all."

With skepticism in his voice, he observed, "You've been watching for a while. You seem a little more interested than just some random guy making sure the area is safe."

That statement hit me like a brick wall. All I could think of was just how long were they watching? Had they observed me when I first arrived? Did they observe me hiding the Symbex? How could I have been so careless that I let this happen?

Not knowing what else to say, I muttered, "I'm just paranoid is all. You know how things can be these days."

I could hear others in the area rifling through my belongings, and quite frankly, I was confused. My mind raced. I wondered if my captors were the OSS. I mean, they had to be. Anyone without a steady supply of Symbex would have either sniped me from a distance or scared me off if they wanted me gone. They'd have to assume I was a carrier of the Sembé virus, yet here they were, scrounging through my stuff, touching everything I owned, and getting down close to me.

"Drone!" one of them shouted as they all scurried for positions of cover under the trees.

Two of them immediately grabbed me by the boots and dragged me into the thickest part of the trees, raking my face through the dirt like a plow.

Now that's telling, I thought. The OWA owned the skies as well as the electromagnetic spectrum. The OSS wouldn't have an airborne threat to scurry and hide from.

As the possibilities of what was going on around me raced through my mind, I heard the ominous buzz of a Scheibel S-100 rotary-wing drone in the distance as my captors immediately began pulling camouflaged thermal-imager-defeating, quick-deploying shelters from their packs, draping them over themselves.

The two men that had dragged me deep into the brush and trees covered me as well, before covering themselves.

I couldn't see a thing as the sound of the drone grew near. To say I felt vulnerable in that moment would be the understatement of the century. I was hogtied and blind with a threat looming overhead while simultaneously being held captive by an unknown foe.

After a few minutes of hearing the buzzing sounds of the rotary wing drone loitering in the area, it appeared to move on, with the sound of its rotors becoming more and more distant until it was gone.

No one moved. Not one of my captors said a word for what seemed like several minutes, before one of them finally whispered, "Let's move."

I could hear the thermal-imaging barriers being whisked off of them, followed by the one covering me being hastily pulled from over me, giving me the relief of fresh air and visibility.

Turning my head to the left, I could see what appeared to be a rag-tag group of militia-type individuals, all wearing a mixed array of camouflage and carrying older generation, primer-fired weapons. Most of them seemed to carry the venerable old AR15, while one carried an AK variant and another had what appeared to be a bolt-action hunting rifle. *Is he their Designated Marksman?* I thought. *Or was it simply the only weapon available?*

As the person carrying the bolt-action rifle pulled the camouflage facemask down from his or her face, long, reddish-brown hair fell into view, revealing the face of a woman in her mid-thirties. She appeared very healthy, which was surprising to me as most of the others I had encountered during my journey had seemed severely weathered, emaciated, and often times, showing signs of the sickness.

"Tamara," one of the men said calmly, "We'll get some distance between us and the path of the drone. You and Raymond stay back a bit and make sure they aren't following. Just because the drone left, doesn't mean it didn't pick us up."

"Will do," she said, propping her rifle, which I could now make out to be a Remington Model 700 on her thigh with the butt of the stock.

No sooner did those words leave her lips than two individuals, I assumed to be men based on their size and grip, picked me up under each arm, yanking me to my feet. One of them leaned in and whispered, "We're not going to cover your eyes just yet because we want you to move fast. If you don't move fast, or if you show any signs of resistance, we'll just shoot you and leave you for the coyotes. You got a problem with that?"

"No. Understood," I assured them.

The group quickly began moving and at a rapid pace. I had a hard time keeping up with my hands tied, tripping, and falling several times from the awkwardness of my hands being behind my back while trying to keep up the pace. I'm not sure if you've ever fallen forward with your hands bound behind you, but trust me, it isn't any fun. I'm pretty sure one of my front teeth was loosened by one of the resulting impacts.

After what seemed like several miles, the group halted as one of them approached me from behind and two others held my arms. The one approaching me from behind reached around and held a damp cloth with a sweet, ether-like smell on my face. He held the cloth firmly as I struggled. The world around me began to fade away...

Chapter Ten

Feeling a nudge and hearing some unintelligible mumbling in the background, I was startled awake. I reacted with such a sudden jerk from the fear of my unknown situation that I felt as if I nearly dislocated my shoulder since my hands were still tied behind my back.

Feeling a nudge from a boot against my side, I heard a voice grumble, but my foggy mind couldn't quite make out what it said.

"Settle down, I said," the voice muttered, this time becoming intelligible in my somewhat coherent state.

As my eyes began to regain their focus, I looked around to see that I was inside some sort of a room. It was a long, narrow space, with what appeared to be metal walls covered in several layers of hastily applied paint. Small LED lights hung from the ceiling, giving the place just enough light. One of the lights flickered as if the unit was failing, giving the room that textbook Hollywood interrogation-scene feel.

Since they had me lying on my side with my hands tied securely behind my back, I couldn't see what was behind me, which was the direction from which the voice and the tip of the boot came.

"Who are you? What's your name?" the voice asked.

"Hank," I hastily replied. For some reason, the image of Hank Williams, Jr. flashed before me as I quickly scanned through my mind for a suitable alias.

"Hank, who?" the voice asked, prodding me once again with the tip of his boot.

"Hank Johnson," I muttered, almost cracking a smile as I thought of the former Congressmen who went by that name, who during a congressional hearing, expressed his concerns that Guam would capsize if too many people occupied the island.

"Uh-huh," the voice grunted, letting me know he did not believe my first attempt at identifying myself.

"Well then, Hank, what brings you to our neck of the woods?"

"I'm just passing through," I replied. "Do you mind if I roll over? The circulation to my left arm is getting cut off in this position."

Without even the slightest verbal response, the person's boot pressed against my right arm and rolled me over onto my back, allowing me to thrust my weight to the right, now lying on my right side.

"That's all the favors you get for now," the voice declared.

Looking up, I saw a man with a medium build wearing a mismatched outfit of camouflage and an OD-green face shield concealing his identity. A Kryptek camo-camo patterned ball cap was pulled down tightly against the face shield, preventing even the slightest identification of hair color, if the man even had any hair.

"Just passing through, huh? To where?"

"Away," I replied. "As far away as I can get from anyone else."

"Well, you did a lousy job of that. Can you tell me why it is that the OWA seems to have an interest in you?"

My heart nearly skipped a beat when the interrogator uttered those words. My mind raced with the possibilities of what might be occurring. Was this the OSS in some sort of clandestine disguise? I'd heard of OSS operators carrying out false-flag operations while acting as a civilian militia in order to turn the survivors that might lend them support against them, making the OWA out to be their savior once again.

I remembered back to when they first captured me, and how they didn't seem to be at all afraid of me possibly being a carrier of the virus, but then remembered their fear of the drone. The drone would have clearly been an OWA asset. Was their fear of the drone part of the elaborate ruse?

My head pounded with the hangover induced by whatever it was they had used to rob me of my consciousness, making it difficult to piece the puzzle together in my mind.

"What do you mean? I asked. "About the OWA having an interest in me, that is?"

Kneeling down before me, the man said, "Don't play with me."

"I... I just don't know what you mean. I've not seen any OWA or OSS personnel. Why would they appear to have any interest in me?"

"Sit him up," directed a female voice hidden in the darkness.

Almost immediately, two large men picked me up from underneath my arms and sat me in a chair directly under a light. "Are you kidding me?" I asked.

"Kidding about what?" the female voice inquired.

Looking around, I said, "This is a little cliché, don't you think? I mean, it's straight out of a cheap Hollywood movie. The dark space, voices hidden in the darkness, sitting me under a light with my hands tied behind my back while you try to intimidate me? It's literally something you'd see in a B-rated movie script."

Reaching up and taking hold of the low-hanging light that dangled from its wires above me, the female shined it in her own face and said, "There, is that better? Now, cut the bullshit."

The light revealed the attractive woman that I had seen earlier. She was dressed like the others, but stood out in the crowd with her tuft of reddish-brown hair hanging out beneath her cap. I must admit, I was taken aback by the sight of her. She was very well kept, and, well—a sight to behold for my weary eyes, if I may be honest.

Releasing the light and allowing it to swing back and forth in a very disorienting manner, she said, "Now, tell us why the OWA has such an interest in you."

"I'm sorry, but you're going to have to clarify that. I really don't know what you mean. I've not seen any OWA."

"The drones," she replied. "We noticed a shift in the routine patterns of the drones that patrol the area. The pattern they have been following indicates a grid search is being performed. We've calculated the probable location of their target of interest and narrowed it down to the area where you were apprehended. The rotary-wing drone was confirmation of that. They were getting close. Those are short range, low-level drones that are used only once their target has been acquired for confirmation."

That threw me for a loop. If this was true, how could I not have noticed the drones overhead? Then again, I had traveled mostly at night, which would have prevented me from getting a visual on them if they ran without lights of any kind, and the newer generation of drones can fly at altitudes that would prevent me from hearing them. I supposed they could have been using thermal imaging to track me, isolating me somehow from the other targets in the area, such as random survivors and wildlife.

"I'm sure it wasn't me," I replied. "They'd have no reason to be looking for me. You must have just missed the person or persons they're really after."

No sooner did I utter that lie than one of the men standing in the darkness grabbed me by the arm and jerked my shirt sleeve up so quickly that it tore.

"Then tell us where you've been getting your Symbex," the woman demanded.

Looking to my arm, I realized that while I was unconscious, they must have found the tell-tale signs of frequent and prolonged use of Symbex injections. When an employee or supporter of the OWA reported for work, they'd get their daily injection of the drug via air gun in order to save on needles. Over time, a noticeable mark would be present around the injection site. It wasn't overly obvious, but could easily be found by a trained observer.

This only deepened my concerns about who my interrogators were. If they knew I had been receiving Symbex injections, then they knew I was a carrier. If they knew I was a carrier, they would know their proximity to me would be life-threatening to them, unless, of course, they too were receiving the life-saving drug.

Playing to the idea that they may have access to the drug, I said, "I'll make you a deal."

"I don't think you're really in a position to be making deals," the woman said.

"I think I am," I replied smugly. "If you give me a dose of Symbex, and promise me that you'll give me access to a continuing supply, I'll tell you anything and everything. If you don't, I'm as good as dead anyway, so what good would talking do me? I mean, you're clearly carriers, or there is no way on Earth you'd be standing in this confined little space with me."

From all of the interrogation training I had received during my career in law enforcement, I could see on her face that her hand had been revealed. She either had to put her cards on the table or fold. She knew I was right. She knew I understood that I would die without access to Symbex and that I must have figured out they would too without access. So, what did I have to lose? Any method of execution would undoubtedly be preferable to the slow, agonizing death the Sembé virus would cause if not suppressed.

Breaking the Beast

As she began to speak, a heavy metal door swung open as several men rushed into the room. Looking at the door and how it swung from metal hinges on what would be the corner of the room, I thought, *what the hell is this, a shipping container?*

"We've got a breach!" the man said with excitement in his voice.

Before she could respond, I could hear the muffled sounds of gunshots in the distance and oddly, above me.

Without saying a word, everyone around me sprang into action, with two of them jerking me off the chair and rushing through the room and out the open steel door. It appeared I was in what could only be described as a series of connected shipping containers, though the low light made any sort of hasty mental investigation difficult at best.

Sliding an old, well-worn sofa out of the way, the woman said, "Go! Go! Go!" as one of the men opened a makeshift door or hatch cut into the floor by use of a cutting torch.

They quickly lowered me down through the hatch and then followed closely behind. There were at least six of them with me, the woman and five unidentified male comrades of hers. Beneath the shipping container, there was a small, cramped tunnel that was lit only with the headlamps that my captors immediately donned. This was something they had clearly drilled and trained on; as they each carried out the process of what seemed to be an emergency evacuation without a single word being spoken between them.

It was challenging to navigate the tight confines of the tunnel with my hands tied behind my back, and my tripping and falling was clearly slowing them down.

"Cut him loose," the woman ordered.

Two of the men responded, with one of them holding me still while another cut the ties used to bind my wrists.

The man cutting the ties whispered in my ear, "I dare you to give me a reason to see you as a threat."

Once my hands were free, the group continued through the tunnel, and we could now hear gunfire coming from inside the maze of shipping containers above us as it echoed through the structure with a hollow, metallic sound.

After what seemed like a hundred yards, the group stopped, and one of them began opening a crudely-made overhead hatch, allowing the crisp, fresh night air to wash through the tight confines of the tunnel. Each of them immediately turned off their headlamps as the first climbed up and out of the tunnel, motioning for the others to join.

As I exited the tunnel with them, the moonlight revealed that we were in some sort of industrial area, in what I could only assume was Chattanooga, but then again, I had no idea how long I had been out or where they had taken me.

Using hand signals only, the group began to work their way quickly along the shadows of the buildings as a helicopter flew at a high rate of speed directly over the rooftops of the metal warehouse-style buildings, causing everyone to duck and cover.

"Let's move," one of them said as shots rang out from the alleyway just across from us, taking the man off his feet with what I could recognize from the report as a CX91 carbine.

Chills ran up my spine when I realized it was the OSS who was upon us.

With the realization that I must be with some sort of resistance militia, I took cover as they immediately returned fire, only to have two more of them be cut down before my eyes.

With only the woman and one of the militiamen remaining, the woman shouted, "Move! Move! Move!" as an OSS operator rounded the corner, taking a shot at her sole surviving companion, striking him directly in the throat, and sending me crashing backward and onto the ground. As her friend fell, she had managed to raise her M4-style AR15 carbine, engaging the threat, striking him several times in the abdomen and pelvic area.

As the man writhed in pain on the ground, I pulled his CX91 from his bloody grasp and began to raise it as the woman's barrel now bore down on me.

As she prepared to fire, the threat that had engaged us from across the alley emerged into the moonlight, giving me more than an adequate target. I pivoted to my left, took aim with the CX91, and sent several of the 6.2mm rounds flying, taking him off his feet and out of the fight.

Ensuring that I didn't turn the weapon back toward the woman, I turned my head to see her still pointing her weapon at me, seeming to be in disbelief as I said, "You can kill me later. Let's get the hell out of here."

Chapter Eleven

It felt like we had been running for hours, but with several massive blasts that I could only assume were OSS airstrikes on the woman's allies behind us, she was relentless. I hadn't run that long and hard in as long as I could remember, or possibly ever. She led me into a heavily-wooded area just south of what appeared to be an old, abandoned and overgrown baseball field complex.

Crashing through the brush, she led me between two large evergreen trees, feeling around through the fallen needles and cones on the ground. Finding what she had been searching for, she said, "Help me," as she began to pull on a handle to lift what appeared to be a door.

Slinging the CX91 across my back, I took hold of the handle and pulled hard, revealing a vertical ladder that descended into the darkness below.

"C'mon," she said, slipping the sling of her AR15 around her back and climbing down.

As I climbed down the ladder, I paused and looked around for a moment, and then closed the door above me.

Reaching the bottom rung, I was pleased to see that she had switched on a small LED lamp.

"We've got loads of solar rechargeable batteries for these things," she said as she placed it aside, attempting a smile.

I tried not to stare, but I could tell she was anguishing inside. She turned away and wiped her face to hide a tear that trickled down her cheek.

"I'm sorry," I muttered, feeling totally useless at the moment.

Waving me away, she dug deep to regain her composure and said, "Any of us would have gladly given our lives if need be. And although I'm not lying back there bleeding out from a bullet wound, they've taken my life as well. It will just happen over days or weeks instead of minutes."

"What do you mean?" I asked.

Snapping her head toward me and making eye contact, she said, "You know good and well what I mean. I don't know where you're getting your dosage, but my link to survival is gone, now."

"Did your friends have access to Symbex?" I asked, half wondering aloud.

"Who the hell are you?" she snapped. "You were spying on us from the ridgeline, and now that your friends arrived, every one of us you were spying on are dead or dying! And now you're asking questions like that!?"

I could see her hand squeezing the grip of her AR15 tightly as rage began to build within her. Her eyes glanced to the sling around my neck and she slowly began to stand. "Just how the hell did you manage to fire that weapon?"

I immediately knew where she was going with that. I had been chipped for what seemed like forever and had fired the CX series of weapons for so long as an ODF officer that it was second nature to me. But to someone on the outside, the fact that I could fire the weapon at all with its smart weapon technology was an indicator of my affiliation with the OWA and ODF.

"It's a long story," I mumbled as I watched her raise her weapon to the low ready position. "If you give me a chance to…"

"A chance to what? A chance to get more information on us?"

"Look, I don't even know who 'us' is," I assured her. "Besides, you saw me use their own weapon against them. I could have easily turned it on you."

"Acceptable losses," she growled. "The OWA wouldn't mind eating a few of its own to advance an agenda. That's been proven again and again."

She had me dead to rights on that one. That was one of the most accurate statements ever said. "I defected. I'm trying to find the resistance, whoever that is."

She scoffed at the suggestion and said, "No one would walk away from a steady supply of Symbex, food, shelter, and safety to live like a rat in holes underground, to be hunted day in and day out by their former comrades."

"No one sane, that is," I rebutted.

"No, I've got you figured out. We've seen a sharp increase in ODF activity and patrols, as well as a radical shift in observation-drone flight patterns. That's how we calculated your approximate position on the ridgeline. We've learned the ins and outs of their practices. Without a technologically-equipped foe, the OWA has gotten a little sloppy with their tech-based ops, allowing us to pattern them and gain useful insights into their operations as a whole. I've got you pegged. You were an undercover forward observer, with drones tracking your progress. You were probably feeding information back to the drones above. That's how they found us. That's why my friends are dead," she said as she raised her weapon, pointing the rifle directly at my chest.

"No!" I insisted. "They're after me. They probably only found you because you captured me and took me back to your facility."

"Why are they after you? They wouldn't put all of that effort into a defector."

"They would if that defector had a large supply of Symbex, and intended on delivering it to someone in the resistance who could replicate it and begin to produce it outside the OWA's grasp."

At that moment, she and I both had the same epiphany. I could see it in her eyes, and she could see it in mine.

"I was the cheese," I declared.

"And we were the mice," she said, lowering her weapon.

At that moment, I realized how I had managed to successfully travel as far as I had, with little resistance once I left the zones. They were watching me from above. They were tracking me, hoping I would lead them to whoever it was out there that I was planning on meeting. I mean, I really didn't have a plan. I had no idea who I would find or where they would be. I only knew I needed to try.

They didn't know that, though. No, I'd imagine at first, what Ronnie and I had done was a shock to them. I'm sure those ODF officers who engaged us were doing their jobs and truly trying to stop us, but once the higher-ups got involved, the order was probably given to let me go, but to keep a close watch on me in order to catch a bigger fish, and hopefully, an entire school of fish. I felt like such a fool.

I looked to her and said, "It's Tamara, right?"

Taken aback by my statement, she hesitated and said, "How…"

"When you found me on the ridgeline, someone called you Tamara."

Rolling her eyes at the realization of the lapse of OPSEC, she reluctantly said, "Yes. Yes, it is. And you are?"

"Joe. Joe Branch," I said, reaching out my hand.

"So, Joe Branch," she quipped, returning the handshake before turning to sit down on a small fold-out camping chair. "Tell me everything, Joe Branch. How exactly did you get yourself into this mess?"

I felt conflicted inside about telling my story. Was this too soon? Was this the right person I needed to be sharing this information with? I still had many questions that needed to be answered, like where she had been receiving her supply of Symbex? I was curious whether everything I had been told about life on the outside was true. I mean, they're obviously still healthy.

I took a deep breath and decided to take a chance. Maybe by explaining my situation fully, I'd be able to glean some useful information from her as well. It was a gamble I was willing to take.

For the next half hour, I explained to her my journey from being a Capitol Police officer who was essentially conscripted into service as an ODF Security Officer, and how I had worked my way up to lieutenant.

While I was telling the story, I had to pause and wonder if my recent promotion was guided somehow by Ronnie's hand, to get me to where I needed to be so that I could help him. After all, he did know me from my days with the Capitol Police. Shaking it off, I had to accept that there were things that I would now never have answers to.

I went on to explain how I had inadvertently become aware of the OWA's actions, both past and present, and how when presented with Ronnie's plan, well, how I just couldn't say no.

I detailed our acquisition of the Symbex and the research data, as well as our big getaway and our struggles afterward. I even explained to her the horrors I saw once we were free from the zones. Those horrors were new to me, although while I told her the stories, I knew she had seen them all repeat themselves over and over again. I was truly preaching to the choir. It was like I was the new kid being dropped off in the jungle of Vietnam, telling the harrowing tale of my first encounter with the VC to a seasoned veteran.

Once I was finished with my story, and how it had led to them finding me, I asked, "So, tell me. Who are you with, and how are you getting by? You're clearly no stranger to the wonders of modern, tyrannical medicine."

Taking a deep breath, she said, "I'm with... or *was* with, a small group of people, who like you, knew of the atrocities and couldn't sit back and do nothing about it. I was a nurse before it all began. The others... my friends who we lost tonight, had various skills in different trades as well. We all had skills that retained value in the eyes of the OWA."

"So you're with the OWA as well?"

Her eyes quickly met mine with contempt. "No, I was never 'with' them," she snarled. Regaining her composure, she explained, "Well, at first, I guess. As a nurse, I thought I was doing the right thing. I thought I was helping humanity during the most significant medical crisis humankind had ever known. I was... I was doing my part. Or, like you, so I thought.

"It didn't take long for me to begin to see how the care we were giving was being directed from above. Some patients were priorities, while some were tolerated, but seen as nuisances, and others were simply steered away. Deviations from that were not tolerated.

"By that point, they knew we understood how we couldn't live without their benevolent hand, feeding us the lifesaving drug. Entire communities were left to die the most miserable death, while those with the right connections were given every possible resource.

"My false sense of service to humanity quickly turned into a feeling of conscription. I was no longer a volunteer; I was property."

Feeling that the two of us shared more in common than we initially knew, I nodded and said, "I'd imagine there are more than a few of us out there who had that realization set in over time."

"Were there others? That you knew, that is, who felt the same?" she asked.

"Things are a little different in the D.C. area," I explained. "Life is pretty good. The OWA does a good job taking care of its loyalists. For the most part, they could live there their entire lives without ever seeing hardship. As long as they were loyal and played by the rules, that is.

"There were others who I felt were pretty good people who were 'transferred' to a new assignment without notice. The more I came to grips with the reality of things, the more I began to wonder just exactly what those transfers entailed. People seemed to know not to speak their minds. Just play along, and life would be fine.

"Ronnie was the first person to ever truly speak his mind to me about the OWA. That was a conversation I had wanted to have for quite some time. I guess he could see it in me as well."

Looking into the darkness for a moment, she said, "Perhaps if I had been assigned to a hospital or clinic in such a place, I'd have never been pushed in the direction I was. Perhaps I would have simply done like the others you describe, going through life with blinders on, being glad my masters took such good care of me.

Shaking her head, she said, "But I wasn't. I was regularly being transferred to other locations, seeing the worst that could be found in the outer edges of the zones. Taking in those the OWA chose to care for and turning away those it didn't.

"Watching families with children I knew I could have saved be turned away crushed my soul. I cried myself to sleep every night. I became so depressed and traumatized that I wanted to take my own life. Then... I met Phil."

"Who is Phil?" I asked.

"Phil was one of the men you watched die tonight," she explained while drying her eyes with her shirt. "He was the best of the best."

"You were close?" I asked.

"Not in that way," she replied, dismissing the notion of anything other than a professional relationship.

"Phil caught me just as I was about to step over the edge. Figuratively, that is. I was done. Then, he gave me hope. He convinced me I wasn't alone. He showed me there were others out there who had looked the beast in the eye and were not going to take it anymore. He gave me hope again. He gave me a purpose."

Seeing the fire that still remained in her eyes despite her heartache, I said, "I'd venture to guess he merely helped you see your purpose. I believe it was there all along."

She smiled at my silly little statement, and it warmed my heart. She had suffered a traumatic loss tonight, and her morning was far from over. But there we were, still in the middle of it all, and still needing a way out.

"The group you were with," I hesitantly asked. "Were they militia? Were they part of a larger organization?"

"In spirit," she replied. "We knew there were others out there who felt the same as we did, and we hoped our efforts somehow contributed to the greater good, but the way things are these days, long-distance communication just isn't possible with the OWA's dominance over technology.

"Did you ever watch reruns of Hogan's Heroes when you were a kid?"

I laughed and said, "My dad used to watch that show all the time."

"That's how we saw ourselves. We would fall in line during the day, then lash out at the OWA, helping others escape their grasp at night or at any other opportunity we could, really."

"Were all of you in the medical field?"

"No. Phil was in transportation. That's how I met him. He was a trucker before it all went down. Until recently, he drove for the OWA, hauling people and supplies to areas of interest. Others worked in logistics, vehicle and equipment maintenance, and such. A large organization such as the OWA needs far more than just tactical operators and soldiers to maintain its foothold.

"We were all assigned to the same mobile response taskforce. We were used to essentially maintain order and loyalty among the communities and populations the OWA needed outside the zones, providing services and material support where needed."

"Did you have access to Symbex?" I asked. I couldn't help but wonder why she hadn't tried a move such as Ronnie and me.

"No, they had thugs like yourself guarding it at all times. I never held a syringe in my hands outside of a secure location, with an entire OSS mobile unit watching every move I made. We discussed such things several times, but it just didn't seem possible. On top of that, we had reason to believe one or more attack drones were circling above at all times in order to prevent any Symbex from slipping away from their grasp. I have no doubt they would have killed every single person on site if an incident ever occurred.

"We also heard stories of medical personnel who stepped slightly out of line with their handling of Symbex. They seemed to make examples out of such people."

"Like what?" I asked. "What do you mean, examples?"

Pausing, she said, "I'd rather not talk about it right now."

"Of course. I'm sorry," I said, feeling about two inches tall.

"Long story short, we knew what we could and couldn't successfully accomplish. We resolved to simply do what we could, when we could, until a situation presented itself to join up with another resistance group to do something bigger, you know, to make more of an impact."

Taking a deep breath, I exhaled, and said, "Well, it looks like that day has come."

Chapter Twelve

For the next hour or so, Tamara and I discussed our options. She was well aware that she could no longer return to her former life inside the OWA. The bodies that had no doubt been retrieved by the OSS would lead them back to her and others within their unit. No, that bridge had been burned. And without the OWA's steady supply of Symbex for its minions, she would soon begin to feel the effects of the virus and would start to suffer the same horrible fate she'd watched far too many others face.

When asked how much Symbex I had, if it was still where I hid it, I simply kept telling her plenty, without going into too much detail. I had every reason in the world to trust her, but we all had developed trust issues these days and tried to keep some things to ourselves. Perhaps it gave us a feeling of control in an otherwise uncontrollable world. Or, perhaps the biggest betrayal in human history had forced us into a corner of doubt and mistrust. Either way, I simply said, "enough."

I explained to her how the original plan had included Ronnie and myself, so we would have plenty of available doses to keep ourselves alive while pressing on with the mission at hand, especially if we scaled back the frequency, which would be risky but possibly necessary if things got dragged out too long. Now, all we had to do was retrieve it, which would be easier said than done.

"This is your turf; you clearly know it better than I do. What do you suggest?" I asked, seeking her input on how to retrieve the Symbex I had stashed before being captured by her and her fellow freedom fighters.

After thinking it over for a moment, she answered, "The hunters."

"The hunters?" I repeated, confused by the vague statement.

"There are a group of hunters in the area that travel by horseback. The OWA tolerates them, as they are merely feeding those in need with their harvest. We don't know much about them, but we've watched them from a distance on many occasions. They're armed only with primitive bows, which is probably why the OWA leaves them be. If they carried anything that could be seen as defensive in nature, that wouldn't be tolerated."

"If you don't know much about them, how do you know they feed people in need?"

"Like I said, we've observed them for quite some time. We've tracked them several times, following them from a safe distance," she explained.

"Safe distance?" I asked. "I thought you said they carried only primitive weapons."

Shooting me, *the look*, she said, "For one, who knows what they're hiding? And two, it's not just for our safety, it's for theirs as well. We are carriers, and making contact with them, even inadvertently, would be dangerous for them since they have no supply of Symbex to fight off the virus once contracted."

Nodding that I understood, trying to avoid another *look*, I said, "So, you're saying we disguise ourselves as hunters, then attempt to recover the Symbex without being noticed?"

"Yes, exactly. If drones are patrolling, the observers on the ground will be able to spot any suspicious activity and call in for an intercept. If they see two hunters on horseback, it'll appear routine."

"Whatever we do, it needs to be right away before more OSS arrive to sniff out and crush any other dissenters. And they will. They won't let this go unanswered."

"I guess you'd know that as well as anyone, wouldn't you?" she chided.

I have to admit, she had me on my toes. I didn't know whether she truly saw me as an ally, someone who shared her own mission, or as a threat that may be temporarily convenient. Was my inherent mistrust getting in the way of reading her properly, or was it her mistrust of me that was getting in the way? It was likely a little of both, but at that stage in the game, it was probably for the best.

Letting someone in close would either lead to betrayal or heartache. There really weren't many other likely options anymore.

She went on to explain how a local man named George had been rescuing abandoned horses from farms where the owners either couldn't take care of them or had died off and were simply no longer around. He took the horses in, nursed them back to full strength, and then he worked with them, using his decades of horsemanship experience to help them become fine saddle horses once again.

If through his working with them, he found them not to have previously been saddle broke, he would train them to pull a cart or a plow. He tried to see to it that every horse in his care had value for its next owner, ensuring it had a productive future, and not simply to be seen as a protein source.

She explained how he was sympathetic to the cause, yet refused to get involved directly. He didn't want to be pushed out by the OWA and have to leave his horses behind for a fate that would almost certainly result in slaughter.

The OWA tolerated him because he provided a means for the local population to provide for themselves without the use of technology, which was something they seemed to be tightening their grip on. After all, the only steady source of gasoline and diesel was through the OWA and was for official OWA use only.

Survivors had to scavenge for what they acquired, and that supply seemed to be just about exhausted. What remained to be found was often beginning to varnish from a lack of stabilizers having been added to them before the collapse.

She explained that we could sneak onto his farm and take a few horses.

"You mean to steal them?" I asked.

"It wouldn't be stealing," she explained. "Like I said, George is sympathetic to the cause, but can't risk being suspected and doesn't want to contribute directly to our support. He said if we were ever in need, to simply take what we wanted, and to leave him a sign that it was us in the form of a knot. That way, he would know it was us, and would not pursue the matter."

"A knot?"

"Yeah. Each horse corral has rope for catching and haltering horses. He said to wrap it around the post in a specific manner that only he would recognize. To anyone else, it was just a length of rope hung around a post. No one else would ever think twice about it."

Handing me a small pack she retrieved from the corner of the room, she said, "Here. It's got three days food and water, as well as a basic first aid kit, a knife, a solar-rechargeable flashlight, and a single person emergency shelter that doubles as a thermal imagining cloak as well. It's heavy and will sweat you like you won't believe on a warm day, but it'll help you evade your friends from the OWA. We'll each take our own pack. We have several of these go-bags stashed in numerous places in the area for just such an occasion."

"Where's my stuff? The pack I had with me when you so politely invited me down to your dungeon," I asked. "There were a few important items in that pack."

"Sorry, it's gone," she said bluntly. "It's gone, along with my friends."

With no further protest on my part, I picked up the CX91 and said, "All right then, let's get moving."

"Not with that thing you're not," she barked. "It's bad enough to be caught with a weapon, but do you really want to be caught with a weapon taken from one of their dead comrades?"

"Good point," I conceded, "but do you really think it matters at this point? After what went down tonight, the OSS won't be tolerating any armed civilians. Being armed at all will be a death sentence."

"Still," she said, standing her ground. "That thing isn't going with us. Take this," she said, tossing me a Sig Sauer 556.

"It was a police carbine in its previous life," she said. "It runs the same ammo and mags as my AR, so we'll be able to run the same rounds, just in case."

"Oh, yeah. I remember these," I said as I admired the weapon. "I always loved gas-piston-driven rifles. They run so much cleaner than a direct impingement AR."

"You probably won't live long enough to get it dirty, but okay," she said dismissively.

"Just don't try to wish that into being," I joked, to see her crack a half-hearted smile. Man, I still couldn't figure her out. Maybe I never would. *Oh, well, get your head back in the game, Joe,* I thought to myself as I followed her up the ladder and back out into the moonlit night above.

Chapter Thirteen

I followed Tamara as she slipped stealthily through the darkness, avoiding the moonlight wherever she could. She moved with grace and skill through the abandoned suburban neighborhoods on the east side of Chattanooga. *No wonder they were able to sneak up on me while I slept,* I couldn't help but think while I watched her move. She was nearly silent and moved with such agility and precision that she barely disturbed a thing around her, while I felt more like an elephant tromping through the woods. If there was a twig to snap, I stepped on it. In one back yard, I even tripped and fell over a toy dump truck that was hidden in the overgrown grass of an abandoned home. Don't get me wrong, I hadn't survived up until that point by being a big, clumsy oaf; she just put things on an all new level for me.

In retrospect, I imagine her being an OWA insider doubling as an insurgent required her to operate at a very high level to avoid capture. She and her late friends had obviously been doing that for a while and had no doubt perfected their craft. It was their interest in me, a watched, pursued man that had been their downfall. I hoped like hell not to be the cause of such losses again.

After working our way east for what felt like an hour, Tamara positioned herself in the shadows of a backyard privacy fence, staying well clear of the moonlight. She motioned for me to move up to her position, so I joined her.

"Okay," she said, beginning to lay out her plan. "We're on Ooltewah Road. If you head south," she said, pointing, "you'll see Houston Lane. Just before Houston Lane, there is a line of trees that follow a fence to the east that separates many of the properties. That tree line will allow you to move to where I need you while remaining under the thick cover of the branches. Once you're clear of the neighborhood, head up the hillside a few hundred yards."

"Wait, we're splitting up?" I asked.

"Yes. If George sees you, he may shoot without bothering to ask you why you're prowling around his property, stealing horses. He knows me, and I'm going to remove my hat so he can see me clearly from a distance," she said as she pulled the cap from her head and let her hair down.

I must admit, I was captivated at that moment by her beauty. She was a very attractive woman. It's not like I had gone an extremely long time without seeing a woman; the D. C. area was still populated by many healthy, attractive people. It was the opposite of the post-apocalyptic nightmare that most of the country and the world had become. But there was something about her....

Snapping her fingers in front of my face, clearly seeing that my mind had been derailed, she continued, "Like I was saying, George will more than likely recognize me. His horses are behind his home in a large barn in a pasture."

Looking around, I said, "I have a hard time picturing horses in an area such as this."

"This is one of those places that was in the middle of a development boom just before the virus was unleashed. George was one of the last holdouts, who refused to sell his land to the developers. He hated being surrounded by cheaply built, cookie-cutter homes, but would have hated leaving his old family farm even more."

Curious, I asked, "How could this George fellow have remained so close to what was surely once a densely-populated area without getting sick?"

"I never said he wasn't a carrier," she countered. "George travels on horseback to wherever the OWA mobile support teams, such as mine, are operating. He petitions them for a dosage based on his work providing working animals for survivors and is awarded a dosage just frequently enough to keep him going. The virus has been allowed to advance enough for it to show, however. He's not what he once was, but he struggles through the pain and presses on with life.

"After tonight, I worry about what will happen to him. If this area is declared to be an insurgent safe-haven, the OWA will pull out, taking its life-saving Symbex treatments with it. They'll either allow the virus to run its course through the remainder of the population, or they'll have their OSS thugs make what remains of life here a living hell. The suffering from our misstep here is far from over."

I knew her misstep was me. I knew she regretted her group's decision to track me down more than words could describe. Her friends were dead, and a community that she truly cared for, that was hanging on by a mere thread, would now almost certainly join their fate.

With that realization, I resolved in my heart to not let their sacrifices go to waste. Tamara and I would recover the Symbex Ronnie and I had smuggled out of D.C., and we would get it into the hands where our lives, and the lives of the people in this town, would be vindicated by breaking the OWA's grip on all of humanity.

Once she had finished explaining her plan to me, we parted ways, and I made my way to the hillside where she had directed. It didn't take long for me to reach our intended rendezvous point. At least, I hoped I was in the right place.

I could see the top of a barn off in the distance to the northwest from my position on the hillside. I assumed that was the barn to which Tamara had referred. I watched it closely for the next half-hour or so, listening carefully for signs that something may have gone wrong. I tried to work out a reaction plan in my mind if that were to become the case.

As I thought, I felt as if I had two different voices in my head, each pulling me to a different plan of action. One was trying to convince me that if something were to go awry, such as the OSS coming down on her while we were separated, that I must help. I must react to her situation and lend her any support I possibly could. The other voice was reminding me of the millions of survivors who may be depending on me to get the Symbex and continue on my way. If I were to react to a situation, I could be killed, and Ronnie's plan would die with me.

Shaking my head, trying to get the thoughts out of my mind, I resolved to simply hope that I wouldn't have to make such a decision, although I knew deep down in my heart I could not put the mission first and leave her behind. I knew that would be the correct thing to do in the grand scheme of things, but dammit, I'd rather not live at all than to be the kind of person who would turn their back on a friend in need.

Hearing movement on the hillside just below my elevation to the north, I gripped my Sig 556 tightly and positioned myself in a way to engage a threat coming from that direction, if need be. I knew, however, that if it was the OSS, they'd have likely presented me with such a distraction all while they approached from a different direction, or more than likely, from all sides.

As my heart rate began to quicken with all of the possible scenarios running through my mind, I caught the silhouette of a rider on horseback, with a second horse in tow.

"Thank, God," I muttered aloud.

I stood and began to work my way toward her, startling her, and causing her to raise her weapon.

"It's me," I whispered.

Riding up to me, she dismounted and said, "I'll take this buckskin paint mare, you can ride the quarter horse."

Handing me the reins to the chestnut quarter horse gelding, she asked, "So, what's your experience with horses?"

"Um, well..." I began to explain. "I guess I haven't ridden since I was a kid, and even then I'm pretty sure the horse was merely following my grandfather as he walked and wasn't paying attention to me at all."

I could see the look of exasperation on her face as she rolled her eyes, and after a slight huff, she dismounted.

"Okay," she begrudgingly began to explain, "This quarter horse is what they call, 'dead-broke'. That means he's got no fight left in him, so he's relatively easy to ride. That's good for a beginner, but if you really need to make him go and go hard, it's gonna require some effort on your part. Let's just hope it doesn't come to that. The buckskin paint was his herd mare, that's why I picked her out of the group. She was dominant to him in the herd, so he should have a natural inclination to want to stay with her, making it easier for you to follow me."

For the next few minutes, she explained the proper way to mount the horse, how to sit in the saddle, how to hold the reins and all of the associated leg, rein, and vocal cues for the basics of riding a dead-broke horse. "We don't have time for you to practice," she grumbled. "You're just gonna have to learn from experience."

Walking back to the buckskin paint, she retrieved a long, slender item and walked back toward me. "Here," she said.

Looking at it, I almost chuckled. She had handed me a stick with a string tied to each end, forcing it to bend like a bow.

"Do I get archery training as well?" I joked.

"It's a prop," she said. "If we're observed, they'll see two people riding horses and carrying bows. At a glance, we'll appear to be the hunters I spoke of earlier. We don't have time for anything else. We just need to hide our rifles under the blankets on the saddlebags the best we can. If anyone approaches us from up close, it'll be obvious, but an observer from a distance or via drone may just fall for it. We don't have any more time to mess around. The sun will be up soon, and that's roughly when the hunters would typically be spotted. Any questions?"

"No, ma'am," I replied sharply. I meant my reply to be a sign of respect for her command of the situation, but for some reason, I felt as if she thought I was patronizing her because I yet again got 'the look'.

She held my horse in place while I mounted. I struggled to get my right boot in the stirrup, having to bend over and hold the saddle fender in place to avoid having to twist my foot too far to get it to align, but once I was in place, I felt right at home.

"I always loved westerns," I said awkwardly, not knowing what else to say at the moment.

She rolled her eyes again, then walked back to her horse, mounted, and rode just in front of me. She looked back, then said, "Okay, let's go."

As she rode away, I squeezed my legs against the horse's sides like she had instructed, but he just wouldn't move. She looked back to see my plight, and said, "Relax the reins. You're too tense and inadvertently pulling back slightly. You're essentially putting on the brakes and pressing the gas pedal at the same time."

Doing as she said, my horse began to go, and Tamara turned and continued riding up the hill toward the ridge. *I've spent way too much of my life in the city,* I nervously thought.

After an awkward ten minutes or so, I began to feel comfortable with the quarter horse and was able to return my focus to my surroundings and any potential threats we may face. Tamara led us toward the area where they'd apprehended me the previous day—at least I think it was the previous day. I still have no idea how long I was out.

Tamara reined to a stop up ahead and signaled me to stop as well. Dismounting, she tied her horse to a tree branch and walked back toward me. As she walked, the sun was now coming up over the eastern horizon, and the rays of light were beginning to shine through the colorful trees of autumn while fog started to form in the valley below as the air began to warm and rise. It was indeed a breathtaking morning and a sight to behold.

"We're close," she said, snapping me back into reality. "We found you just up ahead. Where did you hide your pack?"

Feeling that built-in sense of paranoia began to come over me, I hesitantly said, "It's just a little further past my observation spot. I'll go on from here if you can stay and keep an eye out for an ambush."

Looking me directly in the eyes as if she was reading me, she asked, "You still don't trust me, do you?"

Pausing before answering, I said, "Well, we're talking about the most precious substance on earth right now. There aren't many people who wouldn't kill for it, and you and I both will die without it. I felt the same way about Ronnie at first. I wasn't sure if he had brought me along as an expendable tool, merely something to discard once he had gotten away from the OWA, or if I was truly his partner. That feeling of paranoia eventually passed, just like I'm sure my present paranoia and sense of uneasiness will as well.

"To be honest, though, you were my captor until recently. You've given me plenty reason to believe what you say, that we're both on the same team with the same agenda, but this world... well, it doesn't leave much room for blind faith. I'm sure it will come, though."

"At least you're honest," she replied. "There's plenty room for faith left in this world," she said. "It's just not easy to have faith in mankind. I have faith in these horses, I have faith in nature, and I have faith in God. And, like you said, I may eventually have faith in you—in due time."

I chuckled and said, "If we live that long."

"I'll take a leap of faith in you right now," she said with a smile. "Like you said, I'll stay and provide overwatch while keeping a lookout for drones in the sky above. If anything starts to go down, or if we're being watched, I'll create a diversion so you can get away. Otherwise, if you return with what you said, well, then my faith in you will be a little stronger. If you don't, and you leave me here, well, then our meeting would have been nothing more than a coincidence and not what I had hoped.

"If we become separated, work your way south to a place called 'Old Stone Church'. It's on the map as a historic sight. It's an old civil-war-era church that's been made into a museum of sorts. Meet me in that area. We'll regroup, and then go from there with whatever hand we've been dealt."

She intrigued me with what she had said. I thought it over for a brief moment, then sought clarification. "So, you think we were meant to cross each other's paths or something?" I could see that she didn't quite gather what I was saying, so I clarified. "I mean, based on your faith and all. I've never been much of a religious person. But if you…"

"We'll see," she interrupted with a grin, intentionally leaving me hanging and wanting more. I would be lying if I didn't admit she was good at keeping me on my mental toes. One minute she left me feeling resented, the next appreciated, and the next, well, I can't even put my finger on it. All I knew at that moment was that I was glad I was no longer alone in that cruel, miserable world. I just hoped it would stay that way.

Chapter Fourteen

As I rode off on my own toward where I had hidden the Symbex during my ill-fated nap the previous day, my heart began to race, and I felt a flurry of activity in my gut. If I came upon the site and the pack containing the Symbex was no longer there, it would all be over. The game would be lost. A lot was riding on what happened in the next few minutes, and I felt the weight of it all bearing down on me.

Without Tamara and the buckskin paint for my horse to guide on, he was noticeably a bit more squirrelly. My far-below-novice horsemanship abilities were clear to him as he mistook my accidental bumps and pressures as cues, followed by my intentional cue to steer him in the right direction once I had inadvertently caused him to alter course. "Sorry, buddy," I whispered, rubbing him on the neck. "I do appreciate your patience with me, though."

Once I was within fifty or so yards of where I hoped the Symbex would be, I looked to the east at the glorious sunrise, and it was now shining brightly over the horizon. I almost didn't want to dismount at that moment. The horrible world I had come to know as my new reality seemed to disappear as I admired the beauty and majesty of the natural world, a world that would not change due to the evils of man. It was an odd feeling, but a reassuring one that even if we squandered the opportunities we'd been given on this planet, something of beauty and wonder would remain. Something greater than us would still be here. The sun, the moon, the planets, and the stars would not be at odds with each other, but instead would be adhering to the laws of nature to which they were bound, long beyond our self-inflicted demise.

Snapping out of my moment of bliss, I clumsily dismounted, causing my horse to start to walk off while I still had my foot in the left stirrup. "Whoa, boy," I said, easing back gently on the left rein in an attempt to get him to stop before he spooked, and I found myself being dragged through the woods. I now understood why cowboy boots most often have pointed toes, to allow your foot to slide freely out of the stirrup, unlike my heavily-padded, round-toed hiking boots.

Once he had graciously complied with my request, I removed my foot from the stirrup, and tied his reins to a tree branch, remembering something Tamara had told me earlier. She had explained to tie him only to something he could break free from if he had to, just in case we weren't around to free him later. In this world, nothing was for sure, and leaving an animal tied up to be mauled by predators, or to simply die of thirst while bound to an immovable object would not be the ethical thing to do.

"I'll be right back, boy," I said as I rubbed his jaw.

Once I had dismounted, I did my best to stay beneath the visual cover of the trees, just in case I was being watched from above. I knew that if the OSS operators who had tracked Tamara and her group after they had apprehended me had found the Symbex, they could be lying in wait, hoping for my return. They may or may not have had time to piece it all together, depending on the intel they had gathered before the strike, so I knew I had to proceed as if the worst-case scenario was upon us.

Once the location where I had hidden the pack containing the Symbex was in sight, I knelt and scanned the area, watching and listening for any signs it was a trap. After a few moments of careful observation, I advanced toward the pack. Pulling aside some brush I had used to conceal the pack, I felt tremendous relief. There it was, lying exactly where I had left it, appearing to be undisturbed.

Breaking the Beast

Looking around once more, I took the pack by a strap and quickly pulled it free from the brush and slung it over my shoulder, making my way back toward my horse.

As I approached the horse, instead of feeling a sense of relief, I felt a sense of dread. *This was too easy,* I thought, expecting all hell to break loose at any moment.

I climbed aboard my horse with the pack on my back only to realize I hadn't first untied the reins from the tree branch. "Dammit," I grumbled as I leaned forward to untie the reins, only to hear the buzz of a high-velocity round go right over my back, followed closely by the delayed report of a suppressed weapon some distance away.

Freeing the rein, I quickly turned the horse away from the tree, kicked him in the sides, and began riding for my life in the direction from which I had come.

No! I thought, realizing they must have been watching me the entire time. I immediately changed course, cutting to the left and away from where Tamara should be waiting, not wanting to lead them straight to her, if they hadn't already found her, that is.

Hearing the ominous rotor beat of a ground-attack rotary-wing drone appear from over the ridge behind me, I kicked the horse harder, knowing I had to get as much distance as I could from the drone before it got a lock on me.

I did my best to steer the horse into the thick of the woods, but he appeared to have a different idea in mind, and I didn't have the skills or experience to convince him to do otherwise. He was heading for what appeared to be a wide open game trail, probably also used by the hunters, which would make us an easy target for the rapidly approaching drone.

Reaching behind me, I pulled my rifle from underneath the blanket atop the saddlebags and prepared to make a hasty exit from the now out-of-control situation. The horse was apparently aware that the drone was behind him, and saw speed, not stealth, as his best means of escape.

When I saw a large thicket of brush off to the left, I dove from the horse, hoping the brush would soften the impact and reduce my tendency to tumble. Although I felt I had to make a move, the last thing I wanted to do was to risk damaging the pack in the fall.

To my amazement, it worked like a charm. To my dismay, the brush proved to be blackberry bushes, whose thorns tore at my clothes and skin as I rapidly decelerated and came to a stop. I felt a burning sensation all over my body from the cuts and tears the briars had inflicted upon me.

I had no time to focus on such things, however, and quickly struggled against the clawing sensation of the briars as I freed myself and scurried into the thickest part of the woods near me, hoping to remain unseen by the operator of the drone or its sensors.

The drone flew by at a tremendous speed, closing in on the horse, and opened fire with its onboard anti-personnel weapon, which was essentially a remotely-operated, M134-style mini-gun adapted to fire one of the OWA's proprietary rounds.

I gathered from the horrendous but short-lived cries made by the horse, that the drone had struck its target. I was saddened by what had just happened to my new equine companion, but I buried my feelings deep as I continued to work my way away from the scene before OSS operators arrived on the scene to confirm the kill. Based on the shot I had narrowly avoided just a moment before, they weren't too far from the scene.

Knowing that the OSS operators would be rushing toward the kill site, which was due south of me on the ridge, I turned east and away from Chattanooga, running downhill and seeking shelter in the thick vegetation of the lower elevations.

I ran as fast as I could, jumping over downed trees, brush, and rocks as I went. On the steeper portions of the terrain, I would leap and allow the terrain to pass by beneath me until I made contact with the ground again, making great progress with each stride.

Seeing a small lake down at the bottom of the hill on the east side of the slope, I paused and observed for a moment. There was a farm nearby, but no other signs of possible habitation were evident, at least not at a glance.

After a moment of observing, I thought I could make out a trail that led from the lake in a southerly direction. I couldn't see the trail directly, but it was evident from the slight change in the canopy of the trees in a logical direction from the lake. I wondered what Tamara might have done once it all went down. Did she turn and retreat in the same direction from where we had come, or like me, did she decide that if we were being observed, they would see that as a likely path of travel and lie in wait for an ambush?

I knew Tamara hadn't stayed one step ahead of the OWA and their minions at the ODF and OSS by falling too easily into a trap. With that in mind, I hoped her emergency retreat from the scene would have been similar to mine—over the hill and away from our most recent path of travel.

For the next ten to fifteen minutes, I worked my way as quietly and as stealthily as I could toward the lake. Once I was within fifty or so yards, I could see the path that I had surmised was there. It was a gamble, the way I saw it. I could surely make good time running on a clear path but would be more easily seen by potential threats. I could move more stealthily in the thick of the woods, but I would be moving slowly and would remain within their search grid for far too long.

With that thought, I essentially flipped a mental coin and decided to opt for speed over stealth. I worked my way to the

lake, took one more good look around, and then began a steady
jog, humping the pack Tamara had given me, as well as the
Symbex and my rifle.

After I had jogged for what felt like a half hour, I found
myself at a small, backcountry road bearing the sign, Georgia
2208, along with the intersection of a small road named
Friendship Road. *Well, I'll be damned,* I thought. I was further
south than I had anticipated, but at least now I had my bearings
and could orient myself with the map in Tamara's go bag.

While I took a break under the shade of a large oak tree, I
reviewed the map and traced my finger from my location to our
rendezvous point, the Old Stone Church.

I saw now why she had selected it as our meet-up location.
Two terrain features, both tree-covered ridgelines with good
elevation, came together to the south, right at the Old Stone
Church. Even without a map, it would be easy to find once you
knew roughly where it was in relation to the topography of the
area. The two terrain features formed together with a valley in
the middle, with very little development in the area, allowing me
to work my way to the south while staying down in the thick of
it, helping me to avoid the prying eyes from above.

Maybe that wasn't her plan, maybe I was just giving her
more credit than she deserved and the Old Stone Church was
just something that stuck out in her mind? Either way, it was a
good choice, and hopefully, one that would pay off for us.

Earlier in the day, I had settled into the fact that it appeared
I had gained a partner in this crazy, suicidal mission. Now, I
really dreaded the thought of setting out again, alone. Life would
certainly be better with an ally, especially an ally with her head
on straight. And... there was just something about her. I'd met
so many people in this world who were just going along to get
along—drifting through this new life as if merely an actor or

actress in a play, but her? No, she was different. She was writing her own script.

Anxious to reach the church, I pressed on, using the unique topography of the area to guide me to my destination like an arrow pointing the way. I followed a steady pattern of moving forward, then stopping to listen and observe, especially in the sky above, though my eyes and ears were no match for the technology the OWA used to wield power over the rest of humanity.

I reached the area where the church was located later that evening, just as the sun began to set. I remained at a position of elevation at first, observing the area. The town of Ringgold, Georgia was just to the west of my position, with the Old Stone Church being directly south of me.

It was difficult to see very far from any position in the area, as the terrain was rolling and hilly, with no well-defined mountains or valleys, just a lot of the same in every direction, blocking the view of what was just on the other side of each hill.

The trees and vegetation of the non-paved or cleared areas were also very thick, limiting views as well. I could see what I thought was the Old Stone Church, though. I could see a parking area built for the visitors to the civil-war-era historic site, as well as restroom facilities. I could also see that there was the intersection of several two-lane paved roads directly in front of it, with what appeared to have once been a portable storage-building dealer on the far side of the road.

There were several open areas between my position and the church, but there were also just enough trees to give me a route to pick my way through without having to be out in the open. I debated with myself to decide whether to see those as choke points or as suitable paths of travel. It could quickly go either way if someone were to be lying in wait.

Setting the go-bag given to me by Tamara off to the side, I took a seat on an exposed cluster of roots beneath a large, oak tree, and began to sift through its contents. I pulled the thermal-imager-mitigating shelter from the pack and placed it to the side. I then removed a water-filtration bottle that had been pre-filled and took a drink. Once the water hit my lips, my body cried out for more. I was on the verge of dehydration, I just hadn't given myself time to slow down and adequately assess my condition until now.

Drinking nearly half the contents of the bottle, I placed it aside and removed an OWA-issued MRE. I chuckled and thought back to the first time I had eaten one of those. I guess it was during my previous evacuation-contingency training exercises with the ODF, where we trained to evacuate the OWA bureaucrats in the event the D.C. area were to become compromised by insurgent terrorist activity.

At the time, I thought such things were implausible, but now, I hoped they were probable. Not the terrorist part, mind you, but that the OWA could be sent on the run by a force of patriotic, flag-waving Americans who wanted both their country and their futures back from the despots who had biologically enslaved them.

I thought back to the stories of the colonists of the American Revolution, many of whom were regular people who made significant contributions to the cause, and who'd put their lives on the line to oppose what was seen as an overwhelming force to secure their liberty. Was I doing such a thing?

I didn't kid myself, though. I didn't put myself on a pedestal with the heroes of the past, but I did hope I was at least doing my part to help turn the tides of oppression both at home and around the world. Whether or not my sacrifice would ever be remembered wasn't important to me. I just wanted to somehow contribute to the greater good and wash away all the time I'd served the global beast that was the One World Alliance.

Once my stomach had settled, I inspected the Symbex pack and checked the charge level. The battery packs were at seventy-three percent, which was more than enough to get through the night for a good recharging the next day.

I then removed a single Symbex dosage vial and loaded it into the hand-held portable jet injector, dialed the dosage back to approximately half of what the standard dosage would be, and placed it off to the side while I removed my jacket and rolled up my sleeve to expose my bicep.

With a quick jet of air and the familiar sting of the drug entering my body, I knew I was good for another day or so. *I'll save the other half of this dose for Tamara,* I thought, convincing myself I would surely see her soon.

Sometimes the hope in your heart can be solidified by a simple act of faith. Putting aside the remaining half of the dosage for Tamara may have been one of those acts. I knew the odds of things, and I'd become used to having things not go exactly my way. Still, I had hope, and I'd follow through with her plan.

Realizing there was no way to know if Tamara was in the area if I didn't get closer, I decided to work my way down the hill and around to the east. There was an old cemetery behind the church that ran from the top of the hill located directly behind it, down to within a hundred yards or so of the church property.

Once I had reached the cemetery, I worked my way down the hill, taking cover behind gravestones, also using them as visual concealment until I was satisfied that the route was clear, advancing once again down to the next row of graves.

With the headstones not being arranged in perfect rows, it would be easy to shift my position to avoid giving a clear shot to anyone on ground level. There wasn't much I could do about shots fired from positions of elevation, but hey, I couldn't cover all my bases alone.

Once I reached the bottom row of graves, I got down into the prone position behind a large husband and wife headstone and concealed myself in the unkempt grass and weeds that were several feet tall around each of the stones.

Although I felt adequately concealed from the human eye, I knew the advanced sensors onboard drones or aircraft above would find me if I stayed in that location for too long. Additionally, the thermal-imager-defeating shelter would ruin my camouflage being in the tall weeds and grasses, so I decided to take a leap of faith and move forward, toward the church, to find myself a place to hide for possibly a day or more while I awaited Tamara's arrival.

Looking to the sun that was mere moments from disappearing over the horizon, I decided to leave my position behind the headstone and use those last few minutes of sunlight to find a suitable place to hide without having to use a flashlight that would be far too visible after dark.

Nearing the church, I could see that one of the old, multi-pane windows had been broken, probably by someone seeking to use the old structure as shelter. I approached the opening carefully and stayed close to the outside wall of the church, to conceal my presence from anyone who may be inside.

Reaching the window, I stood off to the side and raised my rifle, slicing the pie around the edge of the window to gain a view inside while covering the interior areas that I was exposing myself to with my weapon.

Seeing no signs of occupation, I placed my left hand on the stone ledge extending from the window, and quickly swung my body up and over, entering the building.

There was just enough remaining sunlight shining through the windows to allow me to see the historical wonder of the place. I read a few of the plaques placed in various places for the benefit of tourists and learned that the building was used as a hospital for the retreating Confederates after the battle of Tunnel Hill.

Blood stains soaked into the old, hardwood floors were still evident from the all those years ago, a testament to its history. As a history buff, my mind raced as I visualized the suffering that must have occurred in this room. A civil-war-era makeshift hospital would have certainly been a place you wouldn't have wanted to find yourself following a battle.

Being a single room structure, there really weren't too many places a man could hide, if any. I walked the length of the room, being required by my paranoia to check under each and every pew. Once I was satisfied that the room was empty, I took a seat on a pew along the center aisle.

By sitting in the center of the room, I could see out of both the north and south sides of the church at a glance. The east and west facing walls, however, had no windows. Turning around and looking at the large wooden double doors behind me, then looking forward toward the pulpit, I decided that I would prefer to sit with my back to that wall, instead. Never sit with your back to the entrance of a room.

I walked up the middle aisle toward the pulpit and noticed the old and very large Bible that sat on the podium. I walked around behind the podium and saw that it was opened to Revelation.

Very fitting, I thought. Though I wasn't personally well-versed in it at the time, I knew the book of Revelation was, after all, about the rise of evil, a great tribulation, and the end of an age. I couldn't help but think of how someone who had been going through the hell inflicted by the OWA would turn to this book, trying to figure out if they were, in fact, living through the apocalypse detailed within its pages.

As my eyes followed my fingers across the page, I heard a female voice say, "Did I miss the sermon?"

Startled, I flinched and reached from my rifle that dangled from its sling as I looked up at the broken window to see Tamara standing there, looking in at me.

My fight or flight response quickly turned to elation as I ran to the window and reached for her hand to pull her inside.

Refusing the gesture, she said, "We can catch up while we're on the move. I want to put some distance in between those bastards and us."

Chapter Fifteen

After leaving the Old Stone Church, Tamara and I moved quickly through the darkness, heading west, wading across the Chickamauga Creek, and following a tree line that bordered several overgrown and weed-ridden agricultural fields before coming to I-75, the major north-south interstate highway that runs through the area.

Stopping just short of I-75, I asked her, "When's the last time you received a dosage?"

Pausing, she said, "A few days, I guess."

"Then, here," I said as I removed the pack and opened it, retrieving the half dosage I'd saved for her. "This is half of a prescribed dose. That amount has been working for me so far. I don't feel any symptoms or anything. If we don't think it's working out, we can up the dosage, but I think we need to try and make this last as long as we can."

"I'm just thankful to God that we have it," she said as she rolled up her sleeve, presenting me with her bicep.

With just enough moonlight available to see adequately enough to get the job done, I took the portable air injector and administered her dose. As she rolled her sleeve back down and squared herself away, I put everything back in its place and shuffled the pack around to my back.

Curious as to what had happened on her end after the retrieval of the Symbex pack went awry, I asked, "So, what took you so long—to get to the church, that is?"

"I had to tie up a few loose ends," she replied vaguely.

"Loose ends?"

"Yeah. I... I had to say goodbye to some folks. And apologize."

"Apologize?" I repeated, unsure of what she meant.

"Yeah. I returned the remaining horse and apologized to George for the loss of the other one, as well as the loss of his Symbex connection."

Still confused, I tried to get her to elaborate, "What do you mean?"

"The OWA is canceling its support program in the area. They say it's because it's too dangerous to operate in an area with proven insurgent activity, but it's really a tactical withdrawal to strangle the resistance's support structure. They're essentially punishing everyone and are going to allow them to die because some people in the area supported our efforts, either by looking the other way or providing direct support, such as how George allowed us to utilize horses at his rescue. He and everyone else will die without the OWA's local viral-suppression support program."

"Damn, I'm so sorry," I mumbled, not knowing exactly what to say.

"Yeah," she replied as she looked off in the distance, wiping a tear from her eye, attempting to conceal it from me. "The OWA intentionally allows these people to die, and we take the blame. It kills two birds with one stone: it dries up our support and rids the OWA of those not loyal to them, even if it costs large numbers of loyalist casualties. That's not a concern of theirs, though. The unwashed masses are utterly disposable to them.

"And once the word spreads to the people near the next regional support facility, the horrors of what will soon happen here will dissuade others from helping our cause. We'll be the villains, and they'll once again be the saviors.

"Luckily, though," she began to say as her tone changed from sadness and defeat to one of resolve and fortitude, "some of the locals want to go out with a bang. They weren't fighters before. They were more of our unofficial support network. Now, though, they see that they need to fight. They don't want to die a slow, agonizing death. They want to land a solid punch on their way out the door."

With my curiosity piqued, I asked, "Do they have a specific plan—for that solid punch, that is?"

"They know you're carrying something important, something that might make a difference, but I didn't tell them what exactly that was. I didn't want to put your mission at risk. There's nothing more valuable than what you're carrying, and people might resort to desperate measures to get their hands on it if they knew.

"They've got five or six running vehicles they plan to use. They'll divide up into three groups: one of those will be carrying us, and the other two will be diversions, heading off in different directions. The OWA has a presence here, but their resources are limited, at least they are for now. That's why we've got to act soon. We need to move before more of ODF and OSS resources arrive—which is a certainty considering the fact that they want to stop you, wherever you are, as well as to provide security for the support-unit withdrawal from the area."

"That's a suicide mission, intentionally drawing attention away from us," I protested. "The ODF will hit them from the air, and they won't even see it coming."

"Maybe. Maybe not. But at least they're standing up for what they believe, in what may very well be their final hour," Tamara said matter-of-factly, as if there was going to be no further discussion on the issue.

I felt conflicted. This was *my* mission. Well, it was Ronnie's, but I had done my part, and had inherited it. But now, it seemed someone else was calling the shots. Someone else was writing my plan of action. I was conflicted by the lack of a solid feeling of control, the feeling I had felt since being on my own after Ronnie's death, but... this was, after all, the goal, right? I mean, I was supposed to somehow find a pocket of resistance somewhere that could help me get the Symbex and the research data to where it could be put to good use.

Even though these folks here aren't the ones to whom I was meant to deliver it, I knew I'd have a much better chance of success if I accepted their help. I also knew my chances would be much better if I had Tamara on my side for the long haul. This wasn't about me and my ego at the moment; it was about something far greater than myself, and I needed to brush my alpha-male pride to the side and see things with a clear head. I needed her, and I knew it.

With that internal argument pushed down deep and set aside, we set out to meet her associates at their pre-planned rendezvous location, which was located in the old Shaw Industries plant, which was just to the west off of I-75 and just beyond what they saw as a choke point created by elevated terrain.

Tamara and I maintained a steady jog, hand-railing I-75 in the woods, remaining out of the moonlight the best we could while making time our priority.

Winded and sweaty, we arrived on the east side of the facility and took a moment to gather ourselves, as well as observing before proceeding. I was exhausted. I was breathing heavily and was dripping with sweat. I looked at Tamara, and she looked as if she had simply taken a leisurely walk through the park. Don't get me wrong, I wasn't out of shape or anything, I think she simply operated at a higher level than most.

I watched as she surveyed the area, brushing her reddish brown hair back behind her ear. The moonlight provided a gentle glow of light on her cheek, and I couldn't help but become entranced by both her beauty and her determination.

She turned to say something, and we locked eyes. I quickly looked away, feeling embarrassed, as if I had gotten busted for something, but what? I hadn't done anything inappropriate. I was merely admiring her. Why did I feel so shy about it?

"Are you ready?" she said, getting us back on track and clearing the awkwardness from the air.

"All set," I said, wiping the sweat from my forehead with my sleeve, and with that, Tamara left our position of cover in the woods and was making her way toward the building, stopping for only a brief second to make sure I was following along.

We quickly dashed across the exposed dirt parking lot on the east end of the facility and made our way to the side of the building, getting close to the wall to hide in the shadows cast by the moonlight. Leaning in close to me, she whispered, "In the center of the building, there is an open area where our contact will be waiting. I was told to expect two vehicles here. The others are supposed to depart from different locations across the area, traveling in pairs. That way, unless they have at least three drones airborne at once, they can't observe us all, possibly following the decoys instead of us. It's a roll of the dice, but it's what we have."

"Sounds good," I muttered quietly as I double-checked the readiness of my weapon and gear.

"Okay, then," she whispered, "Let's get moving."

We quickly made our way around the building to our planned link-up point. Once we reached the corner leading around to where the vehicles were supposed to be waiting, Tamara sliced the pie around the corner while I covered her from behind, scanning the employee parking lot located directly behind the building. Our left flank was exposed to the parking lot as we rounded the corner, leaving me with a feeling of vulnerability that I just couldn't shake.

My heart raced when I saw a tall, slender man in his mid-thirties and wearing all black step out of the darkness from behind a Ford Explorer SUV.

"Chris," she said with relief in her voice as she ran to him. "It's so good to see you here."

"I wouldn't miss helping you for the world," he said as the two shared a warm embrace.

Holding him at arm's length, Tamara looked him in the eye and muttered, "I'm sorry things are ending this way. I wish..."

"Shhh," he interrupted softly. "Look, It's okay. That's how things go these days. I've come to terms with it. We all have."

Changing the subject, he looked to me and said, "You must be the famous Joe Branch I've heard so much about."

"Famous?" I mumbled, confused by his statement.

"You're a regular folk hero these days," Chris explained. "We've heard a lot about you, mostly propaganda from the OWA, I'm sure, essentially labeling you as public enemy number one, offering sanctuary to whoever provides information leading to your arrest. But the way we see it, any enemy of the OWA is more than likely our kind of guy."

"What?" Tamara asked.

"Yesterday afternoon at the OWA Regional Support Facility, when they began packing up shop to ship out, they started handing out flyers. As a matter of fact, I have one right here," he said, removing a folded piece of paper from his pocket and unfolding it.

"Let me see that," she said, snatching the paper out of his hand.

Leaning in to look, I saw a surveillance photo of me taken at what appeared to be the OWA commissary back in D.C. "Well, I'll be damned."

The flyer read, *Sanctuary offered to the individual and family of the individual or individuals providing information leading to the arrest of insurgent terrorist Joseph Branch. Joseph Branch, who also goes by Joe Branch, is wanted in connection with the murders of both ODF officers and civilians alike. He is considered to be armed and extremely dangerous. Do not approach if seen. Contact your local OWA representative immediately.*

"Yeah, they're turning up the heat," he said, reaching out and taking the paper.

Shaking her head, Tamara said, "I guess they're banking on the hope that their withdrawal from the area, leaving innocent people to die, will prompt someone to step up and trade his life for theirs."

"Yep, and after a day or two of not receiving their Symbex, I'd imagine people will be lining up to do it."

Upon hearing this revelation, I felt my stomach tighten, and a sick feeling came over me. "This isn't good," I grumbled under my breath.

"No, it's not," Tamara replied as she placed her hand on my shoulder. "You don't have to worry about Chris here, Joe. He's good people."

"Thanks," I said. "And thanks for helping," I said to Chris as I shook his hand.

"Again, my pleasure," he said. "Besides, those bastards would probably renege on their promise to provide sanctuary anyway."

Turning to another man who had appeared from behind him, Chris said, "Bill here will be riding along with us."

"Bill Bowers," the man said, reaching out his hand. "Nice to meet you both."

Looking around, Tamara queried, "I thought we were supposed to have two vehicles per group?"

"They had trouble with the other car," Chris explained. "The starter has been having an intermittent problem lately, and it looks like it's finally given up the ghost. Sorry, but at the last minute, we didn't have any other running vehicles lined up. It's hard to find one that hasn't already been fried by EMWS equipped drones. If those bastards saw unauthorized vehicle movement, they would fry it without even asking questions."

"That's better than being hit by a drone strike with an air-to-ground missile," I added. "They weren't shy about using those at first."

"I guess now that resources are tighter, those are reserved for known threats," Bill quipped nervously. "The EMWS makes for a handy non-lethal way to deal with the unknowns, I guess. It's also not a consumable item like AGMs and such."

"Come on, guys," Tamara interrupted. "We can chat about tactics in the car."

Nodding in reply, Bill turned and climbed into the front passenger's seat of the Explorer, picking a tactical shotgun up from the floor, while Chris slid into the driver's seat, picking up a short-barreled AR-15 with a pistol brace for a stock from the seat as he sat down, and laid it across his lap.

Tamara slid across behind Bill, and I took the seat in the second row directly behind Chris.

As the vehicle started, the headlights automatically illuminated, followed immediately by Chris saying, "Dammit! I hate those things," as he quickly extinguished them. "If I want lights, I'll turn the damned things on myself. I hate how cars evolved into making those decisions for you."

"You won't have that problem for long," Bill replied.

Wow, that was dark, I thought. *Did he mean that the way I think he did?*

After a brief moment of awkwardness, Chris slipped a set of bifocal night-vision goggles over his head, switched them on, and began driving the Explorer out of the complex. We traveled quietly down Industrial Boulevard and onto I-75 South via Old Alabama Road. I-75 North would have taken us back into Chattanooga, which was an area we needed to avoid for the time being.

Tensions were high in the vehicle. No one said a word. Each just looked out their respective windows as Chris guided us down the interstate as best he could with the NVGs while running dark. Looking up, I said, "Hey, can you open the sunroof?"

Bill looked back at me from the front passenger's seat like he was perturbed by my request. I clarified by saying, "Drones. I figured we could see and hear better with the roof open."

Acquiescing to my request, Bill began to roll the sunroof back as the cool night air swept into the vehicle. I stared up into the sky through the sunroof and was amazed by the clarity of the stars that night. The sky was crystal clear. "It's going to be a cold one," I said. "I'm glad I'm not sleeping on the ground tonight."

With a chuckle, Tamara said, "The night's not over yet."

Just then, I saw one of the stars above us disappear, and then return. My eyes locked onto the star, as I saw another vanish and reappear just ahead of that one. Then it hit me, a drone was flying high overhead, occasionally blocking the view of a given star when lined up directly between us and the star, only to fly on ahead, revealing the star once again.

"Drone!" I exclaimed, pointing toward the sky.

"Where?" Tamara asked, as she too scanned the sky through the sunroof.

Being in the front seat, Bill wasn't in a position to see the area of the sky that we were focusing on, so he rolled down his window, sticking his head out and scanning the sky above.

"Just focus on the stars, you'll see it when it passes in front of one."

"There!" Tamara said. "I see it. It's directly overhead. They're onto us."

As Tamara and I both stared at the airborne threat above us through the sunroof, the deafening report of a handgun fired in close quarters stung our ears as we looked down and were stunned to see Chris holding a pistol in his hand. Next to Chris, Bill lay still, leaning out the opened window, streaming blood down the side of the car as we drove.

Momentarily stunned by the confusion of what was occurring before our eyes, we heard Chris shouting, "Drop your weapons and get your hands where I can see them!" as his pistol was now turned on us. He flipped on the vehicle's dome light and headlights and brought the vehicle to a stop. We saw that he was no longer wearing his NVGs, having removed them while the rest of us were distracted by the drone above.

Tamara screamed, "Chris! What the hell!? What the hell are you doing!?"

"Drop them!" he demanded, and we reluctantly complied.

"I never signed up to fight," he said. "You did. You brought this wrath down on us—you and your traitor friend here. We were getting by. We were all getting by. But now, everyone we love and care for is going to die when the OWA pulls out, all because of you and your stupid cause.

"I'm not going to let my family die because of your poor choices. I'm taking the deal. I'm getting my family the hell out of Chattanooga and to a place where they will provide us with what we need to survive."

Pointing the gun directly at Tamara's head, he then said calmly, "Now, place the pack with whatever the hell they're looking for up here with Bill."

I hesitated briefly, and he shouted once again, "Do it!"

I knew one flinch, one twitch of his finger and Tamara would die right there in front of me. Not having time to think about what to do, I reached over the center console and placed the pack onto Bill's lap.

"Good," he said, "Now, toss your weapons out the window. I don't want your friends at the ODF to come up on the vehicle and see you with weapons on your person. I don't want to take the chance of getting cut down in the crossfire."

Doing as he said, we both tossed our rifles out the windows of the SUV.

As Chris began some sort of half apology, half self-exoneration speech to Tamara, my eyes caught something moving in the sky out in front of the vehicle. It was the drone, exposing its upper surface to the moonlight as it banked and descended toward us.

"That was no surveillance drone," I stated calmly. "It's one of the OWA's light attack drones, and I think we'd all better get out of the car."

"Shut up!" barked Chris, assuming I was creating a ruse to distract him.

I saw a flash of light up ahead as the drone fired on us. At that moment, time seemed to slow down for all of us. Chris could see Tamara's eyes dart toward the distant flash. He began to turn his head as I shoved his pistol upward and way from Tamara, causing his trigger finger to discharge the weapon, firing into the ceiling of the car.

Both Tamara and I reached for our door handles as a great burst of light and an overpowering concussion hit us like a ton of bricks, lifting the front of the Explorer up and flipping it over backward, causing us to roll off the road and down the hill toward the rainwater-drainage ditch that followed alongside the freeway.

After several rolls, the vehicle came to rest on its top and flames began to sweep through the vehicle as I crawled free and into the ditch, having barely managed to grab the Symbex pack that had been tossed back toward me during the missile strike and the accompanying rolls. I could hear Chris screaming as he was engulfed in flames, unable to escape.

"Tamara!" I shouted as I slung the pack over my shoulder, looking around frantically, seeing that her door had been open during the rollover. I scurried up the hill, finding her lying in the road where she had been ejected from the vehicle before it went over the bank.

Kneeling beside her, I shouted over the ringing in my ears from both the gunshots and the explosion. "Tamara! Are you okay?"

Seeing no response, I checked her pulse and felt the rise of her chest as she breathed. "Come on, girl! Hang in there!" I said as I heard the rotor beat of a helicopter rapidly approaching.

With no time to evaluate her injuries before they arrived, I took the chance and picked her up, draping her over my shoulder and began making my way toward the woods.

Seeing my Sig 556 laying on the side of the road from where I had tossed it out, I hooked my foot through the sling, and lifted it up to where I could get my other hand on it, and quickly made my way for the cover of the trees ahead.

Chapter Sixteen

I'm not sure how long I walked with Tamara over my shoulder that night. As a matter of fact, I wasn't even sure of where we were, or how far Chris had driven before the encounter with the drone. My mind was in full-on survival mode. I had to get both of us away from the ODF that had likely arrived with the helicopter.

I hoped the fire disguised the fact that we weren't in the vehicle with Chris and Bill as it burned. I knew they would eventually investigate the scene thoroughly and would discover our absence, at which time, they would be on the hunt once again.

The best I could initially tell without stopping to look at my map was that we were somewhere near Dalton, Georgia, as we had been traveling on southbound I-75 prior to the incident.

Exhausted, I dropped to my knees and placed Tamara gently on the ground next to me and felt thankful that the sun was coming up to my left, which verified that I had indeed been traveling south in the darkness of the night. It would have been easy to get off track navigating the rough terrain in my haste, and I was glad that I had somehow stayed the course.

I quickly checked her over for signs of injury. Her pulse was steady, though her breathing was shallow. I was no medical expert, however, so I really didn't know how to interpret that, other than to know she was still with me.

I felt around on her head and found an area with apparent swelling. I assumed this was from either the violence of the concussion that had hit the vehicle or from hitting the pavement after being ejected while trying to escape. Either way, I had to assume she may have received a head injury, which quite frankly terrified me, considering the fact that I had no medical assistance available, nor could expect any.

I checked her eyes, and they appeared dilated, with one appearing slightly larger than the other. I tried to scan my memory of my emergency medical courses I had received while serving as both a police officer and an ODF security officer, and I vaguely remembered such things being a symptom of a concussion, but I couldn't remember for sure.

Positioning her the best I could, hidden behind an outcrop of vegetation deep in the woods, I stood up and visually scanned the area while retrieving my map from my pack. With the sun's rays now beginning to shine brilliantly over the horizon, I studied the map and compared it to my surroundings.

There was a city to my east and thick woods to my south and west. *That must be Dalton,* I thought as I tapped my finger on the map.

With that revelation, if I were right, that would put the small town of Villanow, Georgia, directly to my west. According to the map, it appeared to be a very rural area with a vast expanse of woods between here and there. It seemed I was standing on the edge of the Johns Mountain Wildlife Management Area, which meant established human occupation would be minimal, with the obvious exception of others who were trying to lay low in the woods, attempting to avoid the infected or the powers-that-be.

For now, we both needed rest. With Tamara's pack left behind at the scene of the crash, I removed the thermal blocking personal shelter from my pack and laid down next to her, attempting to cover us both, retaining our body heat during the cool fall mountain morning, as well as preventing our detection while we slept.

With my Sig 556 rifle lying to my left, and Tamara to my right, I curled up for what I hoped to be an uneventful, much-needed nap.

~~~~

I was startled awake a few hours later. It was Tamara. She was moving around and trying to talk.

"Tamara," I said, placing my hand on her cheek. "It's me, Joe. You're okay. Everything's gonna be okay."

Her eyes flicked open and closed a few times, blinded by the sun's rays shining through the trees with the sun now directly above us in the sky. Using my hand, I shielded her eyes and asked, "Can you speak? Other than the blow to your head, do you feel anything wrong?"

"N... no... no, it's just my head. Oh, damn, this hurts," she said, reaching for the lump on the back of her head with her right hand. Feeling the lump, she recoiled quickly when she touched it.

"Damn, that hurts," she reiterated.

"You're gonna feel that for a while," I assured her. "But don't worry, everything that's supposed to be inside is still inside."

Attempting a smile without much success, she said, "Everything looks cloudy. Is it foggy here? It feels too warm for that."

"I'm sure you have a concussion," I explained. "I'm pretty sure foggy vision is a common symptom of that. Once, when I was younger, I was into riding motocross. I was riding on a muddy track, and the ruts were starting to get pretty deep. Me and this other guy, who I didn't even know, had been fighting for position for several laps. I tried to take him in a sharp turn right before a jump, and my back tire slid over into a different rut than the front tire.

"When I launched off the jump, which was unfortunately a triple, the bike whirled sideways. I threw it away, not wanting to hit the ground tangled up with it, and bounced my grape pretty hard. Thank God for helmets," I said with a chuckle. "Anyway, when I first sat up, I felt as if I couldn't see at all. Then, my vision started returning, but I swear it was delayed. I would turn my head, and it would take a second for the image to follow. It was the strangest thing. That went on for a few minutes before things started to return to normal."

"What did the doctors say?" she whispered, obviously hoping to hear some medical wisdom from my lessons-learned scenario.

"Doctors? I didn't go to the doctor," I answered.

"Men are such idiots," she said with a crooked smile.

"I won't argue with you there," I said as I brushed some twigs out of her hair.

Laying back and closing her eyes, she explained, "I've not had a concussion myself before, but this sure seems like the same symptoms described by all the patients I've aided in the past who were diagnosed with a concussion. Ah, it hurts too bad to think right now, though," she grumbled as she placed her arm over her eyes to shield herself from the light.

After a few moments, she asked, "Where are Chris and Bill?" She attempted to turn her head to look around, but quickly abandoned the attempt due to the pain.

"You don't remember what happened?" I asked, beginning to worry about the extent of her condition.

Thinking for a moment, she replied, "I remember driving, then arguing about something, and that's about it."

Taking a deep breath, I said, "You're friend, Chris, took the OWA up on their offer of sanctuary."

I could see the shock in her eyes. She honestly didn't remember. Giving her a moment to process what I had just said, I continued, "Chris shot Bill in the head right in front of us, then turned his weapon on us. He stopped the vehicle, turned on the headlights and the dome light, and held us at gunpoint. Well, he held you at gunpoint, threatening to shoot you in the head if I so much as moved. He needed me, but he didn't need you, and he used that to his advantage."

Tamara looked crushed. She was genuinely having a hard time taking Chris's treachery in as the truth.

"Unfortunately for Chris, the OWA didn't plan on taking me alive like he thought. They also didn't plan on honoring their offer. They sent an attack drone in for the kill, and its shot came up a bit short, hitting directly in front and underneath the SUV, flipping us over backward and sending us rolling down the hill next to the road.

"When we stopped rolling, the vehicle was burning. The blast must have ignited the fuel lines at the engine. I barely made it out, Chris wasn't so lucky.

"Luckily for you, you had tried to escape when Chris was distracted by the incoming drone, getting your door open just in time. You must have been ejected from the vehicle during the ensuing rollover. You may have a bad bump on your head, but at least you didn't die screaming in a fire."

"Is that how Chris died?" she asked.

I simply nodded in reply. I knew Chris deserved what he got, but she was still in a battle in her own mind between her memory of Chris and what I had just told her.

"Anyway, after the blast, I searched for you and found you up the hill and still lying in the road. I heard a full-sized helicopter approaching, and without the time to consider an alternative, I took the chance of moving you in your unknown condition."

Taking a good look around, clearly starting to feel better than when she had just awakened, she asked, "So, how did I get here?"

"I carried you," I replied.

Still confused, she asked, "Where are we?"

Retrieving the map from my pocket, I unfolded it and tapped my finger on our presumed location, saying, "Right about here, I believe."

"You carried me all the way from I-75 to here while running from the OSS?"

"Yeah, but you barely weigh a buck-o-five, so I managed."

"A buck twenty, but thanks," she replied. "I appreciate it. You could have just taken what you needed and continued your mission without me."

"I didn't, and still don't, see that as a choice," I replied reassuringly, placing my hand on her shoulder and smiling.

Changing the subject, she licked her lips and muttered, "I'm thirsty. Do we have any water?"

"I managed to get away with my pack and the Symbex, of course, but your weapon and your pack had to be left behind. I don't have any water left, but I've got that filter bottle. I'll run down to the creek that's just over that way," I said pointing. "I'll fill it for you. I'll be right back."

Picking up my Sig 556, I laid it next to her right arm and said, "Here. You hang on to this, just in case."

"No," she rebutted. "Take it with you."

"I can run, you can't," I argued. "You're keeping it while I'm gone, and there won't be any further discussion on the subject."

"Yes, sir!" she said smartly, attempting a mock salute, immediately regretting the quick movements involved.

Grinning, I said, "Don't worry. You'll be back on your feet and ordering me around again in no time."

Her facial expression immediately went from somewhat positive and upbeat to downcast. "You think I order you around?"

"Well... I didn't mean it that way," I explained, feeling confused about what had just transpired. I mean, how we treated each other had never come up before. We had been all business, seeing a mission through until its end, no matter what the cost, and here we were discussing our treatment of one another.

"I respect your capability, experience, and your wisdom," I quickly added. "I didn't mean that in a bad way."

"It's okay," she said, changing the subject, which she often does when a conversation brings discomfort for her. "Just hurry back."

Removing the filter bottle from the pack, I carefully walked through the woods toward the creek, which was just over the hill and out of sight. I would take a few steps, then scan the area, looking and listening. I repeated this procedure until I reached the edge of the small, year-round creek.

I knelt down at the edge of the water and had begun to fill my bottle when I saw hoof prints. They were the prints of a shod horse, and they were fresh. Immediately standing up, I looked around again, then noticed a pair of boot prints on the ground just a few feet away. The prints weren't anything like what a tactical operator would wear; they were more of a smooth-soled boot with a pointed toe and a defined heel. A cowboy boot, perhaps?

Thinking of Tamara being back there alone, I quickly filled the bottle and hurried back up the hill toward her. As I knelt down beside her to help her get a drink, she could tell I was agitated about something, and asked, "What? What is it? Did you see something?"

"We're not the only ones who've watered at that creek recently."

"What do you mean?" she asked.

"I saw a set of hoof prints from a shod horse, as well as a set of boot prints. Nothing tactical. Nothing the OSS would wear. It was probably just a traveler, like us, passing through."

"None of George's horses were shod," she said, half wondering aloud. "To keep a horse shod these days, one couldn't be traveling far from home."

Puzzled, I asked, "What do you mean?"

"Even when shod, the hoof grows and needs to be trimmed every six weeks or so," she explained. "That job requires special tools, such as nips, a rasp, and a hoof knife at a minimum, which George used to keep his rescue horses' feet trimmed. But to keep them shod, you need a supply of shoes, a hoof hammer, hoof nails, clinchers, nail cutters, and often times, a forge to beat them into the right shape to match the horse's hoof. That's not something a drifter could carry around in his saddlebags. No, that's an indication of a person who returns to their point of origin at some point."

"So, you think we're on someone's home turf?" I asked.

Shrugging her shoulders, she said, "I mean... who knows? That just seems odd to me. It's not like a man could just ride up to a new town and ask where the village blacksmith is. That was a dying art even before the collapse. It's just a guess on my end. I may be way off base on the whole thing."

Pondering her insight into my observations for a brief moment, I asked, "How do you feel? Do you feel up to trying to walk anytime soon?"

Seeing her try to sit up, I reached out my hand, and she took it, pulling herself up to the seated position.

"Whew," she said. "That made me dizzy."

"Lie back down," I urged, concerned that she might be doing too much too soon.

"No, just let me sit here a while," she insisted, releasing my hand and placing hers on the ground to support herself.

Blinking her eyes rapidly a few times, she said, "Hand me that pack I gave you."

Doing as she asked, I watched as she retrieved the first aid kit from the larger of the two front pockets. Unzipping it, she removed a bottle of Motrin and shook two of the pills out into her hand. Tossing them into her mouth, she washed them down with water from the filter bottle, then wiped her lips.

"Something stronger would be nice, but hopefully the vitamin M will help," she said, placing that pack aside.

"Well," I said, taking a moment to look up at the sky and the position of the sun. "If we're going to be here a little while longer, I may as well charge the Symbex pack. There's just enough light shining through the trees to charge it up pretty quick, I think."

"You do that, I'm gonna take a nap," she said, blinking her eyes again.

"Here, let me help," I said as I reached out my hand, helping her to lie back and onto the ground. I then placed the nylon first aid pack under her head as a pillow and went about my business.

Finding an adequate spot where ample sunlight shone down through the trees, I placed the Symbex pack off to the side and removed the fold-out solar charger from the front compartment. I then plugged the solar panels into the port on the side of the pack.

Catching a whiff of something I didn't' usually smell when handling the pack, I unzipped the main compartment, and to my horror, I realized that even with the extensive padding Ronnie had installed, the life-saving and possibly world-altering supply of Symbex I had been carrying had been damaged in the blast.

I sat back onto the ground in absolute shock. The pack had been in the front of the vehicle when the blast occurred and was thrown violently back, possibly hitting the roof as it went, damaging the contents.

Steven C. Bird

I began sifting through the dosage vials that were now in disarray, *broken, broken, broken, broken...* my heart sank as I searched through them, with each one that I picked up leaking onto my hand, with some being completely destroyed and empty. I finally came across one that seemed undamaged, *please God, let there be more.*

Once I had gone entirely through the pack's contents, I had counted a total of twenty-two vials that remained undamaged. I don't think I had ever felt such an overwhelming feeling of dread like I had at that moment. It was like a dark specter had climbed onto me, and was reaching into my chest, squeezing my heart. I truly felt as if I was going to die, and to be honest, without the Symbex, I was.

The trip had started out with two-hundred vials. Ronnie and I had planned to possibly utilize half of those during our travels, and maybe more. But with only twenty-two this early into the journey...? With that count, even taking half-doses, or every other day doses, Tamara and I would begin to feel the life-threatening effects of the virus within a month, and that's without having any remaining vials to provide to resistance medical researchers—if we found them.

Our valiant effort to break the grip of the beast that was the OWA was over in an instant. And for what? Tamara's friends had died because of my arrival, and now the entire region surrounding Chattanooga would be left to die by the OWA as well.

Our Hail Mary pass to free the world from the OWA's grip had been intercepted. The game was over.

Chapter Seventeen

To this day, I'm not sure how much time had passed from my revelation about the Symbex pack and my willingness to stand up and face Tamara with the truth. She would likely be even more devastated than I. After all, it was she who had lost everything she had in this world thanks to my arrival.

Dread swept through my body as I approached her. What was I going to say? The truth... that's all I had.

"I was beginning to wonder about you," she quipped with a smile.

"You look like you're feeling better," I noted as I sat down next to her.

"A little. The fog is starting to clear, at least. What's wrong?"

She could read me like a book. She knew something was eating away at me—something that wasn't there when I walked off into the woods to charge the pack.

"I have some bad news," I muttered as I stared at the ground in front of me.

"It's the pack, isn't it?" she immediately guessed. "What happened?"

"You probably don't remember, but Chris ordered me to place the pack in the front seat just before the drone strike hit. The idiot thought the OSS cavalry would arrive and he would sit there as the hero of the day with his captives and the prize."

"It's starting to come back to me," she said.

"Well, when the blast hit, the pack must have been ejected from the front and took a few hard hits before we came to a stop in the ditch at the bottom of the hill. All but twenty-two of the vials were damaged or destroyed."

She quickly did the math in her head and reached over and took my hand. After a moment, she said, "What about the data?

Didn't you say there was also research data in the pack? Data that may help the researchers?"

"Yes," I grumbled. "Ronnie had a friend on the inside the OWA's Public Health Service, which should have been called the Viral Enslavement Service. Anyway, his friend worked diligently putting together a set of notes and data that she memorized while on the job, then documented later once she had gone home for the day. Ronnie says there is supposed to be years' worth of research on the little storage device."

With resolve in her voice, she gripped my hand and said, "Then, we still have a job to do."

Turning to her, I smiled. It felt good to have someone who truly felt like a partner in this cruel world.

Returning the smile, she said, "Even if we have to crawl to them on our knees, in the last moments of our lives as the virus overtakes us, we'll get that data in the right hands where it can be put to good use. The plan may not be what it was, but we can still go out proud of who we are, and proud that our lives were used to help others."

I couldn't help myself. I leaned in and embraced her, squeezing her tightly and just relishing in the moment. I hadn't had a feeling of such warmth in my heart in as long as I could remember.

"And at least I won't be remembered as a stormtrooper," I said with a grin.

"You're a hero to me whether we make it there or not," she said as she leaned in and kissed me lightly on the lips.

We sat there for what was probably the next half an hour in silence. I can only assume she was doing the same as I, contemplating our future, present, and past. I thought of where my life could have gone and where it had. I could have still been back in D.C., comfortable, yet knowing the truth, but if I had continued to serve the OWA with that certainty in my heart, I would have been complicit in their deeds. I already felt that I had a black spot on my soul for serving the beast as long as I had, but this—if we could pull it off—would wash it clean again.

I doubt that in her heart she was longing for redemption as I was. She had only served the OWA in a capacity to help others, not to enforce its rule; still, she seemed very at peace with what we faced. She was indeed a person to be admired, and I was fortunate to be facing the challenges ahead alongside her.

Once she decided she was up for travel, we pressed on through the woods to the west. The initial elevation gain to get to the other side of the hill ahead took its toll on her, requiring us to take numerous breaks, slowing our pace dramatically, but at least we were making progress.

"Tomorrow will be better," she said.

"Don't worry about it," I said, dismissing her feeling of holding us back. "It's not like we have an appointment to keep or anything. We'll get to wherever we're going whenever we get there."

"That's the positive Joe Branch I like to see," she said with a smile.

Before I could respond, we heard the nicker of a horse in the distance, and both immediately looked up to see a man dressed in dark brown woodsman's clothing, with a duster-style coat and a brown, floppy full-brimmed hat. The man sat atop the horse at a distance of maybe one hundred yards or so and seemed to merely be staring at us. Neither the man nor the horse moved in any way. He appeared to have a rifle of some sort laid across his lap, but it was hard to tell for sure from our distance.

I reached slowly for my rifle and was stopped by Tamara's hand as she whispered, "No."

"Do you know him?" I asked softly.

"No. No, I don't. We're outside of my area here. But if he meant us harm, he could have shot us without us even knowing he was here."

"Are you sure he's armed?" I asked.

"Why would an unarmed man allow us to see him when we clearly have a weapon? We only know he's there because he allowed us to. Let's not lose sight of that."

The man then turned his horse and disappeared into the woods. The horse and rider moved swiftly and confidently through the trees with the stealth and agility of a deer. She was right. We'd have never known he was there if he hadn't chosen to allow it.

Based on our map, with our current direction of travel, we'd be crossing three to four mountain ridges to get to the other side. However, traveling south or north would take us a long way from our route of intended travel. Deviating either direction for the sake of less-difficult terrain would likely add days to our journey, and those were days we no longer had to burn.

We soon came across a reasonably well-used trail that appeared to have been there long before the Sembé virus had swept through the nation and the world. We explored the trail for a short distance and soon found a white, diamond-shaped trail marker with the symbol of a turkey's foot on it, with the word *Pinhoti* underneath.

"That must be this trail," I said, tapping my finger on the map. Though our map didn't contain any detailed information about the Pinhoti trail, we could see that it zigged and zagged up and down between the ridges in our path of travel. It appeared to have been cut to mitigate the steep inclines, trading slope for mileage.

Unfortunately, most of the trail would add significant mileage to our journey, as it traveled far to both the north and the south, due to the steepness of the terrain. Based on the scale of our map, we would need to travel approximately three miles to clear the wildlife area as the crow flies, but seven or eight miles if we took the trail.

Thinking it over for a minute, I pointed uphill and asked Tamara, "Only you know how you feel after taking that blow to the head. It's your call. We can take the shorter, steeper route or the longer, more flowing route."

She glared at me as if I'd insulted her somehow. "Up and over," she insisted as she began walking straight up the side of the hill.

I wasn't totally comfortable pushing her so hard with what I could only assume to be a concussion, but Tamara wasn't a woman to be argued with. Maybe I was a glutton for punishment, but that was a more appealing trait than I had imagined. Maybe it was the situation, or maybe...

"Well, are you coming?" she quipped sarcastically, already well ahead of me.

By the time we reached the top of the next ridge, my heart was pounding. It had been a much longer, steeper climb than it had looked from the bottom. It's funny how that works. How many times have people uttered the words "it's just over the next hill" or "it can't be much further" only to reach the top to see yet another, and another? More than one could count, I'd imagine.

I knew if my heart was beating like it was trying to climb out of my chest, Tamara must have been feeling the effects of her blow to the head. I had seen her squint and blink a few times, so the pain was more than evident.

Looking around from our position of elevation on top of the ridge, I observed, "Wow, this place is gorgeous."

"Yes, it is," she replied while scanning the area. "If we go down here," she said, pointing straight ahead, "we can cut through those clearings to the south of that ridge in the center, then work our way back up the valley on the next side before cutting across. That would save us one climb and descent."

Examining her proposed route on the map, I said, "That should work just fine. Are those clearings farms?" I asked, trying to make out any signs of habitation in that area. It would have been the perfect hideaway, with the exception of being visible from the top of the Pinhoti trail, of course.

Surrounded by mountains on all sides and essentially cut off from any highways or major migratory routes, it would make a great place to get away from the world, so long as the world didn't go hiking—that is.

"If you look at that cut in the mountains there," she pointed, "a road probably comes into the valley from there. It looks like a one-way-in, one-way-out situation. It would be the perfect setup for blocking the road and keeping vehicle traffic out."

Looking up at the sky, I said, "We've eaten up a chunk of the day already. We'd better keep moving. How do you feel?"

"I'm okay," she quickly answered as if not giving the question a second thought.

I admired her rugged, mission-focused attitude, but I didn't want her to overdo it for the sake of pride or mission accomplishment. Not wanting to hold my tongue any longer, I said bluntly, "Did you fly on the airlines much? Before the collapse, that is?"

"A few times. Why?" she asked, wondering where I was going with that.

"Do you remember that tedious, yet legally required safety brief where the flight attendants would show you how to fasten your seatbelt and put on your life vest, even if you weren't flying over any water?"

"Yeah," she replied, looking even more confused.

"When they mentioned the oxygen mask, remember how they would tell you to be sure to put your own mask on before you helped others?"

Nodding, starting to see where I was going with this, she crossed her arms and continued to listen, humoring me, I guess.

"They said that because if you're struggling to help someone else and forget about yourself, you could pass out and then be no use to anyone. If you get your mask on properly first, then you'll be in a better position to help others."

"Are you telling me to put my mask on?" she asked, giving me 'the look'.

"Yes. Yes, I am. I just don't want you to push so hard that you end up stroking out on me or something from your head injury, especially with the extent of your injury being unclear to us at this point. Overdoing it now won't help the mission if it slows us down or stops us a few miles down the road."

She didn't answer me right away. She looked away, then back, locking onto my eyes. "Okay. It's downhill from here until we reach the valley with the clearings. We'll work our way down easy, and then, at the bottom, we'll find a creek or something to refill our water and take a break. And..."

After an awkward moment, I asked, "And, what?"

"And, I'll try not to be so stubborn. I'll take your advice. I appreciate it. I really do. It's nice to have someone care about you these days. Most people just see you for what they can get out of you. Everyone is just... cold."

"Everyone's in survival mode," I said. "I guess that comes with the territory. Everyone has suffered so many losses, well, I guess we've all been emotionally-hardened, to a point. The one thing I don't think we should do, though, is to focus solely on staying alive while forgetting to live."

She turned to me, almost caught off-guard by my simple statement. I could see her face soften as if she began to lower an impenetrable wall of protection that she used as an armor to keep her emotions safe.

"Look," I continued, "we know the score. We've done the math. Maybe we'll somehow pull this off, but odds are we won't. Let's not waste our remaining time being all business. Let's travel as two companions, rather than two people competing to see who's tougher and who can run up the side of a mountain the fastest."

Smiling, she said, "That's just because you know I'll win."

I laughed out loud for the first time in as long as I could remember. It was a deep belly laugh that almost brought me to tears. I had wanted to be able to enjoy life for so long, yet at this moment, it was the first time it had felt like an actual possibility.

We laughed together for a few moments, and when it finally subsided, she took me by the hand, looked me in the eyes, and said, "You have no idea how bad I needed that," as a tear began to roll down her cheek.

That tear led to another, and then another, and before long, she leaned in and rested her head against mine and began to sob, releasing some internal demons that had long overstayed their welcome.

For the next hour, we sat on the ridge underneath a tree with her head on my shoulder, silently observing the beauty of the world around us. It felt as if it was the first time in a long time we simply enjoyed the presence of someone else, and not just for the physical security it brought with it. For the first time in a long time, neither one of us was alone.

Chapter Eighteen

After our much-needed break on the ridge, we worked our way down the mountainside to the valley below and to the south. Although far less rigorous from a cardiovascular standpoint, I had always hated extended periods of traveling over steep, downhill terrain, because over time, the feeling of having my toes jammed into the front of my boots began to wear on me.

I was elated when we finally reached the bottom, and the terrain flowed gently into the valley below. "First things first," I said. "Let's find water."

Studying the flow of the terrain, as well as a row of trees following the lowest point between the two ridges, Tamara pointed and said, "If I were a creek, that's where I would be."

"Let's check it out," I said, and we began working our way in that direction. Upon reaching the low-lying row of trees, we could hear the faint trickle of water flowing from the higher elevations above.

"See? I told you," she joked with a smile.

Kneeling at the edge of the water, I began to fill the filter bottle as I heard her say, "More shod hoof prints."

Standing and walking toward her, I looked to where she was pointing and visually followed the tracks across the creek and through the trees on the other side.

"Those look fresh," I said, noting the sharpness of the edges in the soft dirt that would have surely begun to wear away if any significant time had passed.

"It only makes sense," she replied. "If we're looking for water, he's looking for water. Out here, if you want to run into someone, it'll be at a source of water."

"Let's drink up, then top the bottle off and get moving," I said, and turned to resume filling the bottle.

After we had both drunk our fill, I topped the bottle off as planned and placed it in the pack.

"I'm feeling okay. Let me carry the extra pack. I feel bad watching you hump both packs and the rifle," Tamara admitted sheepishly.

"You just don't want me to have an excuse as to why you beat me up the next hill, huh?" I joked as I handed her the pack.

"You've got me all figured out," she replied. Looking up the mountain, she asked, "Which way? What do you think?"

I was taken aback at first by her question. I was beginning to see the signs of a partnership. I must admit I, liked it.

"If we go up that way," I said while pointing to the northwest, "I think we'll run into the Pinhoti trail as it works its way back down from the north. We can probably hop on it there to make easy travel over the next ridge.

"That sounds good to me," she said.

Hearing an aircraft flying high overhead, we both looked up to see the contrails of a four-engine jet way up in the upper flight levels. "That's a transport," I said. "Probably a 747. I don't think we have to hide from that."

"It looks like it's heading north to south, I wonder where it's going?" she pondered.

"If it were going into Atlanta, one of the OWA's strongholds, I'd imagine it wouldn't still be up so high. My guess would be along the gulf coast of Florida. There are a few OWA bases down there that require resupply on a regular basis."

"I keep forgetting you're one of them," she said with a sly grin.

"Was! *Was* one of them," I snarled jokingly. "C'mon. Let's get going."

After working our way through the tall brush and grasses in the valley toward where we planned to intercept the Pinhoti trail, Tamara froze dead in her tracks.

I looked up to see the man from before, sitting still and silent atop his horse approximately fifty yards in front of us. He again had a rifle laid across his lap, with his right hand resting on it as if prepared to bring it to bear if need be. "What the hell is that guy doing?" I whispered. "It's as if he's tracking us or something."

Whispering in reply, Tamara said, "He's not acting aggressively."

"Blocking our path with his hand on a rifle is somewhat aggressive, if you ask me," I replied.

Other than the horse shifting its weight around on occasion, the man didn't budge as he stared down on us.

Taking a step forward, Tamara raised her hand to wave to the man.

"What are you doing?" I asked.

"I just want to see his reaction."

The man raised his rifle off of this lap and propped the stock against his right leg, holding it vertically in plain view.

"At least he's not pointing it at us," she noted.

"No, but he's making damn sure we know he has it. It looks like a scoped lever-action from here."

"Let's find another route," Tamara said, acquiescing to the man's formidable body language.

"We've eventually gotta deal with this guy," I protested. "Otherwise, we'll be looking over our shoulders the entire time, wondering if he's out there watching us."

"Good," she replied. "We need to stay vigilant. If we're watching out for him, we'll be watching out for the OSS thugs that are no doubt looking for us by default."

"As long as he doesn't kill us before they do," I grumbled.

"We'd already be dead if that were his plan," she responded.

"Yeah," I conceded. "Especially with a scoped rifle. He could be a lookout, though, exposing himself just enough to turn us and keep us contained until his cohorts arrive."

Her silence expressed her concurrence with that possibility.

We turned and began walking back down toward the valley, working our way to the east to bring us closer to the next mountain we'd have to cross as we went.

We kept a keen eye out, but never saw him following us. Then again, we had never seen him until he presented himself the other two times, so it didn't mean all that much.

With our preferred course offering us reasons to deviate, our new plan was simple, up and over. The sentiment of which could've best been expressed by a deep, "Ugh" from both of us. It was the hand we'd been dealt, though, so it was time to play it.

Making slow but steady progress, we arrived at the top of the ridge just as the sun was setting ahead of us. The trees and vegetation were thick, making it difficult to get a completely unobstructed view of what lay ahead to our west, but any sky devoid of drones or aircraft in this day and age, when you're on the run from the world's only remaining superpower, was a welcomed sight.

Draping our thermal-blocking barrier over a low hanging branch and stretching it out before staking it as tightly to the ground as we could, we settled in for a dinner of expired MREs, courtesy of the foresight and preparedness of Tamara and her recently-departed friends.

We knew the best way to defeat thermal imaging would be to have the barrier directly on top of us on the ground, preventing heat from escaping from the ends, but we desperately needed a chance to just sit back, relax, and eat. We planned on adjusting things once we retired for the night.

Tearing into my meal, I asked, "What did you get?"

"Spaghetti with beef sauce," she replied. "But hey, at least I get the powdered cocoa drink."

Huffing like a spoiled child, I muttered, "I got the vegetarian meal, veggie crumbles with pasta."

"I'll trade you if you want," she said mockingly.

"Pffft! Heck, no. You're not getting my French vanilla cappuccino-flavored drink powder. I can see right through your plan."

"At least you're not eating your last meal at an OWA detention facility," she rebutted.

I laughed, and confessed, "You're giving them too much credit if you think they'd feed a condemned prisoner. No, you'd be lucky if they didn't conduct some sort of sick, twisted, sub-human scientific experiment on you before you died. Your comfort certainly wouldn't be worth the value of a meal. There's no such thing as the Geneva Conventions or other such rules of civilized behavior when there is no formidable foe to negotiate with. Rules like that are hammered out when you actually fear being caught by the other side. No, the OWA thinks they have it in the bag."

With her interest in my past piqued, she asked, "So, as a lieutenant, you must have been privy to private conversations and such?"

"That's what turned me," I explained. "There's only so much truth one can bear and still retain his soul. I was sort of just drifting along, waiting for something, but didn't know what. When Ronnie approached me with his well thought out plan, I knew that was what I was put there for."

"So, you believe in God?" she reluctantly asked.

"Well, it's not that I don't," I stuttered.

Laughing, she said, "But if you stumble over the question of whether or not you believe in a higher power, how could you say you were 'put there' for that? Or is that just a casual, meaningless phrase to you?"

"I... well, I guess... I," I muttered in an unintelligible fashion.

Laughing, she said, "It's okay. Don't strain your brain trying to explain why you felt you had a purpose you were meant to fulfill. The fact you openly acknowledged that you felt something bigger than yourself had called upon you is all I needed to hear."

I knew right then I should never play poker with Tamara. She could read me like a book. I still wasn't sure if it was a good book, though, or just a collection of dime-store novel drivel printed on cheap paper. Either way, for the time being, I was just glad she was reading.

After dinner, we pulled the thermal barrier from over the tree branch and placed it over us like a blanket.

"Do you think we should take shifts?" I asked.

"Shifts?" she repeated as if my question was nonsensical.

"You know," I attempted to explain. "To keep watch."

"Well, unless you're planning on exposing yourself to thermal-imaging sensors and standing guard as a sentry, I don't see the use of it. If you're telling me you're gonna lie here next to me, essentially cuddled up under a blanket, when you're tired, at night, and that you won't fall asleep, well, I call B.S. on that. Let's just get a good night's sleep and worry about tomorrow, tomorrow," she said with a yawn.

It felt irresponsible to me not to post a watch, knowing that we were wanted fugitives, but she was right. It was hard enough staying awake as a sentry at 0-dark-thirty when you've been on patrol all day, but add to that lying down for the night, and well, that just wasn't reasonable.

Acquiescing to her reality check, I lay there, listening to the sounds of the nocturnal creatures, hoping to see the light of day once again.

Breaking the Beast

Yawning, I could hear Tamara whispering a near silent prayer. I couldn't make out what she was saying, but I could tell it was deliberate, to the point, and above all, sincere. She oozed confidence with everything she did and said, and this was no exception. She was truly one of a kind, and I was blessed to have hitched my horse to her wagon.

~~~~

In the midst of a dream, the nature of which I can't to this day remember, I was awakened by the snapping of a twig. If you've ever heard a sound—a single sound—that seemed to tell a tale all its own, this was one of those moments. A mid-level cloud layer had moved in, obscuring the moon, and leaving the woods dark and featureless to the human eye.

With that one solitary sound, I could picture in my mind's eye a boot, frozen in place, with its wearer knowing they may have just given away their position and alerted us to their presence.

I was silent. Dead silent. It was as if even the insects and nighttime critters had been alerted to a potential threat. My own breathing seemed loud to me in the silence of the moment.

Was that a whisper? I thought? Or was I just being paranoid? My heart was pounding in my chest. I wanted to wake Tamara, but I was afraid she would make a sudden movement or sound if I did. Surely, I couldn't wake her and explain the situation to her in complete silence.

Just then, I felt her hand grasp mine tightly. She had heard it too. I didn't just imagine it. Something, or most probably, someone, was nearby.

I heard what I was now positive was a voice. Tamara squeezed my hand two times. In radio terms, two mic clicks were an affirmative or a roger reply. I assumed that was what she was transmitting to me, that she had heard what I feared I had as well.

I knew the reality of the situation. They hadn't just happened upon us. If they were close enough for us to hear while trying to operate stealthily, and no doubt with night vision or thermal, they knew exactly where we were and they were moving into position to overtake us.

Lying there and doing nothing did not seem to be a viable option, but how could I convey any alternate plan to her in our current state of silence and total darkness?

Just then, I heard machine gun fire erupt from a position opposite from the direction I had heard the voices, or thought I'd heard the voices. The machine gun's report was rhythmic and intense. By the sound and cadence of it, it was a belt-fed, as any box-mag-fed gun would've run dry after the number of rounds it had spewed.

Small arms fire erupted from the other side, mostly in bursts from what seemed to be various positions. None of them were shooting at us but were shooting over us. The machine gun was trading fire with several shooters, most likely the ones I had heard creeping up on us in the darkness.

Pulling on my hand, Tamara was urging me to go. I grabbed the Symbex pack, and we belly crawled, being careful to avoid the barrage of rounds that were zinging over our heads. It felt as if we were in the center of a beehive, knowing that if noticed in our retreat, we'd likely feel the sting of many bees.

One by one the report of the small arms weapons were silenced, though the machine gun never relented in its onslaught against them. With a few final bursts from the belt-fed, the exchange seemed to be finished, with the victor being the first to draw blood.

We stood and began to run as a voice shouted through the darkness, "No! This way! More are coming!"

"Who are you?" Tamara shouted, unable to see the source of the deep, gravelly man's voice.

"Trust me, I'm a friend. The OSS just inserted others. They'll be here soon if a drone doesn't beat them to it!"

Not having many viable options, I pulled Tamara by the hand to get her attention in the darkness, "I think we should take him at his word," I insisted.

"Okay," she replied, pulling me in the direction of the voice.

Suddenly, a red light appeared in front of us, and a man, dressed in all brown with a floppy, large-brimmed hat, the same man we had seen on the horse, illuminated himself and stood before us. "Come with me," he said as he extinguished the light.

Following him through the thick, dark woods, we worked our way down the spine of the ridge until reaching his horse. "Climb up, Miss," he insisted.

"What?" Tamara said in protest.

"You're hurt. Get on," the man said. "He and I will run along ahead of you. Link will follow."

"Link?" she questioned.

"The horse. That's his name. Now, quit wastin' time and get on!" the man insisted as he reached down for her foot and helped her slide her left boot in the left stirrup in the dark.

Once Tamara was seated in the saddle, the man said, "C'mon," and began jogging through the woods, working his way off the ridge and into the valley below.

I followed as closely as I could, with the horse pounding away directly behind us. In addition to fearing being shot by the OSS while we fled, I now had to contend with the concern that the big horse would step on me in the darkness, and trample me in the confusion of the situation. Heck, I had barely wrapped my head around what was going on, so surely the horse didn't have it all figured out.

Then again, he seemed to have it all nailed down tight. Maybe it was just me who was playing mental catch-up.

Chapter Nineteen

Reaching the bottom of the hill and entering an overgrown pasture beside an abandoned commercial chicken farm with four of those long, narrow buildings that would each house thousands of chickens being raised for slaughter, the man stopped and took Link by the reins.

Looking up at Tamara, he asked, "Can you ride?"

"Yes. Yes, I can," she replied.

"Do you know how to neck rein? Because that's all he knows."

"Yeah. I'm good."

"My lucky day," the man said as he turned and ran into the open end of one of the chicken houses, only to quickly reappear with two more horses, leading them straight to me.

"I assume you can ride, too?" he asked, looking directly at me.

"Enough," I shrugged, probably overplaying my hand, since my experience was based solely on Tamara's and my quick trip up the mountain to recover the Symbex pack. I had somehow managed to stay on the horse, so I guess that meant I could ride. Though that was more than likely a testament to the horse's abilities and not mine.

Handing me the reins to the smaller of the two, the man said, "Just follow me. We've gotta put some miles between them and us."

As I attempted to mount the horse, it began to walk away before I had swung my other leg across. The man took hold of the horse's bridle and held him still while he grumbled, "Damn it, son. Get on!"

Once in the saddle, the man released the reins, mounted the third horse, and then began riding across the pasture with Tamara following closely behind him.

I couldn't help but hope the horse could see in the dark better than me, because I couldn't see a thing and expected to smack into a fence at any moment at the rate of speed we were traveling.

I opted to refrain from giving the horse too much input, assuming he'd follow his friends easily enough, and it seemed to be working for the time being.

Exiting the pasture, the man led us onto a gravel road and then onto GA 136. Turning west, he ran his horse hard, with Tamara following closely behind him and with me doing the best I could not to fall off as the horse's metal shoes clanked on the paved road, now running at full gallop.

When we reached an intersection with what appeared to be a general store directly across from us and a gas station and several other closed businesses clustered around what I assumed was the remains of the small town of Villanow, we turned left onto Armuchee Road, continuing to ride at what felt to me to be a frantic pace.

As the man began to slow, Tamara and I rode up close to him and heard him say, "We're taking a dirt road to the left and then exiting onto a trail through the woods. Stay close and watch out for low-hanging trees."

Doing as the man said, we followed closely behind and worked our way down the trail for what felt like a mile or so before arriving at a small, dilapidated shack.

The shack appeared to have been either built a hundred years ago or with reclaimed barn wood from that age. The weeds and vegetation were virtually taking over, with a tree branch pushing its way through a gap between two of the hardwood planks. The place was perfectly and naturally camouflaged, which I was sure was why he had brought us there.

As everyone dismounted, he led all three horses into the shack and said, "C'mon!" as he motioned us in.

Once inside, he turned on a small, inflatable solar-powered lantern and used its ample light to remove the halters and saddles from the horses. Once they were all free of their tack, he opened the door, and smacked one of them on the rump, sending them running outside.

"Won't they get away?" Tamara asked.

"I sure as hell hope they do," he huffed.

He then locked the door and led us to a corner of the shack, where he kicked some loose dirt around with his feet to reveal an old metal handle. Pulling on the handle revealed a hidden door built into the floor.

"C'mon," he said, holding the door open with one hand while holding the inflatable lantern in the other. "Grab the saddles and halters and toss them down. We don't want to make things too obvious."

Once all of the tack had been dropped down into the space below, he said, "Okay, head on down, but be careful not to trip over the saddles at the bottom of the ladder."

Though I had my reservations about entering the space ahead of him due to the fact he would be holding the door above us, I swallowed my sense of paranoia and put blind trust in the man. Carrying both my rifle and the pack, I followed Tamara down into what appeared to be a cellar below.

The man then followed us down into the cellar with the lantern, securing the door overhead with a sliding bolt mechanism.

"We need to talk," insisted Tamara, but the man walked quickly across the cellar, seeming to ignore her demands.

"In a minute," he said as he felt around against the back wall behind a rack of shelves containing canned vegetables and meats that appeared to have been there for a very long time, the contents having degraded to an unrecognizable mush.

I could see that Tamara was flustered by his dismissal of her demands, but her attitude was tempered by her curiosity about what the man would pull out of his sleeve next.

Hearing a clunk, the man said, "There we go," and began pulling on the shelves, revealing a hidden doorway. "This thing gets full of dust and cobwebs at times and is finicky to open."

Again, the man urged us to follow, saying simply, "C'mon."

Following him into a passageway behind the dusty old shelf, we entered a tunnel that was finished with cobblestones from the ceiling to the floor. The tunnel was maybe five feet high at the top of the arched ceiling. Hunched over, we trailed behind the man as he led us for what seemed like a hundred yards or so, though it could have been more.

Reaching an old, iron door at the end of the tunnel, the man said, "Here, give me a hand," as he placed the lantern on the floor and began pulling on a large, hinged-loop handle.

With the three of us pulling, the door creaked open and cool, damp air flowed out of the room sending chills up my spine. He then led us into the room, and said, "Okay, now help me get her closed," as he once again struggled to move the massive door.

Once we had it closed and the sliding bolt locked in place, the man walked to a table in the center of the room, which appeared to be a ten-foot by twenty-foot oval, with the same type of stones that lined the passageway making up the floor, walls, and the arched ceiling.

Placing the lantern on the table, he lit several candles and then extinguished his inflatable solar lantern. "We need to save that thing for our way out. It's anyone's guess as to how long we'll have to be down here, but don't worry. We've got plenty food and water," he said, pointing to some old wooden barrels that lined the walls all the way around the room which were barely illuminated by the faint flicker of the candles.

"Please, sit down and relax," he said as he pulled an old wooden chair back from the table and took a seat.

As Tamara and I each took a seat across the table from him, with me leaning my rifle against the chair next to me and placing the Symbex pack in the chair. I was about to explode with curiosity-driven questions when Tamara said, "Okay, who the hell are you, and what happened back there?"

"My name is Robert Casey. I'm part of a group that, well... keeps an eye on things."

"Keeps an eye on things? For who?" Tamara asked.

"Before we get into that..."

Slapping her hand on the table, Tamara demanded, "No! Answer me! We followed you here on hope and faith alone. And quite frankly, because it seemed to be our only option. Now, dignify my simple question with an answer, or we're leaving!"

"You're right!" the man barked. "It was your only option; now, be thankful I presented you with that option and sit back and relax while I explain things to you. I'm not here for my own benefit, so stop your barking at me!"

I could see that Tamara was about to come unglued, but somehow remained calm enough for me to butt in and say, "Look, we don't mean to be rude. We've just had a very rough week, and we have something very important we have to do and a limited amount of time to do it in."

Leaning back in his chair, the man said, "Oh, trust me. I understand what it feels like to have a limited amount of time. But if I may continue, I'll explain."

"Yes, please do," I respectfully replied.

"Now," he continued, "like I was saying. My name is Robert Casey, but my friends call me Bud. I'm with a group that keeps an eye on things and relays certain bits of information to those who may find it useful. It is a rare event when we must step outside of our observer role and become an active participant, but your situation merited that."

"Our situation?" I asked.

"Well, yours," he replied. "But I suppose it's her situation now, too."

I could feel my blood pressure begin to rise. I couldn't tell if he was truly here to help, or if this was some sort of an elaborate, covert interrogation scheme. "Please tell me exactly what our situation is?" I asked.

Looking me directly in the eye, Bud said, "Until recently, you were Lieutenant Joseph Branch of the One World Defense Force."

I felt a tingle run through my body at his utterance of those words. "How the hell did you know that?" I asked, losing my patience and wanting to reach for my rifle. I could see his eyes watching my hands, waiting to see if I was going to make a move.

"Relax, Joe. If I may call you that," he replied, attempting to set me at ease.

I nodded.

"Okay, then," he continued. "You and another gentleman defected from the OWA with some highly valuable items and intelligence." His eyes danced across the room to the Symbex pack in the chair next to me. "I can see you're still hanging on tightly to those things. That's good to see."

"Once the OWA realized what you had done, they chose to monitor and surveil rather than go all out to apprehend or kill you. They hoped you'd lead them to bigger fish. They hoped you'd lead them to fish like me, but that hasn't worked out so well. Now they're ready to put an end to the games and stop you before your treasonous mission actually has a chance to succeed."

I was in absolute shock. I couldn't fathom how this man we'd never met, other than the strange encounters in the woods, knew seemingly everything about me. "Bigger fish like you?" I queried.

"I'll get to that," he said, waving his hand as if signaling me to be patient. "Then, along came Ms. Adams, here."

"Ms. Adams?" I mumbled aloud, turning to Tamara. For the first time since we'd met, she seemed speechless.

After a brief moment, she looked at me and said, "That's my name. Tamara Adams."

"How have I not known that this entire time?" I muttered, still in shock at what was being laid out before us.

"It just never came up," she said softly.

Smiling, Bud said, "It's very fitting for such a patriot such as yourself to bear the family name of a great patriot of the past. But I digress, back to why we're all here right now. Like I said, and as you surely see by now, I'm with an organization who primarily observes and reports, rarely becoming directly involved.

"We're not all that different from you and your recently-departed friends, my dear," he said, nodding to Tamara. "Except, of course, that we have avoided skirmishes to the best of our ability. Such things always lead to a loss of intelligence-gathering capabilities as the flames of fine patriots are prematurely extinguished.

"Now, don't get me wrong, ma'am, I'm not saying your roles weren't needed; they were, and it allowed others like me to continue to operate unnoticed behind the scenes, furthering the cause. You did a lot of good. You righted many wrongs. And while the OWA was focused on grassroots insurgent activity such as yours, others, like me, received less scrutiny."

"The cause?" I asked.

"We serve the same team, Joe, even if you didn't even know the team's name. And at this moment, you're the man carrying the ball, I'm here to help you make your touchdown."

"How exactly do you plan on doing that?" I asked.

"There are many more of us out there, Joe. More than you know. We can help you see this thing through."

Tamara and I looked at each other. It was as if we were having a conversation with no words. I could see it in her eyes that she wanted everything he was saying to be true, just as I did, but we both had been given plenty of reasons to doubt since our journey had begun.

Turning back to Bud, I requested, "Tell us more about the last few days. From the first time we made visual contact with you, until now."

"Okay," he said, shifting in his chair and getting comfortable. Having an idea, he stood up and said, "This might take a while. I'm gonna grab a beer. Would you like one?"

"Are you serious?" I asked. "You have beer down here?"

"Home brewing was a hobby of mine. As you can certainly tell, it stays pretty cool down here, so the beer doesn't get too warm. I also use a lot of hops, just like the British India Corps did to keep their beer fresh without refrigeration."

Appearing from the darkness, Robert handed both Tamara and me a brown glass bottle with an old-fashioned ceramic mechanical flip-top cap. "Here ya go," he explained. "You may as well enjoy it while it lasts. This will be one of my last batches for several reasons, one of which is that my ingredient stockpiles have been depleted.

"How did you keep them fresh this long?" I wondered.

"The magic of vacuum sealing," he replied.

Holding his bottle out to us, he said, "Here's to seeing this thing through!"

Smiling, I said, "I'll definitely drink to that."

As Tamara and I sipped his harsh, hoppy, and unfiltered concoction, he sat back and continued his story.

"I'm gonna start a little further back than you asked," he explained. "Please, bear with me."

Taking a sip, he said, "A little more than a decade ago, I retired from the U.S. Navy as a Chief Cryptologic Technician (Collections). I had worked extensively with the special operations community during the Global War on Terror, and needless to say, it garnered me a lot of important connections back in the real world as a result."

"Is that like a spook?" Tamara asked.

Chuckling, Bud replied, "Yes, they called us spooks. CT's and IS's are basically the enlisted side of the Navy's intelligence community.

"Anyway, after I retired from the Navy, I returned here to Georgia and our family farm here in Villanow, this very property.

"To say my family's roots run deep in the area would be an understatement. My brother and I grew up playing in these old civil war era hideaways. My daddy used to tell us to never show or talk to our friends, or anyone else for that matter, about these dusty, old holes in the ground. I guess he saw the value in having a secret place to run and hide if need be.

"Maybe it was the WWII-era upbringing that made him inherently suspicious of the stability of the world around us. I dunno. But I'm glad he was, because these old bunkers have all but been forgotten, since everyone else who ever knew about them are dead and gone. Most of them from old age and natural causes, long before the Sembé virus was ever unleashed upon the world. The memory of this place simply became lost over time.

"Once the conspirators released the virus and the world began its spiral around the drain, many of my contacts reached out to me, knowing that our trust in each other might pay big dividends, depending on which way the political winds began to blow. Once the actors who became the OWA started to coalesce, we tightened our allegiances and began operating as an underground network of intelligence-gathering patriots.

"Today, there are several loosely-affiliated groups, who together, make up a fairly large and effective resistance. The group I'm with goes by the code name Knowlton's Rangers."

Being a history buff, I scratched my chin and asked, "Isn't that from the Revolution?"

With a look of surprise on his face, Bud smiled and said, "Why, yes. Yes, it is."

Elaborating, I asked, "Weren't they an elite reconnaissance and espionage detachment of the Continental Army?"

"You know your history, Joe," he replied with a nod and a smile. "Since you're familiar with Knowlton's Rangers and such, you'll probably get a kick out of this, too. Each of the aforementioned loosely-affiliated groups that make up the resistance are named after other such historic groups from the Revolution. All the groups combined are referred to by the code name 'Continental Army'. That's not a formal name for the organization as a whole, but I guess you could say it serves as a reminder of what our mutual goal is here. No one should be looking to seek power for themselves. We all merely wish to return power back to the people by kicking the OWA off our shores, and hopefully, someday, off the planet."

I had to smile at the idea. It was brilliant. "What is the formal name, then?" I asked.

He leaned back in his chair and said, "We're the Americans, of course."

Speaking up, Tamara asked, "Why have we never heard of any of this, other than rumors, that is? Why is no one fighting back?"

"Yet!" he replied sharply. "Why isn't anyone fighting back, *yet*? That answer is simple: because we know that unlike with the patriots of the American Revolution, we don't have the same weapons and technology as the tyrannical force we oppose.

"The circumvention of the Second Amendment over the years, as well as the rapid advancements of military technology that was denied to the public, has led to a civilian population that doesn't stand a chance fighting toe-to-toe against a superpower with both airborne and ground-based weapons superiority.

"We have some military hardware and experienced personnel, but when you add their new biological stranglehold on humanity, well, we've got to get into the proper position first. What you bring to the table may prove to be exactly what we need, which is why they are trying so hard to stop you."

Taking a sip of beer, he continued, "But back to your question: our group caught wind of your defection from our network of underground sources. Once you were reported to be in our area, I was alerted and briefed on the situation. I located you by observing both the actions of Miss Adams' group and the ODF, and then kept watch from a distance. Sometimes I kept a watch on you indirectly, by noting the actions of the OWA, and the placement of ODF and OSS assets, and as you saw recently, sometimes I kept watch over you directly.

"When Ms. Adams here and her group got involved, our operational clock sped up significantly, which forced me to become involved more so than normally desired."

Looking to Tamara, he said, "I mean no disrespect by that. There was no way for you to know the ins and outs of everything, especially of a group who had never presented itself to you. That was our mistake, and for that, I apologize."

Tamara simply nodded in reply.

I was again struck by her silence. She had been one of the strongest-minded people I'd ever met, and now she just sat there, taking it all in instead of driving the conversation.

He then continued, "When you entered the woods, I knew an OSS team had been dispatched to find you. I made you aware of my presence on the first occasion to lay the foundation of our alliance, in the event we were forced to meet. On the second occasion, the OSS had been inserted into the area, and I was steering you out of their path.

"On our most recent encounter, well, they had tracked you and were making their move. My ability to be a mere observer had come to an end."

"Were there others with you? It sounded like someone was cutting them down with a belt-fed machine gun or something."

"That was me."

"You had a belt-fed?" I inquired.

"I had one, yes. Unfortunately, I was forced to leave it behind to facilitate our rapid egress."

Just then, our conversation was interrupted by a thunderous boom that could be felt as its shockwave rippled through the ground.

"And so it begins," Bud mumbled as his face turned downcast.

"What? And so *what* begins?" I asked.

Another thud shook us, as he said, "We knew if their OSS detachment wasn't successful, they'd have to up their game. This situation had gotten too far out of hand for them. No, they'll level those woods and everything in the area to make sure you're dead and that your assets are destroyed."

Breaking the Beast

Boom after boom could now be heard, leaving little room for conversation as we each pondered the changing dynamic of the situation, and what it would mean for our objective from that point forward.

~~~~

Several hours later, when the bombing campaign had finally stopped, empty beer bottles littered the table. Barely a word had been spoken during the bombardment. When each beer was finished, Bud would simply replace it with another. Maybe he expected a bunker buster to come pounding into us from above and didn't want his precious brew to go to waste, or maybe he just wanted to numb his mind to his new reality.

After all, this wasn't just another step in the journey to him; it was his home. It was where his family had been since before the Civil War, and now, everything he knew was being destroyed by those who had inflicted an agonizing death upon the population he loved. Just like when I walked away from D.C. that fateful day, he, too, understood everything he held dear would be nothing more than a memory.

Breaking the silence, Tamara asked through a slightly inebriated voice, "Um... where's the ladies' room? That was a lot of beer, and..."

"My apologies for not explaining sooner," Bud said as he stood. "Right over here," he explained, pointing to a curtain hanging in the corner of the room which was barely visible in the poorly-lit conditions. "I have a compost toilet set up over there."

I was thankful Tamara had asked that question, as I had reached maximum capacity as well.

Once we all began winding down for the night, Bud noted, "There are sleeping bags in that barrel in the corner," he explained as he pushed himself back from the table. "They should be ready to use. Pests can't get in there. And there's no need to be in a hurry. Sleep as long as you can. We're gonna have to let the dust settle for a while. We'd get stomped like cockroaches if we went out there scurrying around right now. I'm sure that's how they see us, anyway."

Chapter Twenty

I awoke in the darkness of the bunker with a pounding headache and a desperate thirst. Only one remaining candle flickered, with its wax oozing off the edge of the small metal tray and onto the table where nearly six inches of it used to stand.

I hadn't had a hangover in a very long time, and it was a feeling I didn't miss one bit. Sitting up, I saw a faint view of Tamara in the flickering candlelight, sitting on the floor with her head in her hands and her elbows on her knees.

"How's your head?" I asked, referring both to her hangover and her injury.

"I hate hoppy beer," she replied. "It's always been like a bottle full of headaches for me. It doesn't help that I'm nursing a concussion, either."

"Maybe he has some Tylenol hidden down here somewhere, too," I said, half in jest.

Hearing the heavy, iron door creak open behind us, we both spun around in the darkness to see Bud enter the room carrying his inflatable lantern. "Good morning," he said. "Or good afternoon, to be more precise."

"Afternoon?" I mumbled. "I can't believe we slept that long."

"I can. You two were looking pretty rough," Bud declared. "You needed the rest, and I'm sure nearly passing out from all the beer helped ensure you got it."

"I sure don't feel rested," Tamara interjected. "I feel even worse than before."

"That's the price we pay for drowning our sorrows," Bud replied as he placed three new candles on the table and lit them. Looking up with a smile, he added, "In a letter to a friend, Ben Franklin once said, *We hear of the conversion of water into wine at the marriage in Cana, as of a miracle. But this conversion is, through the goodness of God, made every day before our eyes. Behold the rain which descends from heaven upon our vineyards, and which incorporates itself with the grapes to be changed into wine; a constant proof that God loves us, and loves to see us happy!"*

Holding his finger in the air as if to signify the birth of an epiphany, he added, "If it is wine, or in our case, beer, that is a gift from God to see us happy, the hangover is an act of the devil to take that happiness away.

"I brought breakfast," he added. "It's nothing fancy like sausage and gravy, but it'll do, and it'll help get your aching body back on track," he said, placing several packages of dehydrated meal pouches on the table. "I just need to get my camp stove all set up, and we'll be good to go."

"You wouldn't happen to have coffee, too, would you?" Tamara asked as she massaged the sides of her head with her fingertips.

"Coffee and aspirin," he replied with a chuckle.

"Did you go outside?" I asked.

"No. Not yet," Bud grumbled. "We've got to give it more time. I'm sure they have scouts in the area searching for evidence of your demise."

After we ate a breakfast of rehydrated scrambled eggs and potatoes, I checked the battery level on the Symbex pack and saw a reading of sixty-two percent.

"How much longer do we need to stay down here?" I asked.

"Why, do you have an appointment?" he quipped.

"I need the sun to charge something," I explained, placing my pack in the chair beside me.

"Is that a cooler pack?" he asked.

I reluctantly nodded.

He smiled, saying, "We wondered how you were keeping that stuff from spoiling during your trip."

He clearly knew every detail about both Tamara and myself, so there really wasn't any reason to be keeping secrets from him anymore. Knowing that Tamara and I were due for a Symbex dosage from our limited remaining supply, I asked him, "So, where do you receive your treatment?"

"What do you mean?" he asked.

"Your regular dose of Symbex."

"I don't," he replied as if not giving it a second thought.

Tamara and I shared a concerned glance.

She then said, "I didn't think I had seen you in line at the support center before. How are you getting by if you aren't being treated?"

Taking a deep breath, he looked at her and explained, "There was more than one reason my work was limited to observation and intel collection. I wasn't infected."

"Wasn't?" she repeated redundantly, realizing precisely what he meant as the words escaped her lips.

"You mean..."

Interrupting her, he said, "What would be the point of living in a world where there was nothing worth dying for?"

He then looked at me and said, "Don't worry. Your assets are safe. I won't be asking you for any. It would only serve to delay the inevitable, anyway. You've probably only got enough for a few months between the two of you as it is."

"A few weeks," I muttered.

Quickly turning his head toward me, he said, "We must have been mistaken. We thought you'd gotten away with much more than that."

"Ronnie and I left with two hundred doses. Unfortunately, just the other day, much of it was damaged during a drone strike on a vehicle we were traveling in."

"Damn," he muttered, shaking his head. "I guess we've got no time to waste, then."

"Do you have a plan?" Tamara asked. "What's next? How do we get it to a place where it can do some real good?"

Thinking for a moment, Bud said, "I've got one good option to get you to where you need to be in the time constraint you have."

"What is it?" she again asked.

"If we can get you to Whiteman, they can get you to Warren," he said, still working something out in his head.

Confused, I asked, "Whiteman and Warren? You mean the Air Force Bases in Missouri and Wyoming?"

"Yes, that would be they," he replied. Looking at me and seeing my confusion, he said, "And now you're beginning to learn a little more about your former employer. The OWA has a global reach, without a doubt, but some of the military personnel and assets that chose not to be absorbed are still functioning on behalf of the U.S. resistance."

"But how could they pull that off? As a global superpower, couldn't the OWA simply take them out?" Tamara wondered.

"Normally, yes," he explained. "There are assets, however, at each of those bases that make the OWA a little standoffish."

"Nukes," I declared.

"Precisely," Bud confirmed. "Whiteman has B2 Stealth Bombers, and Warren has Minuteman III ICBMs. Remember, the entire point of having a nuclear arsenal is assured mutual destruction. In other words, if you attack us, you may achieve your goals and destroy us, but you'll die too.

"When the One World Alliance began its rise to power, it hadn't counted on resistance from U.S. military personnel. They had severely underestimated the patriotism of the American fighting man... um, and woman," he said, nodding to Tamara. "Sure, the intel bureaucracies, such as the CIA and NSA were all in, but the military still had intel folks who weren't part of the machine. They were used by the machine, sure, but without their knowledge.

"Once certain aspects of the rise of the OWA came to light, it made its way to the right people in the right places to keep some of our most precious defense assets from falling into the OWA's hands."

"I still have a hard time believing the OWA hasn't made a move to take them out," I grumbled.

"Oh, they have," Bud explained, "but not in a direct confrontation. They've utilized covert operations in an attempt to compromise the resistance defenses, but to no avail, so far. Eventually, they'll find a way. But we're hoping what you have to offer will help us in ways to make that irrelevant. For now, all we have is the crazy man defense."

"The crazy man defense," I repeated, seeking clarification.

"Yes, the crazy man defense," Bud explained. "You see, even if you were a thug in prison, hell-bent on beating someone up to up your street cred, you'd avoid the psycho in the corner who'd likely shiv you in the neck just for looking at him wrong.

"He's in for life without parole, and he's never gonna get out. He really doesn't care what happens to him next. That's the resistance in a nutshell. Our world has already been ruined. We're all facing the death penalty eventually, and we'll shiv you in the neck if you so much as look at us funny, because, well, what have we got to lose? We're basically already dead. But in this case, we aren't merely armed with a sharpened spoon, this psycho in the corner has nukes.

"My guess is the OWA is simply waiting for us to all get sick and die. And without you, that long-game strategy will likely prevail."

Nodding with a smile on my face as wide as I could muster, I asked, "And just how do you propose to get us to Whiteman?"

"By Mustang," he replied with a devilish grin.

"You want us to drive a Mustang all the way to Missouri, all while trying to avoid ambushes, roadblocks, and drone strikes?" I asked sarcastically.

"Not that kind of Mustang," he quipped.

Chapter Twenty-One

For the next few days, we remained hidden in Bud's bunker while we waited for the situation to cool off outside. In some cases, we meant "cool off" in the literal sense, as the airstrikes brought about by the ODF had caused several forest fires that had quickly gotten out of hand.

Tamara and I continued our regular Symbex doses, and each time, we offered Bud a dose as well, but he always refused. "You might need that," he would insist.

The Sembé virus was hyper-contagious, by design I assume, and there was no doubt in my mind that in the close quarters we were occupying, Bud had most definitely contracted the virus and would begin to show signs very soon.

Four days passed before Bud's quick check to the surface resulted in a favorable report. "This is the first day since the bombing began that I haven't seen signs of ODF troops in the area," he declared. "As much as I hate to say it, however, I think we need to give it one more day, just to make sure. There is too much riding on this to find ourselves under the OWA's boot due to impatience."

The next day, Bud checked the surface, and this time didn't return right away like normal. Tamara and I waited for several hours. His trips to the top usually only took a few minutes, thirty at most. We were worried, and rightfully so. Without Bud, we wouldn't know how to find the next contact who would be transporting us to Whiteman Air Force Base, and we'd been burning through our remaining Symbex while waiting for the right time to make a move. No, if something had happened to Bud, it would have been more than just a setback.

Growing impatient, Tamara said, "Let's go up and check it out. I can't just keep sitting down here wondering."

"Yeah, me neither," I agreed.

Picking up the Sig 556, I led the way as Tamara and I exited the bunker room for the first time since we'd arrived. We worked our way through the cramped underground tunnel, lighting our way by candlelight. Once we reached the cellar and carefully and quietly moved the false door disguised as shelving until we got an adequate view of the room.

Stepping out into the cellar with the rifle held at a high ready, I motioned for Tamara that the room was clear. Handing her the rifle, I whispered, "Here, hold this while I climb the ladder and open the door leading into the shack."

Taking the weapon, Tamara gave it a quick once-over to verify its readiness and nodded for me to continue.

I crept up the old, wooden steps until I reached the door above. Pushing on it lightly, I peeked into the shack, which was illuminated by rays of sunlight that shone through the gaps in the planks of the old, dilapidated shack.

Not seeing any signs of threats, I lifted the door open and motioned for Tamara to join me. She then handed the rifle up to me, and climbed the ladder, joining me in the shack.

Even though the shack was fairly dark, we squinted when the sun's rays shining through the gaps reached our eyes. We'd become acclimated to the darkness of the bunker during our stay underground. I felt as if I needed sunglasses just to function as I squinted, trying my best to limit the light that reached my eyes.

Hearing footsteps, I motioned for Tamara to get behind me as I established a kneeling position and aimed the rifle at the door. Mere seconds after hearing the footsteps approach, the door swung open, and I said, "Oh, thank God, it's you!" as I quickly lowered the weapon.

"I give up," Bud said in jest, holding his hands in the air. In his left hand, he had a canvas sack with a blood stain where fresh blood appeared to be seeping through.

"What's in the bag?" I asked.

"Dinner," he replied. Looking around, he then added, "Now, let's get back down below where it's safe."

Once we reached the bunker, Tamara said, "Where have you been, and why didn't you tell us you'd be gone so long?"

Looking at me with a crooked grin, he replied, "You see, Joe? That is exactly why I'm single." Seeing Tamara's expression turn from one of concern to one of scorn, he added. "I know I should have said something. I considered it safe, yet needed to expand my view to get a better look around, so I went scouting about."

"What did you see?" I asked.

"At first, I wanted to just sit down and cry," he explained. "The bombing was devastating. The woods I played in as a child are all but gone. They're burned to the ground. There's nothing but ash and smoldering fires everywhere. And the old farmhouse that both my parents and grandparents were born in, it's lost as well. The old abandoned general store—all of it—gone."

"So... why do you seem like you're in an otherwise good mood?" I asked.

"Because it's time for the next phase of your journey," he replied. "I didn't see any remaining troop activity, and the smoldering fires should make scanning the area with thermal technology problematic, all while the smoke would make scanning the area visually from above equally problematic. We can essentially use their own havoc as cover to make our move."

Placing the sack on the table, he said, "I say we move out at first light. It'll be dark soon, and it will be far too difficult to get around in all that smoke in the dark. But as for tonight, we feast!" he said as he produced two large wild rabbits from the sack.

Confused, I asked, "If it's a true hell on earth up there, how did you catch the rabbits?"

"First of all, a lot of critters had to flee the fires," he explained. "Many of them are out and about, looking for shelter and new homes. Second," he said as he reached behind his back, pulling something from his waistband, "a suppressed .22 pistol is a handy little dinner-getter," he said as he held up a Ruger Mark IV with a suppressor threaded onto the barrel.

Watching as his face turned from an exuberant expression to one of sadness, he added, "If things go the way I hope tomorrow, it will be the last day we spend together because you'll be on your way to Missouri. I wouldn't feel right if I sent you off on such an important mission without a farewell feast."

That night, Bud grilled his harvest on his little camp stove and served it with reconstituted potatoes and carrots. He even went all out and broke out some of his most prized possessions, his salt and pepper.

Once we had finished the meal, both Tamara and I thanked him as he walked across the room and returned with a bottle of red wine. Holding it out to look at the label, he dusted it off and said, "This was a gift from a dear friend. Its vintage is the same year I retired from active duty. He told me to save it for the future, and that someday, I would be able to celebrate some monumental achievement that was linked to my time in the service. I think tonight is that night."

Pausing, he looked at us and asked, "Will you share it with me?"

Understanding that he was going through a flood of emotions with the knowledge that his internal clock was ticking, I said, "Yes, we'd be honored."

"Absolutely," Tamara added with a smile.

He placed the bottle on the table and disappeared once again into the darkness of the corner of the room, and after rummaging around in one of the storage barrels, he produced a decorative wooden box, which he brought to the table. Opening the box, he removed three of the four wine glasses that were safely stored inside.

Handing one to each of us, he said, "My friend covered all of the details."

I rotated the glass in my hand by the stem and saw an engraving of a Chief's anchor, as well as his name and retirement date. Underneath were the words, *In honor of twenty years of faithful, dedicated service.*

Smiling, I said, "I'm glad you didn't stop serving at twenty years. It looks to me like you're still serving your nation well."

"Nevertheless," he said as he paused to maintain his composure, "My permanent retirement is approaching. It was the ultimate honor, and truly the pinnacle of my career, both in and out of uniform, to have helped you on your journey."

He then popped the cork on the bottle and poured a serving into each of our glasses.

Looking me directly in the eyes, he said, "What you've done, and what you're doing, is huge, Joe. It's *huge*. And ma'am," he said, turning to Tamara, "he couldn't have made it this far without you. That, I'm sure of."

Raising his glass, he said, "Here's to both of you! May your mission be a resounding success!"

We each clinked our glasses overhead and took a drink of his wine. For the next several hours, we refrained from talking about the virus, the death, the losses, and just sat around like three old friends. We shared stories of our youth, some embarrassing and some funny, and just enjoyed each other's company. Life outside the zones almost seemed civilized for once.

~~~~

Early the next morning, Bud awoke before Tamara and me and prepared us a hearty breakfast. He pulled out all the stops and opened a can of sausage gravy and heated it on his camp stove. He also reconstituted some dehydrated biscuits, which was basically a crumbly concoction, but it mixed well with the gravy, hiding its dehydrated origins.

After we had both eaten, Bud provided Tamara with a new day pack, and filled it full of dehydrated meals for us to take with us for the journey ahead.

Once we reached the shack above, we each donned a gasmask provided by Bud to mitigate the dangers of the smoke from the still-smoldering fires. He verified that the area was free of immediate threats, and led us out and into the daylight for the first time in over a week. Although we could have kept our distance from the thickest smoke, Bud assured us that staying close to the fires would give us the best thermal and visual cover from any prying eyes, be they flesh or sensor.

Both Tamara and I were shocked by the devastation brought about by the ODF's bombing campaign. We looked to the east, to the mountains we had crossed that were once lush and green, to see that they resembled large piles of smoldering ash. If we'd remained hidden in those mountains and had not been led to safety by Bud, that would have certainly been our fate.

The carnage extended out from there in all directions. Every significant building or structure had been leveled for as far as the eye could see. They clearly wanted to leave us no safe haven in the event we had made it out of the mountains.

Looking back at the old shack, I smiled at how well it was naturally camouflaged. Its having been entirely overtaken by vegetation and trees was no accident. I'm sure it was only visible from the ground, and only if you walked right up on it, facing the front.

We traveled in a westerly direction, moving non-stop for most of the day. Our stay in the bunker had been the perfect opportunity for Tamara to recover from her concussion, allowing her to regain her impressive endurance and stamina. I must admit, it was a much-needed recovery period for both of us, injury or not.

After approximately nine hours of steady travel by foot, we were long past the remains of the small town of Lafayette, Georgia, which was also destroyed during the bombing of the area, and we found ourselves entering an area of rural farmland and cleared pastures after working our way through a cut in the hills via Georgia 193.

"It's not much further," Bud assured us. "It's actually just a few farms over," he said, pointing in a southwesterly direction.

We now found ourselves with clear air above, as the winds were picking up out of the west and carrying the drifting clouds of smoke away from us. With that, our paranoia increased as the prying eyes from above would be unrestricted once again.

"There it is," Bud said, pointing to a hill off to the side of a freshly-cut pasture.

Looking around and unsure of what he was referring to, I asked, "There what is?"

"The hangar," he replied.

"Hangar?" I repeated, still confused.

We quickly made our way across the freshly cut pasture, which was also puzzling, considering the fact that most had become overgrown and weed-ridden. But this one, it was cut down close to the ground. Who'd do such a thing? Was someone in the area still producing hay?

As we approached the hill, something caught my eye. It was the front of a hangar. It looked like a Quonset-hut-style hangar that was built into and blended with the surrounding terrain.

"Okay, now I get it," I said, picking up the pace from the excitement of what may be awaiting us inside.

Seeing a flash of light from the tree line along the back of the hangar, Bud paused, removed a red handkerchief from his pocket, and waved it with his left hand. The light then blinked three times, and Bud said, "Okay, come on."

"Code?" I asked.

"Sort of," he replied. "When prompted, if I waved with my left hand, leaving my right hand free to manipulate a weapon, I would be signaling that I'm not there under duress and I'm still in the fight. If I signaled with my right hand, which would be my weapon hand, it would show that I am traveling under duress, and have been taken out of the fight, being unable to utilize a weapon."

"You don't seem like the kind of guy who'd be leading the enemy to your allies under duress," I observed.

"No, I would hope not, but one can't rule anything out that one hasn't experienced. Also, things can get complicated at times. It's best to have all the bases covered. For example, if they knew of this location, and wanted me to escort them here under false pretenses, it would be better for me to play along and be able to provide a warning to my friend. Again, you never know what circumstances will present themselves, so it's best to have planned for all possible contingencies."

As we approached the hangar, Bud said, "Please, wait here. Let me talk to him first."

"Sure," I replied.

Tamara and I waited as requested while Bud proceeded toward the hangar. When he got to within fifty feet of the hangar, a man appeared from the tree line wearing denim overalls, slip-on boots, and a well-worn straw cowboy hat.

We couldn't tell what the man had said to Bud, but he was clearly pleased to see his dear friend. As he approached Bud with open arms, Bud waved the man off and took a few steps back. The man's happiness quickly turned to sorrow and the look of defeat. As Bud continued talking, the man looked out toward us with contempt.

"I'm not sure this is going so well," I whispered.

"He's basically finding out that we just killed his friend. Bud wasn't a carrier before we came along, and obviously, neither is this man; otherwise, Bud wouldn't have made him stop short.

Nodding, the man turned around and went inside the hangar as Bud turned and waved us forward.

Once we reached Bud, he explained, "That gentleman is Mark Butler. He's a pilot, and he's got a plane that can get you to Missouri. He's one of us, so you don't have to worry."

"He's clearly not a carrier," I noted. "I'm not sure we want to keep infecting everyone from your unit that we meet. It's just not right."

"Don't worry, Mark is going to take all the necessary precautions," he explained.

"Why didn't you?" I asked. "Why didn't you take all the necessary precautions, that is?"

"I didn't have time," he explained. "It was an 'act now or lose you to them' type of situation. Many a soldier has thrown himself on a grenade to save his friends. I did nothing so heroic. So, please, put those things aside and let us help you help us."

Nodding in agreement, we saw Mark exit the hangar wearing a full-body biohazard suit, complete with a fully enclosed hood and filter system.

Once he reached us, Mark barked at us, saying, "Look, I'll do this because it's my duty, but I'm in charge. This is my plane. You'll do exactly what I say when I say it. Understood?"

"Yes, sir," I replied.

"Good," he grumbled. "Now, which one of you is going?"

Looking over to Bud and Tamara, and then back, I muttered, "Um, both of us."

"No. I only have room for one. Who's going? Make up your mind."

"Sir, I implore you..."

Looking to Bud, Mark growled, "This is not going to work."

Exhaling, Bud calmly said, "Mark, please, for me. Can't you try to fit them both? I can't ask that of them."

"They sure didn't have a problem asking you to give up everything," Mark snarled.

"They did no such thing, Mark," Bud replied. "Please, Mark. Can you try and fit them both?"

Mark looked both Tamara and me up and down, and said, "Maybe. Without the rifle, though. Is that the cargo?" he said, pointing to the Symbex pack.

"Yes," Bud replied.

Thinking it over, Mark said, "Okay, we'll try. I'm not making any promises, but we'll try."

"Thanks, Mark," Bud said with a smile.

Bud followed Mark into his hangar while Tamara and I stood outside. Not only did we realize they probably needed some time to discuss things between themselves, but we also understood the fact that our presence wasn't wanted, especially since we were carriers. There was no need for us to contaminate his space any more than required.

A few minutes later, Bud returned, and said, "The good news is he's still on board with taking you. The bad news is he doesn't want to leave until morning. He said it's too late in the

day. You'd barely get there before dark, and if there were to be
an emergency requiring an off-field landing, without runway
lights at alternate airports, or even streetlights to light up the
streets, it would be a death sentence. That, and he can't land in
this field in the dark and doesn't want to spend the night at
Whiteman."

"It's his ship," I replied. "We'll follow his orders and report
to him when he's ready."

Bud then rubbed his jaw and reluctantly said, "There's just
one more thing. He says you have to sleep outside tonight. He
doesn't even want you in his tool shed. He says you'll infect the
tools."

"Doesn't he look at you the same way, since you've been
exposed and all?" I asked.

"He should, if you ask me," Bud agreed. "But I guess he's not
worried if it's not showing signs. If I've not come down with it
yet, the virus probably isn't shedding. You two, on the other
hand, have been infected for so long, well, I guess he sees that
differently. He's not a doctor, but hell, even if there were a
doctor here to explain things, he still probably wouldn't take
their advice. He's a bit stubborn, you could say."

"That's no problem at all," I replied. "Sleeping outside has
become quite a regular event these days. To be honest, I feel
strange sleeping confined by walls. I wake up feeling trapped."

Looking to Tamara, Bud asked, "Is that okay with you,
ma'am?"

"I guess it has to be, doesn't it?" she replied with a smile.

~~~~

Early the next morning, with the wisps of fog still lifting off
the ground, I awoke to see several fawns bouncing through the
woods as if Tamara and I weren't even there. I guess they were

too young to realize humans were exceedingly dangerous to them now. Even more so than before, considering the fact that hunting was no longer a sport, but a way of survival, making rules and regulations null and void.

As I stood and stretched, Tamara folded up the thermal barrier we had regularly used for a blanket as Bud approached with breakfast in hand.

"Good morning," he said. "And here I thought yesterday's breakfast would be the last warm meal I got to cook for you," handing us each a bowl full of scrambled eggs. "Mark has chickens. You sure can't beat those things these days. You don't have to slaughter them, and they still provide you with protein."

We ate as we walked toward the half-underground hangar. Reaching the main sliding doors, Mark appeared through an opening in the middle of the doors, dressed once again in his full-body biohazard suit.

"I'll fire up the tractor and get her pulled out," he said, disappearing inside once again.

"Should we follow?" I asked.

"No," Bud replied, "just wait here with me.

We watched as the hangar doors opened, and once I caught a glimpse inside, to my amazement, I saw a pristine P-51D Mustang named *Rebel Yell*. Appropriate, I thought.

Using an old sixties-era Ford tractor as a tug, Mark pulled the Mustang out of the hangar while Tamara and I stood there in awe.

"She's a beauty, ain't she?" Bud noted with a smile.

"Gorgeous," I replied. Again, the history buff in me was going wild with excitement. "I guess I see now why space is limited."

"Yeah, as with most airshow P-51s, there has been a jump seat added behind the pilot seat. Perhaps if Tamara could sit in your lap, it might work."

"Is he going to fly in that suit?" I asked, referring to the biohazard suit he was wearing.

"I guess he'll have to. That's an awfully confined space to be sharing unfiltered air with carriers," Bud replied. "Mark flew U2s in the Air Force, so he's used to flying in restrictive suits.

"After he retired, he flew the airshow circuit in a little Pitts biplane until he landed a gig flying this thing in airshows around the country. He doesn't technically own it, but the gentlemen who owned it and sponsored the shows passed away soon after the outbreak began, and his family asked Mark to take care of it until everything settled down. It's not like anyone in the family could have flown it, anyway."

"No, I suppose not," I mumbled, nearly drooling on myself at the sight of the pristine old warhorse.

Once the tug tractor had been put back in the hangar, Bud walked up to Mark and said, "Thank you, Mark. I know she means a lot to you, but what these two may be able to do for us will do a lot for all of us."

"I know, Bud," he said, nodding inside the Tyvek hood. Turning to Tamara and myself, with a little less rasp in his voice than before, Mark muttered, "Joe, you climb in the back seat first. See if you can put the pack on the floor under your legs. Like I said, there's no room for the rifle. Leave it. If we make it to Whiteman, you won't be needing it anymore anyway."

Turning to Tamara, he said, "Once he's inside, climb on in and sit in his lap. It'll be cramped, and your head may even touch the canopy, but that's just how it's gonna have to be if you wanna go along."

Doing as Mark requested, I climbed aboard and got myself situated with the pack beneath and between my legs. I could tell by the look on Tamara's face when she looked inside that she didn't look forward to the ride, at least not in these too-close-for-comfort conditions, anyway.

Once she had climbed in, we adjusted our legs as best we could with hers on top of mine, while Mark strapped himself into the pilot's seat up front.

Talking loudly through the hood of the suit, he said, "I know you're uncomfortable, but just be glad you don't have to wear one of these damned things.

"If everything goes as planned, you'll only be back there a shade under two hours. We've got to stay down low to avoid radar the best we can, so it'll take a little longer than usual down in the thicker air. We could go a lot faster up high, but that's how we have to play the game these days."

"Whatever it takes," Tamara replied with a smile. "Thank you for this."

And with a nod, Mark closed the canopy and brought the massive Packard-built V-1650 Merlin V-12 to life. I felt as if I was dreaming. As a history buff, especially a military history buff, the P-51 Mustang was the pinnacle of WWII-era aviation, and here I was, off to save the world, or at least try, in a P-51 that no doubt flew numerous risky missions during the war.

Looking to the side, my elation turned to sadness when I saw Bud waving goodbye. He knew he would never see us again, and he knew that without some sort of miracle, which likely could not happen soon enough, he would not be long for this world. He had nothing but suffering and anguish ahead of him. Mark's bitterness toward us probably reflected his acknowledgment of that fact as well.

Taxiing out, Mark completed his preflight checks, and upon reaching the end of the neatly-cut field, he added power and began the takeoff roll with the tail quickly coming off the ground. Oddly, the field that had once seemed very large no longer seemed quite long enough. Even with ample power on tap, the fence line and trees at the far end of the field seemed to be rapidly approaching.

Just before reaching the fence, Mark pulled back on the stick, and the Mustang roared into the sky. Leveling off just after clearing the trees, Mark began a sweeping right turn back toward his hangar, and with a rock of his wings, gave Bud a fitting salute as we flew by, just before disappearing from his view.

As we flew, Mark explained how we would be skirting between Memphis and Nashville, and then avoiding Saint Louis to the south. He knew the OWA had a presence in nearly every major city but wasn't sure of the extent of their air power at each location. In his opinion, it was best to simply treat every town with an OWA presence as a no-fly zone.

I had never flown that far, that low to the ground before. The view was amazing. I likened it in my mind to a very high-speed train ride. I attempted to glance over Mark's shoulder to see the altimeter, but with the bulk of his Tyvek suit's hood and with Tamara in my lap preventing me from moving around in the very cramped quarters of the rear jump seat, I simply couldn't make it out.

If I had to guess, I would have assumed we averaged one thousand to two thousand feet, but again, that would be a complete guess.

Cutting between Memphis and Nashville, Mark flew low over the Tennessee River, often dipping below its banks and the surrounding terrain. At that altitude, we could see that nearly every town not under the OWA's umbrella of protection was either burned, abandoned, or in ruins. Smaller roads had become overgrown and had abandoned cars strewn all about.

Near Camden, Tennessee, while still flying up the river, Mark had to climb to clear a railroad trestle. In the center of the trestle was a camper trailer, midway across the span of the river. It appeared that someone was homesteading on the railroad trestle high above the river below.

As we climbed to clear the trestle, we saw flashes of light from what appeared to be small arms fire. Apparently, someone was working pretty hard to avoid contact with the sick. I couldn't help but think of the rude awakening they would receive if the OWA somehow put the old CSX train system back in use.

I chuckled at the thought of what the shooter must be thinking, seeing a P-51 Mustang climb over and coming within several hundred feet of his precariously perched home. That would indeed be a sight to behold.

As the Tennessee River eventually merged with Kentucky Lake, Mark turned slightly left, leaving the water behind, skirting just south of Paducah, Kentucky. This allowed us to now head straight for Whiteman AFB while avoiding Saint Louis to the south.

It was somewhere near Cape Gerardo that it happened. A surface-to-air missile streaked by, narrowly missing us. Mark immediately dove for the ground, getting to within what felt like one hundred or so feet, buzzing the treetops.

Yelling to the back, difficult to understand through the hood of the suit, Mark said, "That must have been shoulder fired! Otherwise, they wouldn't have missed us! We may lose them if we stick close to the ground removing us from their view of the sky, but now we know they're onto us! I think the joyride is over! It's gonna be all business from here!"

I'm not sure how fast we were going, but the trees were streaking beneath us, going by like a blur. Mark looked down to his radio, hoping to be able to reach Whiteman from this distance, but noticed the display was no longer illuminated.

"Damn it! They've zapped the radio!" he shouted, meaning that they had evidently deployed the use of their EMWS weapons systems against us, targeting the aircraft with a focused electromagnetic pulse. "Luckily, this baby is so old school, there's nothing else to fry! Old iron has its benefits these days!"

Tamara immediately began pounding on the canopy and pointing. "Over there!"

Looking over his left shoulder, Mark yelled, "Damn it, an attack drone!"

Banking hard to the left and in the direction of the drone, he pushed the throttles all the way to the WEP (War Emergency Power) level and rapidly closed in on the drone.

Seeing flashes of light from the drone's onboard cannons, Mark banked hard right, then pulled hard, climbing nearly vertical as we streaked by the drone.

"We don't have any guns, so I'm trying to give the bastard at the remote station a run for his money, throwing at him what he doesn't expect! Since we can't shoot them, we've got to outrun them!"

Tamara's weight was crushing down on me from the G-load. My stomach began doing flip-flops, and I feared losing the breakfast Bud had cooked for us. Rolling over, and pulling hard to a turn back to the northwest, Mark climbed slightly while accelerating the Mustang past 400 miles per hour.

"By the time that bastard gets turned around and lined up on us again, we'll be pulling away! The most the drone can do is 300! I'm climbing for more speed! The higher we are, the faster we can go! Flying low only helps when you're hiding!"

Leveling off at ten-thousand feet, Mark yelled, "We're gonna just have to make a run for it! Whiteman isn't that far away now!"

No sooner had those words left his lips did we get slammed in the right side by a volley of machine-gun fire from an unseen drone bearing down on us from the north.

Blood splattered on the canopy as Mark screamed out in pain. His right arm had been shattered by one of the rounds that tore through the aircraft.

"Are you okay?" I asked Tamara.

She nodded in reply, then I asked Mark, "How bad are you hit!?"

Releasing the controls with his left hand and holding his left leg against the stick, Mark reached up and unzipped his Tyvek suit's hood, removing it from his head. He placed his hand back on the control, stopping the roll to the left that had been initiated by the aircraft's out-of-trim condition when he had momentarily released the controls.

"That bad," he said, now being exposed to Tamara and me. "It's not just my arm. I'm pretty sure my pelvis is shattered. One drove in pretty deep," he snarled through gritted teeth.

"I'm gonna have to put her down. I'm not feeling so good. I'm not going to make it all the way to Whiteman. If I don't, I'll end up losing it, and we'll all die. I have to..." his speech began to slur, and his breathing became labored. "I have to put her down... now."

Pulling back on the power, Mark began a gentle descent toward a small town just up ahead. I wasn't sure of our exact location, but I knew we were heading in the general direction of Whiteman, and we were at least beyond Cape Girardeau.

It appeared he was heading toward a road just up ahead. He now had the power pulled way back. We could feel the Mustang beginning to slow. Next, he lowered the landing gear, and then the flaps.

"When..." he struggled to speak. "When we stop. Get... get out... Go..."

"Okay," I said, placing my hand on his shoulder. "Thank you."

Approaching the road below, Mark put his left leg up against the stick and released it with his hand, unlatching the canopy and sliding it back. I had expected the wind to be loud and turbulent, but the air glided past us so smoothly, and with the canopy no longer reverberating the sounds from the engine, it was almost quiet and peaceful.

With Mark's coordination and attention slipping, he over-flared and ballooned, causing the Mustang to momentarily climb before running out of airspeed and stalling, dropping down onto the road, bouncing and swerving as the aircraft began to ground loop with the tail swinging all the way around.

Skidding off the road and into the grass, the aircraft's tail struck a tree, nearly shearing it from the fuselage and bringing us to a violent stop.

Tamara began struggling to free herself from the tight confines of the cockpit, and I followed closely behind, tossing the pack down to her once she was on the ground.

I placed my hand on Mark to thank him one more time, but he was already gone. He must have died from internal injuries while in the landing flare. He may have very well been dead before the tires even touched the ground.

Once again, Tamara and I had been delivered to safety by a patriotic American hero who had given everything he had for us and for our cause. We were racking up a debt we felt we could never repay.

"Godspeed, Mark," I whispered as I turned and followed Tamara into the woods.

Chapter Twenty-Two

Running as fast as we could through the trees, we heard several attack drones make high-speed, low-altitude passes, strafing the P-51, eventually igniting its remaining stores of avgas, causing it to burst into flames.

Once the P-51 had been completely destroyed, the drones preformed a circling climb, spiraling up directly over the wreckage, loitering at several thousand feet.

"I wish those bastards would get the hell out of here," Tamara grumbled.

"They probably have orders to observe for a while," I guessed. "I'd imagine they want to see if anyone comes to the pilot's aid."

"Do you think they knew it was us?" she asked.

"That's hard to say. I guess it depends on how early after takeoff they received reports of a low-flying aircraft. They may simply be practicing airspace dominance since non-official air travel is strictly forbidden and assumed to be resistance-related operations."

"Either way," she added. "We're likely to have company soon, so we'd better move on."

"Yes, ma'am," I concurred.

Looking around, I said, "This tree line seems to follow that overgrown farmer's field. That field more than likely bumps up to a road at some point as there wasn't a way into it from the road we landed on."

"Good point," Tamara replied. "Let's follow the trees and see where they lead. Once we get to the road, maybe we'll be able to figure out where we are and form a plan."

Smiling, I said, "My thoughts exactly."

After working our way through the trees, hand-railing the field for what seemed like a half mile or so, we came across a rural road labeled, *MO-50, Loose Creek Hwy.*

"Loose Creek Hwy," I read aloud. "Hmmm, I wonder if that means there's a town named Loose Creek?"

"That or a creek named Loose Creek," she quipped.

"More than likely, both," I replied.

Noting the position of the sun in the sky, we oriented ourselves and began walking west, which would at least be in the direction of Whiteman Air Force Base, if nothing else.

As we entered what once was a quaint little rural town, we saw large red X's spray-painted on most of the houses. They all looked hastily abandoned and in disarray. The area looked like it had been hit hard once the virus swept the nation.

"Is that a gas station?" Tamara asked, pointing down the road to the west.

"Looks like it," I replied. "Let's check it out," I said as I visually scanned the sky for signs of drone activity. It was a beautiful clear day without a cloud in the sky, and with the relatively level terrain throughout the region, a clear view of the sky was easy to obtain.

"Let's go," I said as we began walking further west toward what we assumed to be a gas station.

"I could sure use a Snickers bar," Tamara joked. "What's the odds there is a Snickers bar on the shelf?"

"Slim to none," I replied. I noted Tamara's attempt at humor as being uncharacteristic of her. She was as all business as they come. Was she simply becoming closer to me and showing her true self, or had the stress of everything she'd endured over the past few weeks started getting to her, requiring some sort of off-topic behavior to balance it all out?

"If there is a Snickers bar, you have to half it with me," I said, looking at her out of the corner of my eye to gauge her reaction.

Glancing over at me and catching me looking for her reaction, she punched me in the arm and said, "Not if I get there first!" Catching me completely off-guard, she took off running as fast as she could toward what we could now clearly see was, in fact, a gas station.

Against my better judgment, still paranoid about potential drone activity in the area, I took off running after her, yelling, "But I called halves!"

I scanned the area as I ran. I wanted to cut loose and have a few moments of fun with her, but I knew all too well how quickly smiles can be extinguished by the unexpected in this world. This town looked utterly abandoned, however, so I convinced myself to just let go and enjoy the moment.

Beating me to the gas station that had clearly been abandoned long ago, she jerked the door open and ran inside. A chill ran up my spine as I saw her disappear into the building, urging me to pick up my pace and run even harder as the Symbex pack, only loosely tossed across my shoulder, bounced off my back with every stride.

Entering the gas station, I saw Tamara standing at the empty candy aisle. Turning to face me, she smiled and said, "There was one left, but I ate it as fast as I could."

Looking around the store, we could see that everything of use had been taken. The refrigerated section, as well as the dry goods, had been cleaned out. Well, except for one package of very aged sushi. I guess even in the apocalypse, people weren't willing to trust gas station sushi.

The automotive aisle had been cleared as well. Not one quart of motor oil was left. The display that would have ordinarily carried all of the cheesy knives, you know the ones, the ones with dragons engraved on them with wickedly shaped, cookie-cutter cast Chinese blades, was empty as well. Who bought those things, anyway? I mean, seriously.

I walked over to the ice cream cooler, knowing full well that if anything had been left it would have been melted long ago when the power grid failed, but something caught my eye.

I knelt down, looking underneath, and saw a pocket road map of the state of Missouri underneath the left front leg. Evidently, it had been used to level the cooler to compensate for an uneven floor or something.

Looking over to Tamara, seeing her looking around the room, I said, "Give me a hand."

"What is it?" she asked.

"You're not gonna believe it."

"What?" she again asked, losing her patience with me.

"They leveled the ice cream cooler with a road map," I said, pointing at the floor. "When I lift the cooler, pull it out."

Getting into position, she said, "Okay, go ahead."

Grunting and straining, I coughed, and said, "Damn. This thing is heavy. Give me a hand. Maybe if we lift it, we can kick it out."

With the two of us both in position, I said, "Okay, one...two..."

And then from behind us, we heard a strange man's voice say, "Three."

Chills instantly ran up my spine as we both spun around to see a filthy, wretched-looking man standing before us with a hungry look in his eyes and a pump shotgun in his hands. Calling the man disheveled would be doing a disservice to all disheveled people around the world. He was far from that. He was putrid. I'm not sure how we hadn't smelled him coming from the looks of him.

"Whatchoo lookin' for?" he asked, leaving his mouth open and rubbing his tongue across his front teeth—well, what was left of his front teeth.

"Oh, um, we were just gonna try to get that map," I said, pointing at the base of the cooler. I'd have given anything to have had that Sig 556 at that moment, or heck, any gun, but Mark was right, there just wasn't room in the tiny cockpit of the P-51 that was initially designed for a single crewmember.

The shotgun was pointed straight at me, and his eyes were looking straight at Tamara. "You sure gotchoo a pretty little thang, there," he said, still raking his tongue across his filthy teeth. Licking his teeth seemed to be his favorite hobby because brushing them certainly wasn't.

"We were just passing through," I said. "We'll be on our way now."

"No, you won't," he replied, still smiling. "Whatchoo got in that bag?" he asked, pointing the gun at the Symbex pack.

"Tampons," Tamara blurted out. "I have issues, and we were hoping some may have been left on the shelves here."

Good one, I thought, proud of her quick thinking.

"If that's all you got, I guess I'll take'm. But I don't want you to have to do without your lady stuff, so I guess I'll have to take you, too," he said, waving the gun around, covering us both in a circular pattern.

Based on my years as a police officer, I'd say this guy was two things: first, he wasn't all there, and second, he's wasn't a first-time offender. No, I'd venture to guess he was one of the ones that enjoyed this new world like a pig loved rolling in slop. How he'd not managed to die from the Symbex virus, though, was beyond me.

Had he simply hidden out, awaiting the die off so he could reemerge in the world and wreak his havoc?

"Look," I said, "If you own this gas station, we apologize. We didn't mean to trespass on your property. Like I said, we'll just be on our way and leave you to your store."

"Are you try'n to be slick, boy?" he muttered, spitting as he pronounced the 's' in slick.

"No, sir. I just don't want to cause you any more trouble."

"Oh, she's not causing me any trouble," he replied, taking a step toward Tamara. "It's you who's the problem. Now, why don't you just hand over the pack like I asked? I ain't gonna ask again."

"Okay, no problem," I said, hoping Tamara would see my fidgeting with the pack as a window of opportunity to make a move. If there was one thing I knew for sure about Tamara, she could hold her own in a fight. She didn't need me protecting her, as much as I wished I could do that for her right there at that moment.

As I pretended that the pack was snagged on my clothing, Tamara made her move, grabbing the end of the barrel and shoving it upward as the shotgun discharged, blasting a hole in the dropped ceiling, causing bits of insulated ceiling tile to rain down like cancer-causing snow.

I immediately turned and leaped on the man as he kicked Tamara hard in the stomach, knocking her backward against the ice cream cooler.

I felt the shotgun jerk in my hands as he racked another round in the chamber. I ran as hard as I could toward him, pushing against the gun and forcing him back against the empty candy bar shelf behind him, knocking it over in a loud crash.

With the two of us now wrestling on the floor, Tamara stood over him and drove a fire extinguisher straight into his face, causing the shotgun to discharge as his hand flinched in one last attempt to save himself. I felt a sting and the sensation of a blunt impact as I stumbled, trying to get off the man whose life had just been extinguished by Tamara's fatal blow.

I fell backward, then stood up. I could see the look of shock and fear on her face. She was looking at me. She was looking at my side. I felt around and winced in pain. I pulled up my shirt, and there were but a few small, bloody holes. The man was apparently using clay target loads or something similar.

But how had I felt the impact and concussion of the blast like I had, if only a few stray pieces of shot had hit their mark? I then looked to the Symbex pack hanging over my shoulder, and to my horror, I saw that it taken the brunt of the blast and was riddled with holes.

I dropped to my knees and frantically began inspecting the contents. To my horror, only four doses remained; the rest had been destroyed by the shot, as was our portable air injector.

I sat back on the floor and placed my head in the palms of my hands. Tamara gently placed the bloody fire extinguisher to the side and sat down beside me.

We both knew what this meant. We were due for a dose, but none would be received. The last four remaining vials would be delivered to Whiteman Air Force Base if it killed us, and we both knew it most likely would.

Chapter Twenty-Three

Sitting silently on the floor, leaning against one another, I shook out of the fog in my mind and said, "We'd better get moving. If there is anyone else around, they'll have heard those shots."

I stood up and then held my hand out to Tamara, offering to help, but she simply sat there. I could see depression setting in. I had to get her mind back on track. We still had a mission to complete—a mission that too many others had already died for, or would eventually die for, due to their involvement and support. We couldn't just sit down and wait to die now. We had to press on.

I knelt down in front of her, placed my hand on hers, looked her in the eyes, and whispered, "It ain't over, 'til it's over."

Taking my hand, she stood, dusted herself off, and said, "I'm sorry. You're right."

"You've got nothing to be sorry for. Those same thoughts went through my mind," I assured her.

I picked up the shotgun and looked it over. It was a pre-ban era Mossberg 590 Special Purpose. It had the long magazine tube, and spring-loaded extra shell storage slots in each side of the stock. With nine rounds in the tube, one in the chamber, and four in the stock, fourteen rounds could be carried on and within the gun itself. The four in the stock, of course, had to be loaded by hand once the tube ran dry, but it was at least an expedited method of reloading compared to fumbling around in one's pockets for more.

I searched Mr. Creepy and found six more shells on his person. I cycled the pump action, ejecting a shell with each stroke until the magazine tube had run dry. Six shells had remained in the tube, and with the six on his person, that gave us twelve total.

The shells were a very random mix of loads, from squirrel and bird loads, to clays, to double-ought buckshot, oh, and one random slug. I cycled one round of double-ought buckshot into the chamber, then topped off the magazine tube with nine more. The remaining two I placed in the stock, putting the slug on the left and a shotshell on the right. That way, if a situation called for a slug, it would be easily accessible to hand load into the chamber.

Once we had finally retrieved the map from under the ice cream cooler, we saw that the sun was almost completely over the horizon, and the light was failing fast. We worked our way through the building and out the back door.

Once we were outside, the sun had finally set on our long, eventful day, and it was time for Tamara and me to find a suitable place to spend the night.

We could feel the chill coming on. It was going to be a cold night in Missouri—that was for sure. "Where do you want to sleep?" I asked. "Inside or out?"

"I'd prefer inside tonight if you don't mind," she answered.

"I was hoping you would say that," I said with a smile.

We decided to put a little distance between ourselves and the gas station for good measure, so we walked nearly into town. On the outskirts of town, there was an upper-middle-class home set back in the woods, a quarter-mile from the main road. Behind the house, there was a large garage, an outbuilding for storage, and a greenhouse.

Looking at Tamara, I asked, "What do you think?"

"I'd prefer not to spend the night in someone's house. I don't want to stumble across a scene like you said you and Ronnie did. Any roof over my head will do," she countered.

"How about the garage, then?" I said, pointing behind the house.

"That's fine with me," she said, fighting off a yawn.

"My sentiments exactly," I said as I blinked my eyes to focus. "I didn't get a lot of sleep in the woods last night. Your snoring kept me awake."

"I don't snore," she growled, punching me in the arm.

"Hey, all I know is it wasn't a bear."

"Very funny, mister," she said, seeing through my ruse.

I think we had both started appreciating each other's cheesy attempts at humor. If felt good to... well... feel. It felt good to feel something other than stress, sadness, and duty. It felt good just to feel like you were in the middle of a light-hearted conversation with someone you cared about, and not just another daily struggle for survival.

With it being completely dark in the garage, we felt around until we found a spot of a suitable size, clear of vehicles or other stored items. We then laid out our thermal barrier and settled in for the night. I placed the Symbex pack off to the side, leaned the shotgun up against it, and wished Tamara a good night.

~~~~

When I awoke early the next morning, I felt something draped across my body. It was Tamara's arm. She had evidently snuggled up next to me and wrapped her arm around me at some point during the night. *Maybe she was just cold,* I wondered.

I gently lifted her arm and placed it off to the side. I stood quietly, trying not to wake her. Feeling dizzy, I leaned against a car covered by a canvas car cover and regained my balance.

What was wrong with me? I didn't feel like myself. I felt my forehead, and noticed that I had the cold sweats, and come to think of it, my joints did feel a bit achy the evening before. I guess I had chalked it up as fatigue, or the impact from our crash landing. But maybe it was more than that.

I started thinking about the virus. We had only been taking half doses recently, which was not based on science or medical advice, but on the idea that if it worked, we could stretch our supply out a little longer. After, we had no idea how long our journey would take. And now we had missed a day altogether. Was the Sembé virus starting to rear its ugly head already? Having been inside the belly of the beast from the beginning, I had been shielded from feeling the effects, always having the OWA's health service within reach in exchange for my servitude.

I knelt down beside Tamara and placed my hand gently on her head. She felt a little warm, but maybe I was just being paranoid. With the morning rays of the sun now shining through the garage windows, I unfolded the map we had obtained from the gas station and began to nail down our position. We knew we had been on MO-50, called Loose Creek Hwy, and according to the map, it led into the sleepy little town of—you guessed it— Loose Creek. That was verified by the presence of MO-50BYP, a bypass around downtown, which would be the road we landed on.

Loose Creek was located approximately one hundred miles east of Whiteman AFB. *We can do this,* I thought. *We're almost there.*

As I scanned the map looking for every possible route to Whiteman from our location, I heard Tamara yawn, and say, "Good morning, sunshine."

I smiled and asked, "Are you talking to me or the sunshine?"

Grinning, she said, "Well, the way things have been going lately, seeing each of you another time feels like a victory."

"That's the spirit," I chuckled. "How do you feel this morning?"

"A little sore, but that's to be expected," she answered. Standing and stretching while taking in a deep breath with a yawn, she rubbed her elbow and said, "This lifestyle is taking its toll on me. I feel like I've aged twenty years in two weeks."

"I know the feeling," I replied. "I'm not feeling too great myself."

Changing the subject, Tamara asked, "What's for breakfast?"

"I was just about to fry some bacon and eggs, but then I woke up. Since we only brought the Symbex pack, not expecting to spend the night in Loose Creek, and not having room in the plane for a second pack even if we wanted it, I... I have no idea, but I'm feeling the effects of a prolonged empty stomach."

"There's always that gas station sushi you had your eye on yesterday," she grinned. "You know you want it."

"I'll just let my stomach eat itself, but thanks," I joked as I began looking around the garage for items of use. As my eyes scanned the room, then passed across the canvas car cover, lured to a pair of mountain bikes hanging from the ceiling in the corner behind it.

Hey, wait a minute, I thought as I quickly returned my attention to the car, recognizing the familiar shape of my father's car from my childhood.

"There's no way this is what I think it is," I said as I reached for the canvas car cover.

"What? A car?" she asked.

As I peeled back the canvas, I wondered if my eyes were playing tricks on me as it revealed the glossy raven black paint and signature Shelby stripe of a 1967 Ford Shelby GT500 Mustang.

Removing the rest of the cover and tossing it in the floor, I was in near disbelief. It was immaculate. Along the side of the car was the GT500-labeled stripe with the Cobra badge just above it and ahead of the driver's door.

The car was on jack stands, although its wheels and tires were still installed, probably to help prevent dry rot, I assumed, as they were a retro-style reproduction tire designed to complement cars of that era while offering modern performance. The tread was worn slightly, so the car had been a driver, not just a trailer queen.

Inside, the owner had placed several moisture-absorbing canisters in various places, and even a mouse trap. *That was smart,* I thought. I couldn't imagine storing a collector's car such as this, only to find out a mouse had chewed up the original interior.

I opened the hood to reveal an intact, 428 Cobra Jet V-8, complete with the factory dual-carb setup and all. The engine was clean, but not trailer-queen clean. Again, this car had been a driver. I had much respect for its owner.

Walking to the back of the car, I crawled underneath and tapped on the gas tank, hearing an empty, hollow sound.

"They drained the tank," I said. "That's perfect. We don't have to worry about varnished fuel or rust."

"Perfect?" Tamara repeated. "Are you planning on taking this old thing?"

Looking at her as if she had three heads, I said, "Of course! It's fast, it's EMWS-proof because there are no electronics, it's all old-school. And, it's fast!"

"You said the fast part already," she grumbled, shooting me a scowl.

"Besides, think about it," I said with the excitement in my voice, "It's like it was meant to be. We've used horses, which are mustangs..."

"Wild horses are mustangs, those horses weren't wild," she moaned.

"Yeah, but it's symbolism," I scoffed. "Anyway, then we flew here in a P-51 Mustang! A freaking P-51! And now, the car of my dreams, a 1967 Shelby GT500 Mustang, is sitting here in front of me, perfectly preserved, as if it's begging me to do the last one hundred miles of our trip!"

Seeing that my childlike excitement was not going to be dissuaded, she caved when she realized she was up against a mental brick wall, and asked, "But what about fuel? You said the tanks were drained, didn't you?"

"We'll find some!" I replied with overly optimistic enthusiasm, refusing to let common sense get in the way of a perfectly good, poorly conceived plan. "Besides, we only need to go one hundred miles."

"What kind of mileage does that thing get?" she asked. "That big motor sure looks thirsty."

"Well, not good. I don't know off the top of my head, probably 10MPG or so, but, still, it's just one hundred miles."

Seeing that logic and reason were going to get her nowhere, Tamara exhaled, and said, "Well, let's find your gas."

I grabbed her and hugged her tight, nearly lifting her off the ground. Holding her out at arm's length, I said, "I know this seems crazy, but..."

"Shhh," she interrupted. "No, it makes perfect sense. Let's do it."

I wasn't sure if she really thought taking a classic dream car our last one hundred miles was actually a good idea, or if she was just humoring me, seeing that I needed a mental diversion. If we were gonna make a run to the end zone, I wanted it to be something epic. Going out in a blaze of glory in a Subaru just wouldn't have had the same... well, *pizazz,* for lack of a better word.

If you've ever seen Butch Cassidy and the Sundance Kid, then you understand the romance of how they went down swinging in the end. If this journey from D.C., escaping the belly of the beast with something that can break its back, and with all of the people who willfully gave their lives to see this mission through, and well, I simply couldn't allow it to all end with a whimper.

Before we went looking for fuel, I examined the car carefully to see if there was anything else we might need. Almost immediately, I noticed the battery wasn't installed in the car.

"That makes sense," I said. "If he'd gone through the trouble of preserving the tires and the fuel system, surely the battery would have been on that list as well."

I began looking around the garage, and on the very back workbench, off to the corner on the left, amidst a messy pile of tools and rags, I saw a small solar panel suction-cupped to the window. A wire ran down the wall from the solar panel through a gap between the bench and the wall.

I knelt down and looked underneath the bench and *voila*! There it was. The brilliant former owner of this car had the battery on a solar battery tender. Why not just use a plug-in battery tender? Who knows? Especially if all of this had been done before the outbreak when people still looked at electricity coming through those magical outlets in the wall as a sure thing. Or perhaps he mothballed the car once the world's stability came into question, making the solar charger the logical choice. Either way, I was thankful for his foresight.

Removing the battery from its charging cradle under the bench, I carried it over to the car and very carefully put it into place, connecting the cables and tightening them down.

"Hmmm," I wondered aloud. "Keys. We need keys." Walking over to the driver's door, I opened it and mumbled, "What are the odds?" as I felt around above the visor. "Nope, that would have been too easy."

"I'll go look in the house," I said.

"I'll go with you," she insisted, picking up the shotgun and bringing it along.

Breaking the Beast

Just before we left the garage, I turned and picked up the Symbex pack, which was kind of useless at this point considering I could fit its remaining viable contents in my pocket.

"We can't drop the ball this close to the end zone," I said.

"You and your sports references," she quipped.

"I'm an American; what do you expect? It's part of our language, whether you like sports or not."

Carefully stepping out of the garage, we were awestruck by the beauty of the home. It was a gorgeous, two-story brick house, probably of recent construction, but with the class and style of a classic home from yesteryear, complete with a chimney on each end of the house and a large, covered entryway that visitors could park underneath when arriving at the front door.

"Yep, this is the kind of person you'd expect to own a car like that," I noted.

Visually scanning the area, we saw no signs of habitation or people having been in the area, so we carefully proceeded to the home.

We worked our way around behind the home, looking for the back door, and when we found it, it was evident it had been broken from its hinges. A large wooden post lay next to it with ropes running through holes bored through it as handles.

"Looks like someone made themselves a battering ram," I observed. "And judging from the blunted end, I'd imagine this wasn't its first forced entry." Playing the scenario out in my mind, I added, "So you'd think its owners would have taken it with them to their next target."

I motioned for Tamara to hand me the shotgun and then carefully stepped inside, clearing the room as I entered.

Once inside the mud room, signs of a struggle were obvious. There were bullet holes in the walls that had evidently come from another room inside the home, due to the fact that the holes were exit holes where the rounds entered the room via the drywall, busting their way through.

As we stepped into the kitchen, what would have been a dream kitchen in a different time, I looked at the large, stainless-steel double-doored refrigerator and noticed holes from several small caliber, high-velocity rounds.

As we stepped into the living room, we could see that it was where the final scene had played out. The decayed remains of several individuals were strewn about in their respective death poses, and judging by their attire, they weren't the rightful occupiers of the home.

Looking to my left, seeing the main staircase that led up to the second floor, I said, "We've got to make sure the place is secure. I don't want to get shot in the back while messing around in the garage."

Tamara nodded in agreement, so we proceeded up the stairs. As we ascended the staircase, I couldn't help but notice the photographs hung on the wall on the way up. There were several family portraits, depicting the scene of a loving family of four. I started getting a feeling of déjà vu. *Oh, please don't let me find another tragic family scene,* I thought. I couldn't handle any more dead children or suicidal, loving parents.

Other pictures on the wall depicted the father as a military man in his younger years. One image in particular, was of who I assumed to be the man of the house, posing with a military unit while wearing irregular uniforms and face paint, all holding their weapons with a jungle scene in the background.

Nodding toward the photograph, I whispered, "That explains the invader's lack of success."

Reaching the upper floor, we cleared each room, one by one. At the end of the hallway, we entered the master bedroom. Inside, we found the body of the man who we assumed was in the family portraits and the military photos.

His decayed body was lying face down, wearing blue jeans and a load-bearing tactical vest that was worn overtop a polo shirt. An M4-style AR-15 carbine lay in front of him on the floor with a magazine still inserted.

"I bet the home invasion was a surprise," I whispered in reverence to the scene.

"Why?" she asked.

"He's not wearing any shoes, and those clothes aren't' something you'd wear to a gunfight," I explained. "No, I'd imagine he grabbed his vest and rifle and sprang into action at the first sign of trouble. And based on the fact that his rifle and gear are still in his possession, I'd say he won.

"He probably took a bullet during the melee, then retreated upstairs to say goodbye to his family."

"You think they got away?" she asked.

"There are no other bodies, and he surely wouldn't have been in a position to have disposed of them. And look at the drawers, they're all half pulled open like someone packed in a hurry. My guess is he made it to where his family was hiding just before he died, and then they left.

"They must have left in a hurry if they just left him on the floor," she added.

"Who knows what kind of madness was going on at the time? I'm sure he wouldn't have wanted them to risk themselves worrying about him any longer."

As we briefly looked around the room, I found a photograph on the nightstand of him, his wife, and two daughters. I put the picture in my pocket and noticed Tamara staring at me with a raised eyebrow.

"If we're taking this man's car to finish the journey, I'm taking part of him with us. It was his meticulous attention to detail that left us a car free from dry-rotted tires, varnished fuel, and a dead battery. That, and if things ever get straightened out, and if his family somehow survived, I want to be able to return the car to them. I know, that's nuts. They've probably long since passed. But I'd feel like I was stealing from this man if I didn't at least have the best of intentions."

I glanced at Tamara out of the corner of my eye and noticed she was still staring at me, yet her look had changed from one of confusion to one of adoration.

I smiled and said, "Yeah, yeah, I'm the guy that cries during sad movies." Changing the subject before I got all teary-eyed, I smiled and said, "The OWA's European leaders underestimated the American people's deep-seated beliefs in the Second Amendment. I'm sure when men like him received the weapons confiscation order, he simply moved them from his safe to some other hiding place. Maybe he gave up a cheap shotgun or something to play along, but just think, if the illegal guns we've encountered along the way represent just a fraction of what people refused to turn in, there have to be millions of other weapons out there just waiting to be found."

I then walked over to the AR, picked it up, and began to inspect its condition. Removing the thirty-round standard capacity magazine, I noted from its weight that it was nearly full. I pushed down on the top cartridge, getting just a little movement out of it. I then slipped the magazine into my pocket, and eased back on the charging handle, flipping an unfired M855 green tip round from the chamber.

"It looks like he slapped in a fresh mag and chambered a round once he'd eliminated the threats. Having the presence of mind to keep your weapon ready to go while carrying a fatal wound says a lot."

Tugging around on his vest, I removed two more loaded magazines. "That's ninety rounds total," I said. "That'll do."

Looking back down at the man, I whispered, "Thank you, sir."

She patted my back and squeezed my shoulder, then we turned and worked our way back downstairs. Once we reached the lower level, I began searching for a batch of keys. It seemed everyone I'd ever met had a drawer, or basket or other such things where they kept a pile of keys to nearly everything they owned.

After checking several drawers, I felt around on top of the fridge and found a small glass bowl. Removing it from the top of the refrigerator, I was pleased to find a bowl of change and keys. Sifting through the keys, I found a set of classic Ford keys adorned with a Shelby key fob.

Holding it up for Tamara to see, I declared, "I think it's safe to say these are the keys."

Rummaging around the rest of the property, we failed to find the fuel we hoped the man had squirreled away. With that last box still needing to be checked, we studied the map and got a good idea of our location, as well as the general layout of the small town, in order to try and decide which direction to strike out in search of fuel.

Seeing her face light up with an idea, I asked, "What? What is it?"

"The bicycles hanging in the garage behind the Mustang! We can take those and cover a lot more ground. We can't keep dragging this out. I'm really hungry, and to be honest, I'm not feeling well."

"It may just be the hunger," I said, attempting to divert her fears of the obvious. "But the bikes are a great idea."

Once we had gotten the bikes down and aired their tires with a foot pump stored nearby on a shelf, Tamara said, "I think we should split up."

"Absolutely not!" I argued. "Some of Mr. Creepy's friends may be out there.

"I'm starting to think Mr. Creepy was the last remaining resident of this place. And like I said, we're running out of time. Our clocks are ticking. I feel it."

Seeing that she wasn't going to take no for an answer, I acquiesced and asked, "So, which direction do you want to go?"

Orienting herself to the map, she said, "You go back toward the community center and those chicken farms behind it. Farms always have fuel somewhere, if it's not already been taken, that is. I'll head into town and look for vehicles that may have unvarnished fuel in the tanks. I can take a hose and jug for siphoning. We obviously can't carry enough on the bikes, so if either of us can get at least a few gallons, we can get the car started, then go back to the source for more on our way out of town."

"That's as good of an idea as any," I conceded. "Except for the splitting up part, that is."

"Oh, c'mon. I got by just fine before the mighty Joe Branch came along. I'll take the shotgun, you take the AR. We'll both be able to defend ourselves."

"Touché," I replied, with my pride stinging just a bit.

Chapter Twenty-Four

I felt something wrong in the pit of my gut as we went our separate ways. We'd come a long way to be taking unnecessary chances this close to the finish line. Then again, maybe this was her way of telling me she felt her own clock ticking away inside of her.

With the AR slung across my shoulder, I rode the Trek hardtail mountain bike north and to the northeast on county road 403. It wasn't long before I came upon the Loose Creek Community Center. I stopped at a distance of maybe one hundred yards or so, and just watched and listened.

From that vantage point, the center seemed to be a recreational complex combined with an event hall. There were several overgrown baseball diamonds, as well as a playground outside of the main facility. Seeing no activity, I rode closer, then paused again, watching and listening.

Still not seeing any signs of human activity, I rode into the parking lot and took a closer look. From there, I could see large red X's painted on the doors, which were partially open, if only by a few inches.

I rode closer, and to my horror, I saw chains stretched across the double doors, which had been bolted directly into the block walls from the outside. Those chains weren't being used to keep people out, they were being used to keep people *in*.

Dear God, I thought as I rode up to the doors. Seeing movement, I was startled and quickly brought my rifle to bear, only to see a cat slip through the doors. Seeing me sitting there on my bike, the cat spooked and disappeared into the bushes.

I tried not to think about what a cat might have been doing in there, or had been doing there over the past year or so. I stepped off of the bike and pushed it around to the back of the facility, where I found the rear exit to be blocked in the same manner as the front.

What exactly had occurred here? The darkest parts of my mind had an idea, but I chose to simply ride away and see no more. I had enough haunting images burned into my mind. I didn't need any more nightmares. Besides, whatever had occurred here happened long before we arrived. Probably at the onset of the virus sweeping through the area. There was nothing I could do, anyway.

I rode on to the chicken farm that was located behind a feed store, on past the community center on County Road 403. The doors to the feed store were wide open, and it appeared to have been ransacked long ago. I'd imagine the folks who lived on the farms in the distance, the ones who may have avoided the initial spread of the virus as it came through the area, may have found a need for feed while trying to keep their livestock going through the winter. Especially once fuel became scarce. Running tractors and such to cut and bale hay for the winter would eat deep into their fuel stores with no means of resupply. Seeing nothing of use at the feed store, I rode on back to the chicken farm behind it.

The farm had a sign at the entrance to the gravel road that led back to four long buildings used to house their poultry stock. That sign read, *Johnson Family Farms and Quality Foods."*

I assumed if there was long term fuel storage for generators and such, which a poultry building nearly always had for emergency ventilation and temperature control, it would more than likely be diesel. Still, I figured I needed to check and see, just in case.

Reaching the first building, I leaned my bike against the wall, then turned the knob, and then pushed the door open, stepping back and covering the entrance with my rifle.

A dank smell emanated from the door opening, which had likely been closed for a very long time. Peeking inside, the entire floor was covered with the decayed corpses of tens of thousands of young chickens.

This, of course, was to be expected for animals that were kept in a captive environment where they depended on humans for their every need. The sight made me unsure as to whether I'd ever crave fried chicken again.

Stepping back out into the fresh air, I coughed uncontrollably as if my body was demanding that I purge whatever it was I had inhaled from my system.

I walked along the building, attempting to remain within its shadows. I eventually found the generator I was looking for around back, up against the back wall and directly underneath a huge exhaust fan.

"Yep, diesel," I said aloud.

Giving up on the chicken houses, wanting to hurry and get back to Tamara, I decided to check out the family home and detached garage, which was actually more like a workshop in size. After all, that would be the most logical place for the storage of gasoline-powered vehicles.

Carefully entering the workshop, I saw several ATV's, a fishing boat, and an old Ford pickup truck. It was an F-100 to be exact. Early seventies vintage, if I was correct.

I approached the truck first, removing the fuel cap and taking a whiff. "That's bad," I said, noticing that the contents had an aroma of varnish.

Checking the fuel in the fishing boat, I found it to smell rather fresh. I stood back and thought about it, and since many people winterize their boats, the fuel in the two removable fuel tanks had likely received a stabilizer treatment as part of that winterizing process.

The engine was also a newer four-stroke design, which meant the fuel would be straight gas, with no premix. I'd hit the jackpot. Now, I needed to find a way to transport enough of it back to the Mustang to get her started.

Rummaging through the workshop and looking for a small fuel can or something similar that I could use to carry enough fuel back while riding a bicycle, I stumbled across one of those tow-behind child cars that parents used when riding bicycles with their small children. It's like a little trailer that hitches to the bicycle's seat post, pulling the child along behind.

"Jackpot!" I couldn't help but shout.

After connecting the child trailer to my Trek, I retrieved both of the fuel tanks from the boat and placed them inside where the child would normally sit. I was pretty proud of myself. I felt brilliant in that soon-to-be fleeting moment.

That was when I heard it. I heard the sound of approaching vehicles. I immediately ran to where I could get a view, and to my horror, I saw a convoy of six OWA mine-resistant ambush-protected vehicles, or MRAPs, similar to the one Ronnie and I had used during our heist of the Symbex delivery. And, of course, they were heading straight into town, exactly where Tamara was supposed to be.

Quickly formulating a plan in my head, I rode the bicycle with the fuel trailer following along behind down County Road 403 until I reached the feed store. From the feed store, I cut across on a small dirt connector road to Bradford Lane, which just happened to be the name of the neighborhood street the house with the Mustang was on.

I rode as hard as I could, with the convoy now being long past the house. Reaching the house, I immediately carried the fuel cans inside the detached garage next to the Mustang. I then unhooked the trailer and hopped back on the bike and rode like a madman toward town.

Seeing the MRAPs parked in front of the local veterinary clinic, I ducked behind a row of ornamental trees and laid the bike off to the side, before bringing my rifle up to the low ready. Creeping up as close as I could get, I saw one of the ODF soldiers pushing Tamara's bicycle over to his superior.

If they had been able to determine that it was us being transported by the P-51, any information they found would no doubt be reported directly to a field-grade officer nearby, who could then call in whatever assets they needed to finish us once and for all. And if there were MRAPs in Loose Creek, there had to be more elsewhere. I hoped this was just some sort of routine patrol, but had a feeling it was far from that.

They were clearly discussing the bike, and since I saw no sign of Tamara, I could only assume they were discussing how to go about finding its rider.

I knew I had to find Tamara, but how? If they had found the bicycle, she was definitely close by.

Twisting the zoom on the 1-6X CQB scope on the AR out to 6X, I began working my way back toward the ODF patrol while scanning the area with the magnified optic as I went.

I searched both sides of the road, paying particular attention to the shadows and overgrown brush.

There she is! I thought as I saw a fleeting glimpse of that reddish-brown hair I would recognize anywhere. She was hiding behind a row of trees, directly behind several of the ODF soldiers as they searched the area on foot. It was only a matter of time before they found her. I had to act and act fast.

I knew I needed to ready our getaway car because things were starting to come to a head, and once it all hit the fan, there wouldn't be time. With that in mind, I quickly began working my way back to the home.

Arriving back at the garage, winded and exhausted, I first found a large, rolling floor jack and began removing the jack stands from underneath the car. Once all four tires were on the ground, I found a large funnel and began transferring fuel from each of the six-gallon marine fuel tanks. They were nearly full, which would give us twelve gallons of gas, and for that big engine to push this car one hundred miles in a hurry, well, that would be cutting it close.

Once she was fueled up, I fumbled around in my pocket for the keys and placed them in the ignition. I started to turn the key and looked ahead to see that the garage door was still closed.

Think, damn it!

I exited the car, unlatched the roll-up garage door, and reached up and pulled the release handle, disengaging the door from the chain-driven electric motor.

Once it was free, I pushed upward on the door, raising it just enough for the Mustang to fit underneath. I then ran back to the car, sat down, and said a quick little prayer as I turned the key.

Cranking slowly at first, having to pump the fuel through the empty lines all the way from the tank, the big engine finally coughed and sputtered to life. The entire car shook from the power of the massive 428CI V8.

Pushing in the clutch, I slipped the four-speed manual transmission into first gear, and thought, *well, here goes,* as I eased the clutch out and the powerful car lurched forward and into the sunlight for the first time in a very long while.

I pulled the photograph of the family we were borrowing the car from out of my pocket, and slipped it between the large tach and speedometer, bending it slightly with the tension holding it in place. Looking at the picture, I said, "Wish us luck."

Attempting to keep the powerful car quiet from a distance, I shifted early, lugging each gear while I crept out of the neighborhood. With the MRAPs last being seen on Loose Creek Hwy, I thought if I could get onto County Road 402 before they spotted me, it would give Tamara a chance to make a run for it.

She could use the thick trees in the area as cover, preventing the MRAPs from following her directly, forcing them to turn around and backtrack down Loose Creek Hwy to reach 402 in order to pursue her. Those MRAPs may be able to withstand a good, hard blast, but they weren't much of a pursuit vehicle.

Pulling out onto Loose Creek Hwy, with the direct line of sight between myself and the MRAPs being obscured by a bend in the road up ahead, I took a deep breath, and eased into the accelerator, feeling the visceral power of the classic muscle car.

Shifting past second, and then third, I was impressed. That thing was a beast. Traveling now at about seventy miles per hour, they were bound to hear me coming. That car had a voice, and it was shouting out loud, yelling, "Come and get me!" with each throb of the pistons.

I yanked the wheel hard onto 402 and accelerated toward Tamara's last known location. I reached over and popped the door handle, then downshifted to second gear, nailed the throttle, and felt the full fury of that massive engine as the rear tires broke loose and the car began to slide.

Seeing Tamara make a break for it, running directly toward me, I slid the car into the grass, spinning it around to face her and sliding to a stop with the passenger's door slamming open, bouncing off the hinges. She dove in, and I again nailed the accelerator as small arms fire began ringing out, with the tell-tale sounds of *ting ting ting* as several of their 6.2mm rounds found the car's rear quarter panel.

Accelerating like a bat out of hell, ripping down 402 to the west, I shifted past third, then fourth. We blasted through the town at nearly one hundred miles per hour, dodging parked cars and driving directly through trash and refuse that was blowing aimlessly in the wind. We soon merged back onto Loose Creek Hwy, the same road the MRAPs were located on, but if my plan went the way I hoped, they would have had to backtrack to get on to 402, being unsure of our destination. Either way, the MRAPs couldn't catch us now, but we couldn't rule out other unknown OWA assets that may be in the area.

Glancing over to Tamara, I shouted, "I've got a route noted on the map! It's right there on the floor! Open it up and give me progressive instructions as we go!"

Within what seemed like mere seconds, we crossed the bridge over the Osage River and left the little town of Loose Creek far behind.

Studying the map further, Tamara noted, "You've got a route drawn out all the way through Jefferson City. Are you sure you want to go through there? It's a much larger town. Wouldn't that increase the odds of an OWA presence?"

"I looked at other ways around it, but everything would take us too far off course, and add significant mileage. We've got to hope we can get within range of Whiteman before the OWA has a chance to get aviation assets on station. Time is our enemy. No matter where we are, they'll find us from the air," I explained.

"Here comes Jefferson City," she said as we blasted into town at one hundred and twenty miles per hour.

I felt like I was playing a video game from my youth. You know, the one where you're driving down a near empty road, occasionally having your reflexes tested by dodging a much slower moving car. In this case, however, the cars weren't slowly moving. They were abandoned and parked in random places.

"MRAP!" she shouted, pointing several streets over near the center of Jefferson City.

"They know where we're headed for sure, now!" I shouted without ever letting off the accelerator.

Rounding a corner just before entering Apache Flats, my heart skipped a beat when I saw two MRAPs parked across the road, completely blocking our path. One thing a classic muscle car could do was get going in a hurry. One thing they couldn't do, however, was to stop equally well. Brake technology lagged a bit behind horsepower during the muscle-car-era. With that knowledge in mind, knowing I'd prefer to go into the grass off to the side of the road between MO-50 and the next street over than to slam into a heavily armored vehicle at over one hundred miles per hour, I allowed the Shelby to drift out of the lane and into the grass. The car slid down into the dip in the middle, and then up and out the other side, flying through the air like an old Dukes of Hazard episode.

Luckily, our landing surface was Country Club Drive, which went downhill into a neighborhood, mitigating the bone-crushing impact we'd have had if we had landed flat. Just like on a motocross track, landing downhill was critical.

The car struck the ground, bounced, and then settled back in as I downshifted to third and began to build up our speed once again.

"We're gonna have to get back over! This leads to a dead end!" she shouted over the roar of the engine.

Looking up ahead and to our left, I said, "Hang on!" as I once again entered the grass between the two roads, went back down into the dip, and then launched up the other side, getting airborne once again and coming down hard onto MO-50.

Hearing scraping metal dragging on the ground beneath us, I joked, "I think I owe that family a new exhaust."

Passing the town of Tipton, Tamara shouted out with enthusiasm, "Holy crap! We're already almost halfway there!"

"Those mile markers really tick by at one hundred and twenty miles per hour!" I said with a smile on my face as the car continued to pull hard. "I must admit, it's getting a little harder to hold this thing straight at this speed. I'm pretty sure we bent a few things back there."

"Ya think?" Tamara quipped. "I hope they have chiropractors at Whiteman."

Looking up at the dash, I noticed the only non-factory item the car had was the stereo. An aftermarket retro-fit stereo had been added. "See if you can find us some good tunes," I said, wanting to keep my own attention on the road in a car that seemed to become wobblier by the minute.

"I'm pretty sure there aren't going to be any good radio stations in the area," she sarcastically replied.

"Pffft, c'mon!" I mocked. "That's one of the ones with MP3 data storage. Scroll through and see what he had saved on it."

Powering the radio up, one of my longtime favorite songs booted up and began to play. John Lee Hooker—he was one of the greats, and his song "Boom Boom." It flowed through my veins and sang to my soul.

"Boom Boom Boom Boom, gonna shoot ya right down. Off of your feet," I sang until the song quit playing. "What did you do?" I asked.

"I didn't do anything," she replied as we began bickering like an old married couple. "I didn't touch it. It just went off."

Trying to turn the stereo back on to no avail, she said, "Damn it. They zapped us."

Luckily, killing our music was all they could do to that old car with their EMWS technology. But still, that was enough to let us know they were nearby.

Tamara began scanning the area above us, as I said, "It's probably high and behind, following us. Leading other assets right to us."

"What's the next town?" I asked.

"Sedalia," she said. "It's the last one before Whiteman."

"That means it's their last chance to score," I grumbled. "We can count on a presence there." Thinking for a moment, I said, "Let me see the map."

Handing it to me, she tapped on our current location.

"I've got an idea," I said.

"What?" What's your idea?" she demanded.

"We've got to give them what they don't expect. We're going to alter our course."

"Wouldn't they just consider all contingencies?" she asked.

"Not this," I affirmed.

As we approached Sedalia, I said, "Tighten your seatbelt."

"Why, what are you going to do?" she demanded.

"We're gonna do a little farming," I said. "Now, quickly, what road was it that 16th Street connects to that leads all the way to Whiteman?"

Looking over the map, she said, "Highway Y."

Shooting her a curious look, I said, "Really?"

"Yes!" she shouted. "It says the freaking letter Y with nothing else. They have a lot of roads in the area named after nothing but letters."

Shrugging, I said, "Okay. Y it is, then."

"But how the heck are you going to get from MO-50 to 16th Street? They in no way connect!" she shouted.

"That's why they won't expect it," I declared.

As we approached the last big curve on MO-50 before entering Sedalia, we could see a roadblock up ahead with no exits remaining between them and us, only this time, it wasn't just the big, heavy MRAPs, they had ODF security patrol cars as well, which would give us a little more run for our money.

"Well, here goes," I said as I pulled the wheel to the left, leaving the paved road and heading directly for a set of railroad tracks.

"You crazy bastard!" she shouted as her head bounced off the ceiling.

"I told you to tighten your seatbelt!" I shouted over the noise, just as the car launched over the railroad track, ripping the exhaust that was dangling underneath clear off of the vehicle. The engine's roar was now coming directly out of the exhaust manifold and was deafeningly loud as we launched into an adjacent, overgrown farmer's field.

The windshield cracked right in front of me from the impact, no doubt a result of the twisting and flexing of a body that was never designed to withstand such abuse.

Downshifting, I laid hard on the accelerator, making it deafeningly loud inside the car. The overgrown weeds in the field were higher than I had hoped, smacking the car all around and lashing off of the windshield as we blasted through it all, almost completely blocking our view.

Blasting out of the field and through the parking lot of the Highway M Chapel, we entered 16th Street, and sped through the tight confines of the neighborhood, dodging parked cars and debris that littered the road.

Looking behind us, we saw an ODF patrol car slide sideways and onto 16th Street in furious pursuit. "Show me what you've got, boys!" I said as the passenger in the ODF vehicle began firing on us, shattering our rear window.

Looking at Tamara, I said, "Are you okay?"

"Yeah!" she shouted over the thunderous engine noise.

"Well, don't just sit there! Shoot back!"

Flipping me off, she picked up the AR and began firing a steady volley of shots, striking the car on occasion, forcing it to back off a bit.

Just up ahead, we could see another ODF patrol car traveling at a high rate of speed down South Limit Ave, apparently attempting to head us off. Downshifting into third, I floored the Mustang, pulling the engine long and hard before shifting back to fourth, inching just past them before they slid sideways onto 16th Street.

"Those boys must be seasoned. Those aren't academy level skills," I noted.

Passing the Missouri State Fair Grounds, 16th Street became County Road Y.

"We're in the home stretch!" I shouted as the car pulled long and hard, staying just ahead of our pursuers.

"So, what happens when we get there?" she asked sarcastically. "Do you think they'll just open the gate and let us in with the ODF in hot pursuit?"

"I... well... I guess... they'll..." while I was trying to sputter out an answer to her obvious question, the Mustang began to sputter as well. My heart sank in my chest as she began to lose power, and steam began emanating from under the hood.

"Damn it!" I shouted as I punched the steering wheel.

"Don't blame the car," Tamara snapped. "No car could have survived what you just put her through."

As we rolled to a stop, both Tamara and I quickly looked back to see the two ODF patrol cars rapidly approaching. "Do you want the rifle or shotgun?" I asked.

"You know I like the shotgun," she answered with a smile.

"You're a helluva woman," I said to her as I opened my door and stepped out to face my fate head-on.

Stepping out of the passenger side, she looked at me with a sly grin and quipped, "You're not so bad yourself... for one of them."

Just then, both patrol cars slammed on their brakes, sliding their cars sideways while smoking their rear tires in a frantic attempt to turn and retreat.

"What the...?" I said in the confusion of the moment as a shrieking sound came raining down out of the sky above us.

Both Tamara and I turned to see two A-10 Warthogs bearing down on the patrol cars. With several bursts from their 30mm cannons, the ODF cars were obliterated before our eyes. The A-10s then flew on into Sedalia, pounding the ODF forces that had been lying in wait to ambush us.

Within minutes, we saw a convoy of Humvees approaching from Whiteman. When the Humvees came to a stop, the security personnel stepped out of their vehicles, each wearing full-body biohazard suits, similar to the one Mark had been wearing. One of them stepped forward and stood directly in front of Tamara and me, and asked, "Are you Lieutenant Joseph Branch?"

"Yes. Yes, sir," I replied

He then reached out his Tyvek-suit gloved hand and said, "Our mutual friend, Robert Bud Casey, said we should be expecting you."

Chapter Twenty-Five

The first few days after reaching Whiteman all felt like a blur. They quarantined Tamara and me, providing us with intensive medical care, as well as debriefing us both over and over again, ensuring they did not miss a single detail of possibly valuable intel. I had learned that Bud was still alive, but gravely ill from the Sembé virus when he had last made contact and was now assumed to be dead.

We were then flown by air transport with a fighter escort to what they fondly referred to as the Continental Army Base in Wyoming, formerly known as Warren Air Force Base.

There, we discovered that we were more use to them than we'd imagined. The data that Ronnie had acquired to accompany the Symbex had been more complete than any of us had known. It was essentially all the clues that were needed to lead to an eventual cure.

The antibodies in our blood, being that Tamara and I were both infected carriers, also led to the rapid development of a vaccine that could save the lives of the millions of people around the world who had survived.

In addition, Tamara and I served as the test patients for their research, resulting in a nearly complete recovery for both of us. I say "nearly" because even though we tested negative for the virus, we both just never felt the same again. Perhaps the few hard weeks we spent together before arriving, first at Whiteman and then Warren, had simply aged us.

Aches and pains aside, though, I couldn't have been happier. Tamara and I grew closer as the days went on, and once we were cleared and released from quarantine, we actually began seeing each other on a romantic basis. We did our best to keep things slow, however, making sure that it was what we both really wantcd, and not just some psychological attachment brought about by the traumatic events we'd shared.

A few weeks ago, I was called into the office of the base commander, General Thomas Hill. When I arrived, there were several senior resistance leaders present, representing both the ground and air forces, as well as clandestine operations and intelligence.

"Mr. Branch," General Hill said. "Come on in."

I must admit, I was delighted to no longer be called Lieutenant Branch, as that part of me was now long gone.

Once all but one of the introductions had been made, the remaining gentleman, who wore civilian attire and had a slightly unkempt beard and hairstyle, introduced himself as Colonel Wood, the commander of the clandestine and covert ops branch of the Continental Army known as Knowlton's Rangers.

My face lit up when he mentioned Knowlton's Rangers. Two of his men, Bud and Mark, had given their lives for us. "It's truly an honor, sir," I said, shaking his hand.

I told them the entire story from beginning to end. Well, the Cliffs Notes version, at least. They'd all read the official intel reports and debriefing transcripts. They knew every facet of the events that had occurred. No, this felt more like a room full of patriots who just wanted to have their spirits lifted by such an unlikely tale of luck, combined with perseverance and duty before self.

Don't get me wrong, I personally took credit for none of it. Those positive attributes were laid at the feet of Ronnie, Tamara's friends, Bud, and Mark. I was simply the guy carrying the football. It was the rest of the team that had made it possible for me to reach the end zone.

After our lively chat, Colonel Wood looked me squarely in the eye and said, "We sure could use an advisor on our team who knows how things work on the inside, in D.C. specifically.

We've got some operations planned that will require first-hand knowledge to succeed. Will you help us?" he asked.

"Yes, sir," I affirmed with a smile.

General Hill then called the occupants of the room to attention, which I must admit caught me off-guard. He walked over to me and retrieved a gold oak leaf from his pocket and pinned it to the collar of the polo shirt I just happened to be wearing.

He smiled, and said, "Don't worry, Knowlton's Rangers don't wear uniforms. But you will need the appropriate authority to be an effective advisor and strategist for Colonel Wood, and we don't have time for traditional career progression these days."

He squared up on me, looked me up and down, and then said, "Major Branch. That sounds a helluva lot better than Lieutenant, don't you think?

"And don't worry, Major, Miss Adams, or should I say, Major Adams, has already accepted an appointment as well. With the help of some of our finest, she'll be the leading a unit that specializes in the training and organization of locally-based insurgencies. Her first-hand operating experience will be a tremendous asset to us as we move forward and begin to tighten the screws on the OWA's support network in the near future."

I was speechless. I expected to wake up from this dream any minute, only to find myself sleeping under a tree somewhere, covered with ticks and counting my remaining doses of Symbex.

General Hill then said, "We have one more surprise for you. Miss... er, I mean, Major Adams and a few others are waiting for you in hangar fourteen. I suggest you don't keep them waiting."

My heart was racing. What more could there be? General Hill and the others escorted me to hangar fourteen. When I walked in, I saw a large crowd of resistance personnel who had clearly been gathered for whatever it was they were about to show me.

Tamara ran up to me and gave me a big hug, saying, "I'm so excited."

"Excited about what?" I asked.

"You'll see," she said, wiping a tear from her eye.

A moment later, I heard an engine roar to life and begin to idle. Whatever it was remained out of view outside the main hangar doors.

General Hill approached me and said, "We all tried to think of a gesture we could make to thank you for having the courage to walk away from the comfortable life you had back in Washington. You voluntarily set out on a journey to face what any sane person would have seen as a path to certain death, just to do the right thing, not only for yourself, but for humanity as a whole.

"I read the reports detailing your actions over and over again, and one thing stood out to me. I contacted the base commander back at Whiteman and had her do me a little favor. We put together a team of volunteers who utilized our aircraft maintenance and parts fabrication facilities, and well, let's just say although it's not perfect, they've worked wonders."

He then turned and waved to a man standing by the main hangar doors, who relayed the signal. I could hear the rumble of a big V8 engine ease toward the door. To my amazement, I saw the very 1967 Shelby GT500 that had gotten us to the finish line enter the hangar.

She was truly a sight to behold. She was in far better shape than I remembered leaving her in. I'm pretty sure neither Ford nor Carol Shelby ever intended for her to take flight, nor did they ever intend for her to double as a farm implement, bush-hogging overgrown fields with speed and brute force alone.

I walked up to the car and ran my hand down the fresh coat of black paint. Like General Hill said, she wasn't perfect, but considering she came out of an aircraft corrosion control shop and not a hot-rod paint shop, she looked pretty damn good.

"We had to swap out the wheels and tires," one of the aviation maintenance techs explained. "The other wheels had chunks of metal taken out of them and would've never balanced again, and the tires, well, they were showing cord in several places. How they still had any air in them at all was a mystery to us. How many miles did you drive her again?"

Laughing, I said, "Just a hundred, but it was a hard hundred."

"Clearly," he replied, shaking his head.

"Where did you find parts?" I asked.

"We fabricated much of it, so you've got some exotic materials in there that Ford didn't have available in 1967. For other parts, there are several abandoned junkyards within a few miles of here. Oh, and there's no shortage of abandoned donor cars everywhere you look these days. We had a security detail travel with us while we scavenged. So, please, keep in mind she's got a few non-original parts. That radiator, for example, is out of a compact truck. Maybe someday you'll be able to piece her back together properly."

When I looked inside, I saw the picture of the family who had unknowingly donated the car to the cause. The techs had ensured that it remained precisely where I had put it, only now, it was contained in a small, handmade picture frame, securely attached between the gauges.

They had no way of knowing who those people were, or why I had a picture of them right in front of me during our hundred-mile dash for the base, but they knew they must be of some importance, and treated the picture with the respect it deserved.

The people in that photo represented more than just the family who'd owned the car. They represented all the upstanding American families who'd worked hard, took pride in what they had earned, and fought hard to defend their homes when the time came. There were thousands, or tens of thousands of families all across the country and millions across the world who had faced similar struggles in the aftermath of the horrors inflicted upon them by the OWA, most of whom with stories we will never know.

We will never understand what their final moments entailed, or the heroic efforts they made trying to defend what was right and just until the very end.

I looked around the room, with everyone staring at Tamara and me as if we were some sort of heroes. We weren't heroes in my eyes. We were blessed. That's what we were. There's no way we could have done this alone. I didn't deserve this car. I didn't deserve the adoration of these people. The people who gave their lives to get us here are the ones who should go down in history.

If I somehow manage to survive the fight against the OWA that will surely come, I will make it my mission in life to see that our history books going forward contain their names. Each and every one of them.

~~~~

Once Tamara and I had formally accepted our commissions and were sworn in, we were briefed on intelligence we were previously not privy to. One such piece of privileged information was the organization and operations of Knowlton's Rangers, in particular, the tremendous contributions of operative Robert "Bud" Casey.

After he had gotten a message through to them to expect us at Whiteman and had relayed his condition to them, he still never gave up. Another operative in the area had detailed how he had remained on watch, despite his suffering, and had continued to provide updates on the OWA's activity in the region.

It was also reported that he kept up his spirits and maintained pride and enthusiasm in his work until one day when the reports simply ceased to come in.

Once he knew he was infected, it would have been easy to have given up on the world around him. He could have just crawled down into that hole that sheltered him and resigned himself to his fate. But he stood the watch until relieved by God Himself. I'm sure of that as much as I am anything.

I'm sure he's still watching over us from somewhere. If there is one thing Tamara taught me throughout all of this, is that such faith is truly justified. Despite all the evils in the world, there are far too many things that happen which simply cannot be accidents or coincidences.

Another tidbit of information I had become privy to was exactly why the OWA hadn't used attack drones or air power against us while making that final run for the base from Jefferson City and beyond.

As it turned out, the fine folks at Whiteman were responsible for that, too. I'm not sure exactly how, but I know they played the part of the crazy inmate in the corner who'd shiv you if you looked at him wrong, very well.

And on that day, the A-10s and the nukes that backed their actions made a very effective shiv. Evidently, the ODF officers in the patrol cars had ventured just a little further than was to be tolerated.

Well, folks, I'd love to stick around and tell you more, but right now, I'm ripping through the gears of the Shelby Mustang across the Warren Continental Army base here in beautiful Wyoming with an even more beautiful woman sitting beside me, and we're on our way to the base club for dinner and drinks. A man has to have his priorities, you know.

Oh, and Tamara says to tell you hi. We'll both be seeing you around.

~~~~ The End ~~~~

Breaking the Beast

A Note from the Author

Thank you very much for reading *Breaking the Beast: The Redemption of Joe Branch*. Writing this book was truly a labor of love for me, and I hope it provided you with hours of pleasurable reading as well.

Though this book is a work of fiction and presents an unlikely scenario, I'm sure I'm not alone when I see the possibilities of collusion and conspiracy throughout both business and government. It's the nature of the beast, and it's something that reminds us of its presence on a regular basis, and you don't have to be a tinfoil hat wearing conspiracy theorist to see it.

Joe's saga represents one that many people have undoubtedly faced throughout history when governments, tyrants, and dictators have chosen to use their own citizens to serve them, while carrying out dastardly deeds against their fellow countrymen. And like Joe, I'd imagine there are countless stories out there that we will never hear, about those who chose to draw a line in the sand and say, "no more!" This story is a tribute to them, the ones who stopped merely following orders and stood for something greater than themselves, with most of them paying the ultimate price as a result.

Again, thank you very much for reading, and I wish you all the best in life and every endeavor you pursue. God bless.

Respectfully,

Steven C. Bird

Breaking the Beast

About the Author

Steven Bird was born and raised in the Appalachian coal town of Harlan, Kentucky, where he grew up immersed in the outdoors. After graduating high school, he joined the Navy and moved to the Seattle area, where he served on active duty for eleven years, eventually retiring out of the reserves at just over twenty years of service.

Upon leaving active duty, Steven began working as a charter pilot and a flight instructor. Eventually finding his way into a turbo-prop airline, and then on to a jet airline, he acquired thousands of hours of flight experience before leaving the airline industry to fly for one of America's largest cellular retailers.

Steven's writing career didn't start off with a degree in English and a background in literature. It was during his time with the airlines that inspired his writing with his first book *The Last Layover,* which was written mostly on an Android smartphone. Since then, Steven has published twelve additional books and has discovered writing as his true calling.

Steven and his wife, Monica, live on a farm/homestead in rural Tennessee on the Cumberland Plateau with their three children, Seth, Olivia, and Sophia. They raise cattle, horses, donkeys, sheep, chickens, ducks, and turkeys, in an effort to be as self-sufficient as possible, while exposing their children to the real world that surrounds them.

Steven's passion for the concept of individual liberty shines through in all of his works, as it does in his daily life. Join him in the stories he weaves through the following books and series:

Breaking the Beast

The New Homefront Series:

> The Last Layover: The New Homefront, Volume One
> The Guardians: The New Homefront, Volume Two
> The Blue Ridge Resistance: The New Homefront, Volume Three
> The Resolution: The New Homefront, Volume Four
> Viking One: A New Homefront Novel

The Society Lost Series:

> The Shepherd: Society Lost, Volume One
> Betrayal: Society Lost, Volume Two
> The Tree of Penance: Society Lost, Volume Three
> Them: Society Lost, Volume Four

Erebus: An Apocalyptic Thriller

Jet: Dangerous Prey

The Edge of Civility

Free Preview of EREBUS: An Apocalyptic Thriller – Available Now!

Winner of the 2018 Audiobook Listener Awards Thriller of the Year!

Breaking the Beast

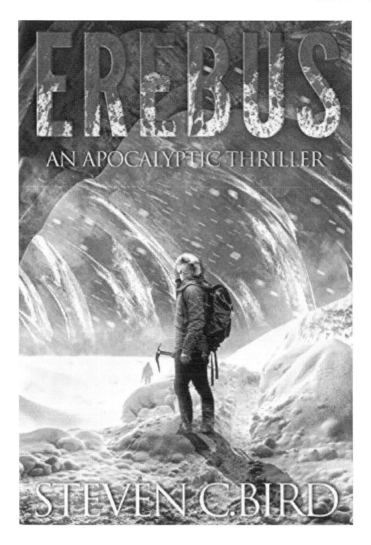

Breaking the Beast

Introduction

In 1841, when the British vessel H.M.S. Terror first charted Antarctica under the command of explorer James Clark Ross, the crew laid eyes on a volcano reaching 12,500 feet above the surface of the frozen ice of Antarctica. Ross and his men saw the huge white plume rising from its crater at the summit, and it has been erupting ever since. Mount Erebus, as it was later named by explorer Ernest Shackleton, was named after the Greek god Erebus, the god of primeval darkness. To anyone who has visited the mountain and its incredibly harsh environment, this name is found to be more than appropriate.

Today, on the steep and icy slopes of Mount Erebus, can be found a rugged team of scientists, researchers, and mountaineers carrying out their work in one of the harshest and most remote parts of the planet, at a facility known as the Mount Erebus Volcano Observatory, or simply MEVO. These professionals, tough enough to brave the extreme climate of Mount Erebus, include experts in the fields of gravity and magnetotellurics, volcanology, geophysics, and even astrobiology. These doctorate-level professionals travel each year from several major universities such as Cambridge, Missouri State, the New Mexico Institute of Mining and Technology, and the University of Washington in order to study Erebus, as well as the unique environment it has created for itself in one of the most remote places on Earth. They are assisted by a professional mountaineer, as well as graduate students from their respective institutions who study under them.

The researchers at MEVO, when not on the mountain at the research camp simply called the Lower Erebus Hut, are based out of McMurdo Station. Mac-Town, as McMurdo Station is fondly referred to by its residents, was founded by the U.S. Navy in 1956. What was initially called Naval Air Facility McMurdo is now simply McMurdo Station. McMurdo Station is currently run by the United States Antarctic Program and is governed by the Antarctic Treaty, signed by forty-five world governments. The Antarctic Treaty regulates daily life at McMurdo, as well as the research conducted there.

In many respects, the inhabitants of McMurdo Station are on their own on the vast and remote continent of Antarctica. This is especially true during the winter months, when most of the station's one thousand residents return to warmer climates, leaving behind a skeleton crew of only two hundred to face the rigors and potential horrors of life at the bottom of the world—alone.

Chapter One

Mount Erebus Volcano Observatory (MEVO)

Holding on tightly to the core sample drill as it bored into the side of one of the massive ice towers that reach high into the sky, Dr. Hunter focused on his task at hand with relentless determination. Standing over him like giants from ancient-Greek mythology, the ice towers, formed by condensing air as it vents from one of the many fumaroles on Antarctica's largest and most active volcano, Mount Erebus, reach as high as sixty-feet above the ground.

With the frigid arctic winds atop Mount Erebus pounding his body, his coat buffeted violently as he struggled to maintain his footing. His beard, nearly full of ice and snow, clung to his face like a rigid mask as he wiped his goggles, attempting to see the drill as it bored its way into the ice before him. The season's expedition was about to come to an end, and he could not afford to leave without the core samples he desperately needed in order to complete his research.

"Doc, we've got to get moving," Mason yelled through the howling winds, placing his hand on Dr. Hunter's shoulder as if to urge him away from his work. "If the storm gets any worse, we won't be able to see well enough to make it back to the hut! It's already damn near zero visibility."

Ignoring the plea, knowing his task was nearly complete, Dr. Hunter yelled, "Got it!" as he pulled the core sample gently from the tower of ice. Without saying a word, he patted Mason on the shoulder, and they began their hike through the pounding weather to their snowmobiles, to return to the Lower Erebus Hut before the mountain claimed them, as it had tried so many times before.

~~~~

Entering the Lower Erebus Hut, Mason slammed the door shut as quickly as he could to keep the fierce frigid winds at bay. Everyone in the room turned to look at the two ice-and-snow-covered men. Having just returned from the summit with Dr. Hunter's core samples in hand, they placed them gently on the floor and began to dust off the fresh snow that covered them, in preparation for removing their heavy outer layers of protective clothing.

"I was starting to worry about you two," said Dr. Linda Graves, a forty-four-year-old astrobiology researcher with the University of Washington.

"So was I," replied Mason, as he began peeling off his balaclava and removing his many layers of clothing. Mason, or Derrick Mason to be exact, was a graduate student of geochemistry at the New Mexico Institute of Mining and Technology (NMT).

As a student of Dr. Nathan Hunter, the Principle Investigator for the expedition and a professor of geochemistry at NMT, Mason had been hand-selected to come along on this year's expedition to Mount Erebus. Dr. Hunter not only chose him for his academic prowess, but also for his abilities as a seasoned mountain climber and avid outdoor adventurer. Mason was an experienced hunter, long distance hiker, mountain climber, and most importantly of all, a survivalist at heart. There were plenty of students academically up to the task, perhaps even more so than Derrick Mason, but Dr. Hunter refused to let his research be slowed by having to babysit a graduate student who wasn't physically up to the extreme conditions that Antarctica, and specifically, Mount Erebus, thrust upon those ill-suited for the challenge.

With Derrick Mason, however, he had a stout, twenty-eight-year-old outdoorsman that he knew could be counted on when things became challenging and treacherous on the volcano.

Peeling off his gloves, Dr. Hunter quipped, "If we were gonna leave without one of our critical core samples, what would be the point of coming? I'm not waiting until next year to come back just to fill in the gaps, and I know you didn't come all the way from Seattle to leave just yet either—all things considered. Caution is wise, but risk yields rewards."

"That it does," joked Mason, rubbing his face in an attempt to return warmth to his skin. "But it's days like this that remind you of the fact that Shackleton named this mountain after the Greek god Erebus, the god of primeval darkness."

"Did you get what we were looking for?" Dr. Graves asked.

"I think so," Dr. Hunter replied. "I still want to get down as far as I can into the fumarole on the north side of Tramway Ridge and get a sample before we leave. But today's cores contain some of the material we were looking for."

Changing the subject, Dr. Hunter looked around the room, and asked, "Any word from Mac-Town?" referring to Antarctica's McMurdo Station.

"The first helicopter will be here in the morning," answered Jared Davis, a volcanologist and a junior member of the research team from NMT. "We'll have them available through the end of the week, but after that, Mac-Town will be buttoned up for the winter. The last Air Force C-17 leaves Saturday. If you've not done what you need to get done by then, you'll either have to leave it behind until spring or be stuck here with the wintering-over crew at Mac-Town."

"I suppose so," Dr. Hunter replied. "Now, getting back to the important business at hand, what was for dinner and is there any left?" he asked, looking around the crowded and cluttered living area and seeing dishes piled high in the kitchen sink. "It looks like we missed out on whatever it was."

Brett Thompson, a Homer, Alaska native and the team's mountaineer and safety specialist, spoke up and said, "Neville made us a pot of his famous Worcestershire stew."

"He made what?" asked Mason with a confused look.

Neville Wallace, a tall, lanky, curly-haired British graduate student who had accompanied Dr. Gerald Bentley, the Co-Principle Investigator and volcanologist from the University of Cambridge said, "I simply concocted a basic vegetable stew from what was left of the fresh produce, before it spoiled. It was already getting a tad bit long on the shelf, so I opted to put it to good use. To mask the rather dismal condition of the ingredients, I kicked it up a bit with what was left of the Worcestershire sauce. It wasn't anything to write home to mum about, but it filled the void."

In a deflated tone, Dr. Hunter replied, "Wasn't? I assume that means it's all gone."

"I told Lester and Ronald not to go for seconds until you had returned and eaten your share, but you know how those two buggers can be," Neville said, poking fun at the two men who had finished off the rest of the soup.

"Oh, well... we'll survive," said Mason as he plopped down onto the only empty spot on the old, worn-out sofa. "I was in the mood for some sort of canned meat anyway. As a matter of fact, I'm so hungry I could go for one of those one-hundred-year-old cans of mutton still on the shelf in Shackleton's Hut."

Tossing him a can of pickled herring, Dr. Hunter said, "Here ya go. It's not century-old mutton, but it'll do. We're scraping the bottom of that sort of thing, too," he said as he searched for food in each of the nearly empty cabinets.

"If something happens and the helicopters don't show up soon to give us our ride back to Mac-Town, we may have to decide who we're gonna eat first," chuckled Mason, as he peeled open the can.

"I vote for Lester and Ronald then, since they ate the last of the soup," said Dr. Jenny Duval, the official camp scientific assistant. "It only seems fair."

"Hey, now!" replied Lester Stevens, an engineer brought along as the team's lava-lake-imaging technical guru.

Lester Stevens and Ronald Weber were the resident non-scientific technical experts, and though they had never met before traveling to Antarctica, the pair often seemed as if they were long-lost brothers. The others frequently joked that they spent way too much time in the hut and needed to get out on the mountain more. They often teased about the two having a fictitious mental condition they called *MEVO Fever* from being isolated on the mountain for too long. If anyone in the camp had it, it was truly those two jokers.

As the rest of the group settled into their nightly routine of watching old black-and-white science fiction movies, Dr. Walter Perkins, a researcher from Missouri State University who specialized in gravity and magnetotellurics, stood and waded through the tired bodies strewn about the floor. The researchers lay about the hut with their heads propped up on boots, jackets, or whatever they could find to help them see the television. To an outsider, it would appear to have been the scene of some apocalyptic movie where the dead lay scattered on the floor wherever they had fallen.

Approaching Hunter and Mason, he asked, "Dr. Hunter, would you like me to put your samples away in the cold room while you two finish your five-star cuisine?"

"Thanks, Walt, but we can get it," Dr. Hunter replied. "There's no reason for you to get the chills after warming up from your day out and about. The two of us are barely thawed, so we won't even notice."

Looking to Mason, watching as he devoured his canned meal of compressed fish, he said, "Actually, Derrick, I can get it. I'm hitting the sack after that. Get your stuff together and be ready to accompany me to Mac-Town in the morning when the helicopter comes. We'll get our samples on the next transport and then head back up to the summit when we return tomorrow afternoon. I saw something interesting that I want to check out."

"Yes, sir," Mason replied sharply. Taking another bite of pickled herring, he turned and asked, "What did you see?"

"We'll talk about it in the morning; it may be nothing."

"Roger that," Mason replied, turning his attention back to his half-eaten can of fish.

~~~~

Early the next morning after the weather had cleared, Dr. Hunter looked off into the distance, scanning the horizon for the arrival of the helicopter that was scheduled to transport his core samples back to McMurdo Station. Once at McMurdo, they would arrange to have the samples loaded onboard a U.S. Air Force C-17 for transportation back to the states where he could continue the analysis of his samples in a proper laboratory environment.

"There they are!" shouted Mason over the howling winds of the clear, arctic morning.

Looking at his watch, Dr. Hunter replied, "It's about damn time! We're cutting it close. We barely have time to get them on today's flight. We haven't got time for delays."

Upon landing, Dr. Hunter and Mason loaded the crate of core samples, as well as some other gear that was packed and ready for shipment, on board the Eurocopter AS350. Once everything was securely lashed to the floor, the pilot was given a thumbs-up and they were quickly on their way.

During the flight, Mason couldn't help but look across the frozen continent, thinking of how, strangely, he would miss it during their time back in New Mexico. Antarctica, a place that to a casual observer may seem to be merely empty, cold, and harsh, somehow endears itself in the hearts of those who spend time there. There is a beauty and peace about the frozen continent that feels like home to a wandering soul, and a wandering soul he was.

As the helicopter approached McMurdo Station, a research base that more closely resembled an industrial mining town than an environmentally-friendly research facility, Mason's mind switched gears as he chuckled to himself, thinking, *then again, I could use those warm New Mexico nights right about now.*

After landing, Dr. Hunter and Mason quickly unloaded their core samples and placed them on a forklift for transportation to McMurdo's Ship Off Load Command Center.

Walking into the facility behind the forklift, Dr. Hunter and Derrick Mason were immediately greeted by George Humboldt, a logistics specialist at McMurdo. Pulling his scarf away from his mouth, George said, "Dr. Hunter, I'm glad you made it."

"Have we missed it?" Dr. Hunter impatiently inquired.

"No, but unfortunately, the flight is delayed until tomorrow due to mechanical issues." Pointing at the crate on the forklift, he asked, "Is that the samples we spoke of?"

"Yes. Yes, it is," Dr. Hunter replied with tension in his voice. "I can't stress enough how these samples need to remain frozen at all times. They contain...well, they contain material that is critical to my research. I just can't do without them."

"Don't worry, Doctor," George replied. "It's no problem at all. I don't think I need to point out that transporting ice samples is a fairly routine task for us here at McMurdo."

"I know. I know," Dr. Hunter replied. "Forgive me, but I believe I'm onto something special and if my samples are lost for any reason, it will be a setback that will require me to wait until next year just to catch back up."

"Every sample from every research team is important, Doctor. But you have my word that I will ensure that exceptional care is given to yours. By this time tomorrow, your samples will be well on their way back to the U.S., and will be in good hands."

Patting Dr. Hunter on the arm, Mason interrupted by saying, "C'mon, Doc. George has a handle on things here. Let's get some lunch before we head back out to MEVO. I've been looking forward to a hot meal after what we've been down to for the past few days."

Nodding in agreement, Dr. Hunter said, "Yes, of course. Thanks, George," as the two men turned and began their walk toward the station's cafeteria.

~~~~

Completing the paperwork for Dr. Hunter's shipment, George watched as Mason and Dr. Hunter left the facility. Turning to see Vince Gruber approaching with the forklift, he chuckled, placing his clipboard on top of Dr. Hunter's samples.

Stepping off the forklift, Vince said, "They always wait until the last minute. Every year, it's the same damn thing."

Patting Vince on the shoulder, George smiled, saying, "Yep. They all think their work is more important than everyone else's, too. You'd think these ice samples were tubes of gold the way that guy acts. He's one of the worst. He's always uptight about his stuff. He could carry it on the plane his damn self, if it were up to me."

Pausing to look around at the vast amount of cargo they had yet to load, George continued, "Oh, well. You'll be home in

Florida soon, and I'll be back in Philly eating a real cheesesteak, not the sorry excuses for a sandwich they have here. Let's just get on with it and mark our last few days of the season off the calendar."

~~~~

Arriving at the station's cafeteria, still referred to as the galley due to McMurdo's roots as a naval facility, both Mason and Dr. Hunter grabbed a plastic tray, a large and a small plate, and silverware as they began working their way through the hot food line. Plopping a heaping scoop of barbecued pulled-pork onto his plate, Mason said, "Man, I've been looking forward to this."

"I know what you mean," replied Dr. Hunter. "MEVO is like a second home to me, but when provisions begin running low, it's not like we can run out and get more. Being based on the side of a major volcano has its inherent limits."

As the two men sat down and began to eat, they were approached by Dr. Raju Tashi, a particle physics researcher from the University of Wisconsin. "Dr. Hunter, may I join you?" he asked.

"Of course, Raj," Dr. Hunter replied. "And this is one of my best and brightest graduate students from NMT, Derrick Mason," he said, gesturing to Mason. "Derrick, this is Dr. Tashi. He's one of the particle chasers out at the IceCube facility. They're researching neutrinos. Pretty exciting stuff for a particle chaser."

"Pleased to meet you," Dr. Tashi said to Mason with a smile as the two shook hands.

"Likewise, Doctor."

"How are things going at IceCube?" Dr. Hunter asked.

With a look of excitement on his face, Dr. Tashi replied, "Excellent. Our experiments with the high-altitude balloon went very well. We're excited to get back to Wisconsin to study our results in more detail. We have wrapped up our operations for the season and are all awaiting transportation back to the states. And yourself? How are things at MEVO?"

"Excellent as well," he replied. "Although I wish I could say we've wrapped things up as you have. No matter how much I accomplish, I always feel a step behind the mountain. There is so much to learn. So much to explore. And of course, as soon as you're on to something good, Erebus throws you a curve ball and a critical piece of equipment gets smashed by a crater bomb or the like."

"Well, at least you haven't been smashed by a crater bomb yourself," Dr. Tashi said with a chuckle.

"He came close a few times," Mason said, looking to Dr. Hunter with taunting smile. "Last week, a crater bomb the size of a Volkswagen almost nailed him.

"Is that so?" asked Dr. Tashi with a raised eyebrow.

Placing his glass of tea on the table while poking around at his tray for the next bite of food, Dr. Hunter responded, "Let's just say Erebus doesn't give up its secrets without you having to earn them."

"I don't envy you for that," Dr. Tashi replied. "At IceCube, all we have to contend with is the cold."

"Well, gentlemen," Mason said as he pushed himself back from the table with a satisfied look on his face. "I'm gonna grab dessert. Can I get anyone something while I'm up?"

"Frostyboy is down again," Dr. Tashi said in a tone of frustration, referring to the cafeteria's famous soft-serve ice cream machine.

"No! Ah, damn it," Mason said, exasperated by Dr. Tashi's news.

Patting Mason on the back, Dr. Hunter laughed and said, "Don't fret about it. By next week, you'll be getting yourself a scoop at Cold Stone Creamery from that cute blonde who has her eye on you back at NMT."

With that, Dr. Hunter stood and said, "It was great seeing you again, Raj. Are you coming back next summer?"

"That has yet to be decided," Dr. Tashi replied. "If not, keep in touch. I'm sure we'll cross paths again. We may not be in the same field, but science is a small world."

Shaking his hand, Dr. Hunter smiled and said, "You take care. And yes, yes, it is."

Chapter Two

Mount Erebus Volcano Observatory

As the helicopter touched down near the Lower Erebus Hut, snow and ice crystals swirled around them as the twenty-five-mile-per-hour wind gusts pounded the craft. Shoving open the door and holding it against the violent winds, Mason signaled for Dr. Hunter to exit the still-running helicopter. Once Dr. Hunter was clear and on his way to the Lower Erebus Hut, Mason shut the door firmly and signaled to the pilot that they were clear. Before the two men reached the door of the facility, the helicopter pilot had lifted off and was on his way back to McMurdo Station and the comforts it provided.

Closing the door securely behind them, Dr. Hunter looked around the room and asked, "Where is Linda?"

Looking up from his work of packing up some of the team's sensitive data-recording equipment, Ronald answered, "Linda? Oh, Dr. Graves. She and Brett went back up on the mountain this morning just after the two of you took the helicopter out to McMurdo."

"I hope they hurry. It's getting late. There isn't much daylight left as it is," Dr. Hunter said with a noticeable uneasiness in his voice.

"They'll be fine," Mason replied. "Brett is a top-notch mountaineer. I wish I had just half of his climbing skills."

"You find your way around the mountain pretty well," Dr. Hunter said as he walked over to the coffee maker.

"I'm an outdoor junkie, but I'm your average outdoor junkie," Mason replied with a thankful smile. "But Brett—he's hardcore. That's why I know they'll be fine. Besides, Dr. Graves is a fitness freak. She can scurry up a vertical ascent and be looking down at us from the top, while the rest of us are stopping to catch our breath a quarter of the way up."

With a chuckle, Ronald added, "And Doc, you know better than to let her catch you uttering words of concern about her. She'll rip you a new one."

Smiling as he took a sip of hot, black coffee, Dr. Hunter said, "You're right about that, Ronald. She's not one to tolerate a male counterpart's acknowledgment that she's a lady."

~~~~

Opening her eyes and seeing nothing but darkness around her, Dr. Graves realized she was lying flat on her back. With her head pounding from the impact, she paused for a moment before she attempted to move when she heard Brett yelling down to her from above.

"Dr. Graves!" he shouted. "Dr. Graves, are you okay?"

With his words echoing off the walls throughout the ice cave, it was disorienting and difficult for her to tell from which direction his shouts were coming. Sitting up, she felt herself become dizzy and light-headed as she replied in a weak, shaky voice, "Yeah. Yeah, I'm fine—I think."

"I can barely hear you!" he shouted. "Are you okay?"

Mustering the strength to shout back, she yelled, "Yes! Yes, I'm okay!" She instantly regretted her efforts as the intensity of her throbbing headache increased with each word she uttered, as if the words were bouncing around inside her head.

"I'm coming down!" he shouted.

Struggling to get to her knees, Dr. Graves reached for her headlamp, only to find that it had been irreparably damaged in the fall. Pulling her hand-held flashlight from her pocket, she flicked it on, only to discover in amazement that the walls of the cave around her contained traces of grayish microorganisms, unlike anything she had ever seen.

Hearing a rope bounce off the wall behind her, she turned and pointed her hand-held flashlight skyward and into the small, tubular vertical fumarole shaft from which she had fallen into this previously undiscovered chamber deep beneath the ice. Seeing Brett's climbing rope, she shouted, "I've got your rope. Come on down. I'll belay you from here."

Within a moment, Brett Thompson, the MEVO research team's professional mountaineer, appeared above her with his feet dangling as he descended into the dark chamber. Brett, still an Alaskan at heart, had been in and around large mountains his entire life. Standing six-foot-two with a slim build and sandy brown hair, Brett had always been popular with the ladies. However, his heart belonged to the extreme environments created by the mountains.

After working as a guide on Denali since his mid-twenties and having climbed the likes of Everest, Kilimanjaro, and the Matterhorn, Erebus seemed like the next logical place for his mountaineering career. It had yet to disappoint him in that regard.

Dropping into the chamber in front of Dr. Graves, he said, "You scared me half to death. That fumarole has to be at least one-hundred and fifty feet nearly straight down."

"Thank goodness for helmets," she said, tapping her gloved knuckles on her head. "That, and I tried to ball up the best I could to create drag on the sides of the ice tube to slow my descent. That way, it wasn't really a fall so much as it was a slide—at least until I reached the opening in the ceiling here. That part was a free-fall."

"Either way, I'm amazed you're up and walking," he said, scanning the chamber with his headlight.

"Hand me one of your sample containers," she said, reaching out to him as she began to look closely at the life-forms that appeared to be thriving on the chamber walls. "We've stumbled across something special here. It's hard to tell exactly, given the conditions, but I don't think we've documented microbes such as these before."

Handing her the container with the lid removed, Dr. Graves took it and immediately began collecting specimens with her Zero Tolerance brand folding pocket-knife, a gift from her brother that she carried with her at all times. "These walls are almost wet to the touch. What temperature is it in here?"

"I'm showing thirty-three," Brett replied, looking at his thermometer with his headlamp. "It's almost warm enough to remove a few layers of gear."

"Don't," she quickly replied. "These chambers have all sorts of gasses flowing through them, and we don't have any O2 with us. We may find ourselves having to egress in a hurry, and you won't have those few precious seconds to spare."

Screwing the lid back onto the container, Dr. Graves said, "Turn around. Let me put this in your pack, if you don't mind."

"Of course," he said, allowing her to stow her precious sample safely in his pack.

"Do you hear that?" she asked.

"What?"

"Nothing," she replied with amazement. "It's so quiet down here. Everything is so still. In most of the caves and tunnels created by the fumaroles, you can see the light shining through the walls and ceiling from the sun above. You can hear the wind pounding the mountain. But here, there's nothing. It's silent."

Looking around, he said, "Amazing, isn't it? I'm not sure we've ventured this deep before."

"Of all the trips we've made into the ice caves, I've never noticed that particular vent."

"The one you fell into?" he asked.

"Yeah. It's like it simply appeared."

"The heat from the mountain mixed with the cold ice above can do some crazy things," he said. "Helo Cave, and others like it that are close to the surface, appear steady to us because they have the cold to keep them solid. This far into the volcano, though, who knows what hot gasses come and go, cutting a swath through the ice only to have it fill in and refreeze later before we've had a chance to discover it."

Walking over to Brett's climbing rope that dangled into the chamber, Dr. Graves asked, "Do you have your ascenders?"

"Yes, ma'am," he replied.

"Get them set up while I take a few more samples. We'd better get going. Who knows when the next blast of hot gasses will come rushing through."

~~~~

Looking impatiently at the clock that hung on the wall in the Lower Erebus Hut, Dr. Hunter began to speak when the door opened, allowing a rush of frigid arctic wind to enter, blowing papers off the table in front of him. "Linda, so glad you two are back. How did it go?" he asked, attempting to mask his concern.

"It's a long story," she confessed, "but it's one you'll want to hear."

****I hope you enjoyed this free sample.****